DATE DUE

APR. 16. 1992 RET.			
NOV. 13. 1994 RET.	JUN 0 4 2007		

AIKI

AIKI

A NOVEL BY

JOHN GILBERT

DONALD I. FINE, INC.
New York

For
SUE, SKIP & CÉSAR

Men who live by violence,
shall die by violence. This
is an ancient law.

LAO-TZU

All men fear suffering, all men fear pain. Knowing
this, and that you are like unto them, do not strike
or slay.

SHAKYAMUNI

CHAPTER ONE

BIMBI had seen nothing but poverty all his life. Brooklyn poverty. He had been born an Untouchable; he had been born poor. When you were born poor, you knew nothing else, you dealt with nothing else. The poverty was always there, holding you down, pressing against you, allowing you to see nothing but its grim face. The world beyond Brooklyn—Queens, the Bronx—that was something you cared not to deal with.

And so it was that Bimbi became a victim of his caste, his life falling into a pattern typical of youths of that time. He spent his early years roaming the streets, searching for a true fight-guru, someone who would guide him in the ways of the warrior spirit. He never listened, though, and was forever making enemies rather than friends. The one person in whom he could place his trust was his older brother José, who had established himself as a top commando in the army. Bimbi had always wanted to follow his brother's path—be a soldier, a warrior. But he had been chosen by Mother Nature to be the youngest son, and with one brother already dead in a street fight and another serving in the military, he was forced to bide his time and look for other options.

Chief among Bimbi's options were the Arena League Farms, camps set up within the cities for the purpose of training youths whose goal it was to fight in the Arena. It was to the Arena League Farms that Bimbi was now preparing to go so that he could fulfill his dream of becoming a warrior.

Though thousands of Untouchables were recruited every year for the war games, only a select few were considered sufficiently skilled to compete in the Arena spotlight. Once having attained that position an Untouchable was assured of lasting fame: his name would be spoken wherever people congregated; the details of his life made public knowledge; and, in time, if he managed to survive his preliminary bouts, he might even earn a match against the greatest and most formidable competitor of them all: Mantis. Every Arena contestant wanted a shot at the Grand Champion and Bimbi was no exception.

"I intend to kill Mantis!" Bimbi told José.

They were walking on the south side of old Ocean Parkway, territory that belonged to several rival gangs. They had just left a local Humor's Bar, where you could pop an emoveer pill and then space out on the light show. José wasn't popping the pills like in the old days, though. Bimbi had found him very different this time home.

"So you're going to kill him, huh?"

"Yeah—I mean, he's gotta go. *Somebody's* gotta put that dude away."

José motioned his brother forward. "And you're gonna be the one to do it, right?"

"Yeah, sure," Bimbi said. "Why not?"

José suddenly stopped short.

"Just tell me one thing. Before you can take on Mantis, you gotta become an Arena champion yourself, right?"

"Yeah, that's what I've been tellin' you."

"So how are you going to become a champion if you don't know the first thing about fighting?" José asked.

"I can fight."

"You need a fight-guru first. You got one? Huh?"

Bimbi hesitated. "Well, not yet..."

"No, you ain't got one," José said, "because there aren't any good ones around. The only trainin' most people can get is in the army, and that's bullshit, too."

"What... what are you talkin' about?"

"I'm sayin' that fight-gurus, and the army, and all this crazy talk about bein' a great warrior is bullshit, plain and simple."

José began to shift about on his feet as he glanced around. "I mean, look at me. I'm twenty-six now and I've killed thirty—maybe forty—guys: East Germans, Cubans, Russians, Africans. You name it, I've killed it. So where's that gonna get my soul in the end?"

They were standing on the corner now, Bimbi looking somewhat bewildered as a fall wind picked up and two figures began to scan them from a nearby tenement. José spotted them and, again, coaxed his brother forward.

"Let's move."

"What're you talkin' about? What's a soul? That's church shit. I don't believe in that."

"That's your problem, you don't believe in nothin'. You don't even have enough common sense to realize we're cruisin' Enrique's turf right now."

"Enrique can shove it."

"He does that, he's gonna do it with about five guys behind him. Let's head this way."

José pulled his younger brother across the old parkway, past dozens of derelict vehicles, onto the opposite side of the street.

"Look," José said, "if I do one last thing before I get it, it's gonna be to set you on the right course."

Bimbi looked at his brother, amused.

"Get it? What—you plannin' on dyin' or something'?"

José grabbed Bimbi by the collar. "This ain't no fuckin' game. Now, listen to me. All this stuff they been feedin' you on TV—about the Arena and guys like me in the army—it's all lies, man.

They're usin' us. This uniform here, man—it's a monkey suit. Those dudes who go into the Arena, they're even bigger apes. You been duped since you was a little punk to believe that the wars and the Arena were right."

"But it's fightin'," Bimbi protested.

"And fightin's wrong, don't you see what I'm tryin' to tell you? It's wrong when you turn it into a sport." José released him. "And look at you, poppin' them sodac pills. You know what they're doing to you?"

Bimbi grunted. "They make me feel good, see things."

José shook his head. "They're messin' with your senses. The drug goes into your pineal gland, makes you want to look at TV."

"Why?"

"'Cause the TV's got cathode rays. I found out about it while I was in the army. The pineal gland affects your eyes and ears. When you take sodac you make that gland want to feed on things like TV, and video games, and neon. That's why the government makes those pills. They turn you into a 3-D clown."

"I don't get it," Bimbi said.

"Don't you see, bro? We've been manipulated, used." José backed off and began to rip the medals from his uniform.

"What're you doin'?"

"I don't need them no more, 'cause I'm through. I ain't home on leave. I've deserted. I'm out, finished."

Bimbi stared, wide-eyed. "Deserted? What're you, crazy?"

"No, man—don't you *see*? There are more and more of us doin' it now, you just ain't hearin' about it yet. You can't fight the system by playin' its game, and that's exactly what you'll be doin' if you step into a ring."

Bimbi looked at his brother as if he did not recognize him. He shook his head.

"I don't read you, bro."

"It ain't gonna be easy to walk away from it—not at first— because they've been conditionin' you all this time. That's what them pills are all about."

"So what do you want me to do?"

José was about to answer when he noticed four figures across the street, cruising the shadows like cats. He reached into his pocket and handed Bimbi a credeer card. The card was blank.

"What's this?" his brother asked.

"If you hold it under some neon, you'll see some symbols."

"So?"

"So take it to the Slope Arcade, first alleyway south. There'll be a sign there with the same symbols on it. Remember this name: Capitan. Ask for him."

"Who's he, a fight-guru?"

"Something better," José said. "Never mind that now, we gotta move outta here. You still got them nunchaks on you?"

Bimbi opened up his coat and revealed the weapon. They both could see figures moving closer now, spreading out and hiding behind the derelict cars. The two brothers moved swiftly down a side street, Bimbi pausing now and then to look at the card.

"What's this all about?" he asked again.

"Just take it where I told you and remember one thing: it's the system that's setting up the trouble. It ain't the cops, or the corporate serfs, or even the Professionals that are keeping us down. It's the system itself. The system's everybody's enemy—"

Before José could finish they had rounded the corner into another side street. There were six figures standing there, all dressed in kung fu black with spike bracelets. Standing at their head was a tall, snakelike youth whose long black hair was done up in braids.

It was Enrique.

"Welcome, bros," he said. The gang members began to circle.

"This is six to two," José said.

"One to one," Enrique retorted. "We make this a duel, between me and your big-mouth brother there."

José immediately stepped in front of Bimbi. "He don't want to duel you."

"Sure I do."

"Shut up," José said, and then he quickly shoved Enrique.

Five shivs snapped out like cat claws as Enrique pointed his finger menacingly.

"Lemme tell you something, José. Your bro there, he don't know when to shut up. We took him in our gang, taught him our secret code, then he ran out."

"Yeah," said another hood, "he betrayed us."

"Only 'cause you weren't no true fight-guru," Bimbi protested, "like I thought. I don't want no part of any gang that pushes old people around."

"Like shit."

"That's what they do, José. They roll old people for their sodac pills."

"I *am* a fight-guru," Enrique shouted.

José burst into laughter. It was all a farce, this scrawny little street punk asserting himself and his own scrawny little brother doing the same—two little boys surrounded by a gang and all of them hooting and acting like apes on a slum side street in the middle of nowhere. All the campaigns of glory José had undertaken, all the suicide missions, all the para-drops—at the moment they seemed as worthless as the torn uniform he now wore.

"Fight, fight, fight. You're punks, all of you," José said. He pointed at Bimbi. "You, too—just another punk."

"So says the big general."

It was Tomaso, Enrique's largest man, his lieutenant. He stepped forward and whipped a pair of nunchakas out of his back pocket.

"How about if soldier boy and me fight a duel first?"

José smiled wryly, then stepped back a bit.

"You guys—you never learn. What you wanna prove, bro?"

"We don't gotta prove nothin'," Tomaso said. "You gotta prove. I'm your size, you fight me."

It was hopeless. José knew there was no reasoning with this kind of street ignorance. He shook his head, turned to Enrique, then nodded, resigned to the whole affair.

"Okay. A duel. One on one. Your best man and me."

"Caballero."

José turned to Bimbi and swiftly pulled out his brother's pair of nunchakas. Then, without notice, he swung around, aiming at Tomaso's head. Tomaso dodged back and the fight was on. Assuming a very martial stance, the tall hoodlum began to circle José, who merely stood like a prizefighter, nodding and motioning for his opponent to attack.

"Come on, cut the kung fu shit," José said under his breath. "Let's get this over with."

Excited, Tomaso charged, missing his opponent completely and sustaining a blow to the side.

"Give up?"

Enraged, Tomaso charged again, swinging his weapon about madly but to no avail.

A patrol car could be seen slowly pulling up in the distance.

"Cops."

"That's their problem."

Bimbi attempted to signal the car, but José waved him down.

"The Man stays outta this."

"Right on," said Enrique.

Inside the patrol car the two officers on duty watched the fight with amusement. Like most of the police, they were drawn from the ranks of the corporate serf structure, workers imprisoned by the credit system. Since they were only one caste above the Untouchables, and at least partly addicted to sodac themselves, it was predictable that they would watch the fight as if it were just another TV show.

"Who you bet on?" the first officer asked.

"Ah, the soldier boy. Looks like he's got more goin' for him."

They watched as José continued to tease Tomaso, dodging his blows and waiting for him to attack. Every now and then José lashed out with a rod of his nunchakas and nipped Tomaso in the ribs.

"He's good."

"Yeah...Say, run the scanner on him."

"What for?"

"Maybe he's one of them deserters we been hearin' about. You know, one of them 'Aiki' guys."

"That's just rumor."

"Maybe. Let's run the scanner on him anyway."

The second patrolman adjusted the forward scanner. In a moment a magnified image of José's face appeared on the screen.

"So?" he asked. "You recognize him or what?"

"Did I say I did? Run his image back to the station."

Tomaso charged again, panting like a bull, his nunchakas smashing against a derelict car window and catching in it. José moved in swiftly, crashing his knee into the hood's groin and sending him to the ground. He swung around and looked at Enrique.

"And that's that," José said.

Enrique suddenly pulled a .38 out of his jacket. Everybody froze.

"What's this?"

"What it look like...?" Enrique stuttered, his hand trembling.

"You got cops there—"

"So—" and suddenly the revolver went off, the shot piercing José in the solar plexus, throwing him against the car. Blood gushed from his chest. Bimbi screamed and rushed forward as Enrique and his four other men took flight. Tomaso slowly staggered to his feet but was unable to run as the patrol car zoomed through the maze of derelict vehicles toward the scene.

By now information from police headquarters had appeared on the scanner: JOSÉ ARGUAYO, 5TH AIRBORNE, PRESENTLY AWOL AND BELIEVED TO BE SECT MEMBER, CODE: AIKI.

The patrolmen hurried out of the cruiser, stepped over Tomaso's slumped figure and approached Bimbi. He was sobbing as he held his dead brother in his arms—sobbing and watching as José's blood glowed across the gritty pavement. The blood of a hero. It looked the same as any other blood.

Bimbi had just learned his first lesson.

CHAPTER TWO

IN the days when the martial arts were at the height of their popularity—when a dojo could be found on every city block and the dream of every youth was to some day become a famous fighter—Sten Johnson was recognized as one of the great champions. His face covered scores of martial arts magazines; his style of Okinawan Gung-Ho Karate-Do was widely emulated; and his dojo was considered among the best. Sten had gained particular fame for a strong right hook that lifted his opponents off their feet and sent them hurtling back through the ropes.

But Sten Johnson had his problems. Sten's first problem was that he was famous; his second problem was that he was one of the figureheads of an institution marked for destruction.

Karate and the other martial arts, though dedicated to the spirit of combat, were also paths directed toward self-discipline and wisdom—paths that the government needed to close off if it hoped to instill in the Untouchables a love of violence. It was not the government's wish to whip up a fervor that could not be controlled. That would only serve to tax the system even further.

Rather, what it sought to do was heighten the Untouchables' aggressiveness and hostility until, reaching a fever pitch, it demanded an outlet. And then, lo and behold, an outlet would be provided, the only acceptable one: the "war games." In that way, the government would be assured of a continuing supply of troops to carry out its militarist policies.

As a first step in the process of erecting this new social order, the government chose to undermine that system which, more than any other, was responsible for the people's beliefs. It set up a program called Demo-A, which would have as its joint goal the complete eradication of the martial arts infrastructure and the establishment in its place of a gruesome spectacle known as "Arena." Demo-A agents were instructed to work their way into positions of power and authority within the martial arts hierarchy, placing themselves in a position to take over when key individuals were "removed."

As it turned out, the instrument of Sten Johnson's destruction was a cunning female agent. Ordered to take the karate champion as her lover, she did exactly that, gradually gaining his trust until he was receptive to her every suggestion. One suggestion involved drugs. Though hesitant at first to introduce foreign substances into his body, Sten was eventually persuaded to take small quantities of sodac plus, and as the female agent's influence grew and the quantities of sodac became larger, Sten's dependency finally became total. The karate champion was turned into a juicy lollipop to be suckered by the government and its fighting agents.

Unaware that this new dependency had left him grossly unprepared for combat, Sten accepted a challenge to fight from none other than Mantis himself, who was working at the time as an agent for Demo-A. Posing as a T'ai Chi boxer, Mantis completely overwhelmed the karate champ, knocking him unconscious before a large Coliseum audience. As the saying goes, the bigger they are, the harder they fall. . . . Sten's defeat turned him into the most lamentable of derelicts: the athlete gone sour. Within months his school was closed and his students gone, leaving him with only one consolation: an awareness of the true nature of things. For as Sten sat back and watched Demo-A slowly usher Sport Arena onto the scene, he realized that he had been duped, not defeated. True, he was at least partially responsible for the whole disgrace, but he also saw that he had been the victim of a system that cared as much for the sanctity of human life as a mindless child cares for the insects he crushes under his feet. Though he had yet to recover his former strength, Sten made it his business to seek revenge, not just for himself but for the people.

Sten's first step was to attach himself to the minor league string of managers that controlled the Arena's schedule of fights and dives. This string of small-time bosses had been designated by the government "U-2," and it was U-2's business to monitor and handle the flow of contestants from the beginning stages up to the most advanced level of competition. (At that stage the U-1 string took over.) U-2 was, in effect, the filter through which undesirable Untouchables with revolutionary attitudes were swiftly strained— sometimes through bribery, sometimes through drug payoffs, sometimes through murder. It was U-2's task to make sure that U-1 was not handed any stars who would make bold declarations to the media. With the war games demanding more and more recruits every day, the old enjoinders against "rocking the boat" or "upsetting the status quo" applied more than ever.

Sten's long-range plan was to enter U-2's influential circles, learn what he could, work his way through the minor leagues up to Level One, then swiftly dispose of Mantis and declare freedom for the people. Naively, he never realized that in attaching himself to the office of Abe Goldman, U-2's head honcho for the New York area, he had lowered himself to the status of a punch-drunk boxer who fills and empties ringside pails.

Given a job as a delivery boy, Sten shuttled from one smoke-filled office to the next, carrying with him drugs that were to be used by the promoters as negotiating gifts. It was a disgusting world that he had been drawn into. And yet, it had at least one compensation. While Sten's boss, Abe Goldman, was one of the most ruthless and powerful of the U-2 chieftains, he was also noted for the personal attention he gave his staff. It was Abe's distinct policy to make his employees aware at the outset of the general nature of the business they were entering, after which time they could choose either to leave or stay. If they stayed it was with the understanding that their personal lives were no longer their own.

"If you screw up, I get blamed for it," Abe repeatedly reminded his staff. "So don't dare screw up."

Abe had known of Sten before his fall, and felt some sympathy for the situation in which the ex-champ found himself—perhaps there was something inside the old promoter that longed to see the *karateka* fully healed and back in the ring. Not one to indulge in drugs himself, or be fooled by anyone, Abe personified the image of the tough Jewish gangster. Short, stout, wielding a fat cigar, he had gotten his start as a gunman during the great coke Wars of the late nineties, serving some time in the slammer for his misdeeds. After making parole, the tough little spitfire began to branch out on his own, becoming in time an influential drug trafficker. It was years later that Abe helped set up the U-2 system.

Although never a yes man, Abe always knew where to draw the line concerning his own ambitions and his position within the general scheme of things. It was likely that his early years in the pen made him hesitant to work his way into the U-1 string and its close connection with the government. In any case, Abe chose to remain a kingpin within the second string, eventually hiring Sten without the slightest inkling that the ex-champ harbored dreams of revolutionary glory. Such dreams were anathema to Abe. He could not afford them, either personally or financially, and it was for this reason that he summoned Sten into his office one afternoon after learning from his lieutenant, Charlie, that Sten had been tampering with U-2's computer files. Sten was inquiring into the whereabouts of Mantis's new penthouse in Manhattan, Charlie had reported, and that spelled trouble.

Abe swung around in his seat and aimed his cigar at Sten as the huge warrior entered the doorway, his image filling all four corners.

"I want to talk with you," he said.

Sten pulled out a pack of gum and started to chew. It was the *karateka*'s habit, when nervous, to chew gum and look down at the floor.

"Yeah?"

"I just heard somethin' about you snoopin'."

"Snoopin' where?" Sten asked.

"Through files," Abe said calmly. "Charlie came in this mornin' and found the computers warm."

"Yeah, so—?"

"So things had been messed around with. If you play with the computer, it tattles."

"I didn't play with nothin'," Sten said. "I don't even know how to turn it on."

"That's a lie," Abe said, rising from his seat. "I caught you once, watchin' us program the machine. A kid could turn this on."

"Yeah, well, I ain't no kid and I didn't turn nothin' on."

Abe lit his cigar again and sat down. There was a pause. "Why do you want Mantis's address?"

Sten shifted uncomfortably.

"Why do you want it?"

"Who says I do?"

"You do, I can see it—in your face. Besides, the computer ratted on you. This machine here freezes the info you want and then takes a face-print. Here, take a look."

Abe hurled a face-print of Sten across his desk. The *karateka* said nothing.

"Goof off on me is one thing—lie to me is another. I could fire you for this."

"So... fire me."

Sten sat down and began to crack his knuckles. Abe shook his head and leaned back in his chair. "What's up with you, kid? Why'd you want that address?"

"I wanted the address, I got the address."

"Yeah, but why?"

"Because... I'm gonna go meet him."

"What for, to shake his hand?"

"No...to challenge him."

"Great. Great news," Abe said. "Challenge him to do what, play poker?"

"No...to fight."

"Fight? What're you—crazy?"

Sten got up from the chair. "Abe, I used to be the best."

"*Used* to be," Abe said.

"And whether I'm outta shape or not doesn't matter. All I need is some good trainin' and I could take him on. I could fight."

"Sure, sure you could fight—sure you could take him on." Abe rose from his chair and began to fiddle with the dials on his desk. He watched as the blinds to his office slowly began to angle, partially blocking the sunlight. Abe had a thing about sunlight. He turned to Sten and grinned. "And after you took him on, he'd kill you, plain and simple."

"You don't know that," Sten said.

"I *do* know that," Abe said, biting angrily into his cigar. "You were a karate champ, you fought with gloves and by the rules. In the Arena—you're down, you're dead. Real simple. Your neck is in the hands of the mob. If they want to twist it, all they gotta do is lower their thumbs."

Sten slumped moodily into his chair as Abe leaned back and took another puff on his cigar.

"Look, why would a decent guy like you want to get hooked up with the Arena? Tell me that."

For the first time since the discussion began, Sten seemed amused.

"Decent? Me decent? Don't put me on. I'm a delivery boy for your shit. Don't ever call me decent."

"You're decent in here," Abe said, pointing to his heart. "I always kinda hoped, with the right encouraging, that you could beat your drug habit, put your life back together."

"I want to fight for the people."

"You want to fight for the people, you're gonna lose your head. This ring here, it's for animals like Mantis and this nut from

France that's comin' to challenge him. Ease off, kid, this ain't your game."

"I could make it my game," Sten said.

Abe rose from his seat again, his face beet-red. "What—I gotta beat it into you? Look, this game here, this game runs on blood. Muscle, skill—it all means nothin' in the end. The Death Ring has one rule: go for the kill."

"I could do it—"

"Face facts, for your own good. You ain't a killer. Be thankful for that."

"I could learn."

"Killing ain't somethin' you learn, it's somethin' that's in you. So stay away from it."

"But I—"

"Don't argue with me," the tough little gangster said. Abe got up and walked around his desk. He looked at the blinds. Still too much sunlight. He adjusted the dials again, then looked back at Sten, thinking....

Back in the old days, when Abe was a hit man for the coke tribes, he had never much liked taking contracts. But the nature of the job suited his general conditioning: no questions asked, everything business, strictly impersonal. It was conditioning Sten didn't have. Guys like him were soft at heart, had emotions, got personally involved—the last place they belonged was in the Arena. At its best, the Arena supported killers who did a job, who were not caught up in personal emotions. You win, you make money; you lose, you die. You don't fight for the people. The Death Ring was never staged to be a political platform. It *never* could be one, because the people who watched the matches, who lusted for blood, were not interested in hearing speeches. This thing with Sten had to be nipped in the bud now. The last thing Abe needed was a guy like Sten making waves, getting in front of the media. He aimed his cigar at the *karateka*.

"I want you to make me a promise."

"Promise?" Sten said. "What kind of promise?"

"To stay away from Mantis. I know you got his address. Stay

clear of it. If I give you an I.D. permit, I don't want you causin' no trouble in Manhattan. You do your work, you come home. You behave yourself. I want you to make me that promise. You make me that promise or you're through, you're fired."

Sten smirked. "You threatenin' me?"

"Yeah, kind of, call it that. Put it this way. I'm guidin' you the hard way, for your own good."

There was a long pause, Sten looked down at his biceps, then up at Abe.

"So what do you want me to do today?"

"I didn't hear you promise."

"What, I gotta kiss your feet? Ain't I got some pride left?" Sten flushed.

Abe settled back in his chair, feeling an unfamiliar twinge of sympathy. He wondered how he, a killer in his own right, could feel for Sten the way he did. He must be getting old.

"You gotta drop somethin' off in Manhattan. It's waiting for you on Charlie's desk, with an I.D."

Sten rose from his seat and turned to go.

"Forget the past, kid. Forget Mantis. And I'll tell you one thing more and then we'll forget all this. You mess with that guy, you're gonna be cruisin' a one-way ticket to heaven. Got it?"

Sten grinned. "Yeah, sure. I got it." Once more his image filled all four corners as he passed through the doorway.

"That's just what I was afraid of," Abe said aloud, as he adjusted his blinds once again.

No more sunlight.

CHAPTER THREE

STATE crematoriums had been erected to handle the growing number of dead Untouchables. Funeral rites were left up to the individual's family, after which the bodies were picked up by state vehicles and officially disposed of. In time, as the death rate increased and things grew more complicated, the S.C.s began to move about on wheels. Bodies were then disposed of on the spot, and tombstones or markers were replaced by an official ledger, which simply recorded the death and the name of the deceased.

So it was with the funeral of José Arguayo, Spec 5, U.S. Airborne. Placed on the finest blanket the family could find, José's body was surrounded by candles and portraits of Lord Christ and the Holy Mother. Señor Arguayo had run off many years before, and now young Bimbi found himself the only male figure present, clutching his sobbing mother and sisters as other relatives prayed nearby and two army officers examined the body.

"We don't need you here," Bimbi told the uniformed men.

"Just routine," one of the officers said politely. "Making sure this was our man."

"You could have checked him outside, when the truck came," a relative said.

"You better go, *cabrones*," Bimbi said.

The two officers completed their paperwork, matched José's fingerprints against the prints they had on file, then politely saluted the soldier's family. As they exited, the chanting and prayers resumed.

Bimbi sat for the longest time, numb to the sobbing and the prayers and the flickering candles. He knew his brother was going to be wheeled out soon, to be disposed of as his other brother had been years before—like fodder. It filled him with a sense of rage. Everything out there was like a big mouth ready to eat you; the only way you could stay alive, it seemed, was to fight. Fight and kill. If you didn't kill you didn't survive.

The wailing and prayers continued, the candles danced on the cracked walls....

But the Arena...the Arena and the army were there to help you, weren't they? The Arena and the army were a way of fighting out of the trap. So what did José mean?

At least you counted for something in the Arena and in the army. Sure, they wanted you to fight, but you had to fight anyway just to survive. Why not use the Arena and the army as a way of striking back? A way of staying out of the jaws of the monster and its killers?

Its killers...some of them were coming to get José—his body, at least. He would show them. He would show the whole stinking world. The world that wanted to eat him, the world that he was angry at, confused at, filled with hatred for...because it wanted to eat him....

"I'll eat *you!*" he shouted.

Bimbi stormed out of the apartment, smashing the door behind him. Outside, on the darkly lit street where he had been raised, he kicked over a trash can.

"Hey," someone yelled.

Bimbi yelled back. "Fuck you."

He kicked the can again just to let everybody know he meant business, then flinched as he spotted the crematory wagon rounding the corner. People—mostly kids—began to follow it; it was always entertaining to watch the "ashmen" collect and then dispose of the dead bodies in their infamous "smoke trucks."

"Assholes..."

Bimbi knew what was about to happen. He could already see his mother wailing and clutching at the blanket-covered body, and the ashmen heartlessly prodding her for the signature that would give them permission to burn José's remains then and there. He could see it: the filthy frigging ashmen with their masks, prodding her, demanding that she sign.

As the truck rolled nearer, something in Bimbi snapped. Perhaps it was the accumulation of all those drugs, perhaps it was a sense of moral decency that had finally demanded an outlet after so many years, but as he saw the ashmen pull up in front of the tenement and don their masks, Bimbi grabbed hold of a trash can and hurled it at the smoke truck.

"Yo!"

As the can bounced off the front grille, one of the ashmen cried out and shook his fist. Bimbi responded by picking up the trash can lid and hurling it like a frisbee. It struck the truck's windshield and shattered it.

"Dirty bastard."

"I'm cut, shit—!"

"This is C.W. 5 here, mayday—we got a nut on our hands, Cooper and Fourth. Repeat: *mayday!*"

The two ashmen scrambled from the truck, one holding his cut face, the other drawing out his mace gun. He fired the gun at Bimbi and the spray hit him in the chest. Bimbi began coughing madly, then crashed into several trash cans and fell on the pavement, choking, gasping for air. The ashman with the mace gun approached him.

"You sonuvabitch punk," he shouted. "Wanna choke some more?"

But before the ashman could fire, he was hit by a brick hurled by one of Bimbi's neighbors.

"Christ!"

The ashman fell to his knees and his mace gun clattered across the pavement. Another local kicked it away. Sirens could be heard in the distance.

"Bimbi—run!"

"Run, Bimbi—run!"

The sirens were closer now. Bimbi staggered to his feet, saw the writhing ashman before him, then caught sight of an approaching patrol car.

"Run, Bimbi—run."

Though still dazed, Bimbi quickly made his way through the maze of back alleys, zig-zagging in and out so as to escape the squads of police who followed. The drugs he had recently taken clouded his brain. He began to imagine lines of patrolmen on every street, and at the head of each line there were blood-hounds—robot bloodhounds, their barks sounding like sirens. He was still running, pursued, through streets he had never seen, when he came to a *bodega*. In the window, resting on all the groceries, was a brightly colored portrait of the Holy Mother. It made him think of his own mother. Where was she now? Was she back at the house worrying about him, thinking he had been arrested? The thought urged him on.

Bimbi continued to run, sensing after a time that José was with him. He was an angel now—an angel in uniform, *el uniform del Padre*.

"*Pues, me voy, hermano mio—al cielo!*" José the angel seemed to say. "*Recuerde el signo...*"

The sign...José's card with invisible signs. Bimbi began to remember. The card...

He had been running for some time now. He stopped.

Gathering his breath, he looked about. He recognized the area. It was the Slope. He was sweating, confused. He reached in his pocket and pulled out José's credeer card—the card he had never stopped carrying since the night José was killed, the card the police officers had asked him about when they searched him. Why?

Exhausted, he leaned back and scanned the opposite street.

There was an arcade.

There was neon.

He was having a sodac lapse and he needed cathode, neon. Needed to focus. He crossed the street and went in.

Inside the arcade it was all a blur, but the machines were on and you could focus once you stuck your head inside them. It was crowded. Bimbi began to panic. He needed a machine. There *had* to be one empty. It was all a blur and then... he found one.

He stuck his head in and inserted the credeer card.

Everything was clear now. He was in the jungle, but it was all clear. He could see Cubans, and then he saw the Uzi-9. He was armed, ready for them—a commando, yes. The Cubans were after him. They were spreading out and surrounding. Moving in for the kill. There was one now. Bimbi's hands reached for the trigger. He fired. The Cuban went flying back, blood everywhere. Bimbi's position was known. He ran, trying to escape. There were more Cubans. They were approaching and...

Everything went blank.

Confused, Bimbi frantically turned the dials. There was more darkness, then suddenly the screen flashed the following message:

"Credeer card, Code Militex 2001 2ac, hereby is terminated and no longer valid."

The screen went blank again and the machine spit out the card. Confused, Bimbi inserted it once again. And again there was darkness and then the same message:

"Credeer card, Code Militex 2001 2ac, hereby is terminated and no longer valid."

Once again the card was returned. Bimbi pulled his head out.

Things were not as blurred as before. There were definition and borders to the arcade now. He looked at the card angrily.

"Permisso..."

People wanted to pass. As Bimbi moved forward, the card in

his hand passed under some neon and he spotted the three strange symbols:

```
---- o ---- o
---- o ---- +
```

Looking at the symbols, he began to grow dizzy, feel sick. He quickly made his way outside, onto the street.

"First alleyway, south," he remembered his brother saying. "There'll be a sign there with the same symbols on it."

Bimbi started to walk.

The alley José had referred to was cornered on one side by an old abandoned warehouse, on the other by a string of dilapidated old brownstones, long past their prime. Some of the buildings had been gutted, others had been bricked up. But there was one that had a sign in front of it, suspended by chains on a pole, like in the old picture books Bimbi had seen. It read:

```
---- o ---- o
---- o ---- +
```

Bimbi approached the old brownstone slowly, the credeer card tight in his hand. He stared at the sign. For the longest time his mind seemed to hover in a trance. He had the strangest feeling that he was home.

But, no—that was too easy. Bimbi was not used to feeling things easily. Life was a struggle. It was a fight. He had never had a teacher before. What reason was there to think that he could just walk into some place and find one now?

"Fight-guru, my ass," he muttered, looking at the sign.

He had the shakes now, but he felt wild, strong—capable of ripping everything and everyone apart. He looked at the sign again.

Then he picked up an empty bottle that was nearby. It was

made of Duraplast, nice and hard. Once again he looked at the sign.

"Fight-guru, huh? We'll see..."

Bimbi hurled the bottle at the sign. There was a large thud. Once, twice... three times more Bimbi hurled the bottle at the sign and each time there was a larger thud. He picked up the bottle for the fifth time and held it in his grasp.

"I don't believe in nothing!" Bimbi shouted, and again he hurled the bottle at the sign.

"Nothing! I don't believe in nothing! *Nothing!*"

Bimbi stumbled back then, exhausted, and fell to his knees. He had said his piece.

CHAPTER FOUR

ONLY ten seconds before Bimbi first struck the strange sign with his plastic bottle, Capitan Alzerras had rolled over onto his back, luxuriating in the first deep sleep of the day after a night spent tossing and turning. He had been, for reasons he could not explain, consumed by images of the Arena. It was odd, because Capitan was very much an opponent of the sport, an "old-timer" nearing his forties who had devoted the early years of his life to the martial arts and then seen them trampled by the government. The images of the Arena were very strong, however. Capitan saw himself in the pit of a vast coliseum, fighting for his life.

For a long time the images would not leave. And when they did leave, he was kept awake by the stirrings of his latest sweetheart, Carmen, a lady ten years his junior. It was hours before Capitan finally began descending into that great realm of consciousness called sleep—and then a large thud invaded his brain and snapped him abruptly awake. Carmen immediately began to squirm next to him.

"What the hell's that?" she said.

"Cats..." Capitan answered, attempting to roll over, and then the large thud was heard again.

"Cats..." muttered Carmen, "sounds more like a tiger."

Another thud, followed by: "Nothing! Nothing!"

Capitan raised his head wearily and looked up toward the heavens.

"This is highly unfair, you know, really."

Another thud. And more cries from outside. Carmen rolled over angrily.

"Who're you talkin' to?"

"Uh...my guardian angel." Capitan wiped the sleep from his eyes as Carmen bounced up, her ample breasts shaking.

"I'm gonna go out and kill whoever's there."

"Calm down....I didn't teach you to think that way," Capitan said. Another thud was heard. Capitan winced and grabbed his head. "Bastard."

Carmen poked him. "Either you go out, or I go—"

"Enough," Capitan said. He hit the lights.

They were in a loft in a giant studio area that had been converted into a martial arts academy. Capitan began to descend the ladder of the loft, attempting, rather clumsily, to put on his yoga pants en route. He felt as though he were suffering from insomnia, or just plain lack of sleep, or something. All these violent images coming to mind now—what was the reason for them?

Thud!

"Jesus!"

Capitan went to the door and stared through the peephole. He saw an Hispanic kid on his knees, apparently sobbing.

Carmen leaned over the edge of the loft. "Well...what is it?"

"Uh...cats." Abruptly, Capitan opened the door.

Bimbi swiveled around and spotted Capitan, standing barechested in the doorway. There was a long pause as the two summed each other up. Bimbi rose to his feet, approached Capitan, and pointed a finger at him, saying with a high degree of flair and intelligence:

"You asshole."

His great diplomacy announced, Bimbi turned and proceeded to kick over some garbage pails, lined rather conveniently, Capitan thought, along the side of the abandoned warehouse. Capitan watched stoically as Bimbi smashed one can after the other with a series of very talented roundhouse kicks. After he was finished, he again approached Capitan.

"Come on, you want to fight?" Bimbi asked. "I'll kick your face in."

"Well, I certainly don't doubt that," Capitan said, "so let's call it a day."

Confused, Bimbi began a new set of antics. The young Hispanic pranced around the alleyway, doing kung fu kata, imitating Chinese lions and tigers and birds. Capitan stood there calmly, shaking his head.

"Look," Capitan said finally, "I kind of have a dislocated shoulder, and I'd like to get some sleep—"

Bimbi began screaming loud, shrill, militant war cries.

"Okay," Capitan said. "Let's talk."

Bimbi struck a wild combat pose.

"This," he said, "is talk."

Capitan nodded, resigned finally to the whole affair. Barefoot and bare-chested and dressed only in his yoga pants, he stepped out into the night air, motioning the strange young Hispanic forward. Bimbi smiled, thumbing his nose imperiously, and then struck quickly with his foot. Capitan entered like lightning, jacking Bimbi's leg up before it could make target. He pulled gently, and Bimbi crashed in a lump upon his own head.

"Ow..."

"Had enough..?"

Bimbi rose, stunned. He shook his head and began to circle Capitan as the senior warrior stood calmly and waited for his junior partner to strike. This time Bimbi charged with his fists. Capitan quickly sidestepped him and shoved him into the garbage cans. Carmen appeared at the door, ready for combat. Capitan turned to her and grinned. "Just like old times, huh?"

Bimbi quickly charged again, but Capitan once more side-stepped him and redirected his attack—toward Carmen. Carmen quickly side-stepped herself, sending Bimbi spinning—back to Capitan. Bimbi had never seen this before. It was as if he were trapped in a maze, a web. Confused, Bimbi lashed out again with his fist. Capitan responded with a swift shot in the guts.

"Sorry," Capitan said.

Bimbi staggered forward, then fell to his knees.

The fight was over. Capitan turned to Carmen. "Kind of like when *you* first came to me," he said with a smile.

Not amused, Carmen shoved her lover aside and walked over to Bimbi. He looked up, a dazed grin slowly crossing his face.

"Who the hell do you think you are?" Carmen asked.

"Man..." Bimbi muttered, "I'm damaged."

Capitan came over and stood beside his woman. Bimbi rubbed his sore gut. "I don't know *who* I am," he said. "My stomach hurts."

"It'll feel better in a minute," Capitan said.

Bimbi forced a smile. "Hey, bro, you think you could teach me that stuff?"

"He doesn't teach punks," Carmen said.

Bimbi's face flushed, his eyes growing watery. "I ain't no punk," he told her. "I was sent here."

Capitan studied the boy for a few moments. All in all, it had turned out to be a strange night. Very strange. But his heart was moved as he watched the young Hispanic try to hold back the tears.

A sudden wind picked up, whipping down the alley and prodding the half naked warrior back to his senses. He offered Bimbi his hand.

"My boy," Capitan said, "you were sent to *me*."

"I was?"

"He was?" Carmen asked.

"Oh, yes," Capitan said. "Sent to me, and God-given." He laughed as he brought the young man to his feet. "I don't know how I know this, but you were sent to me, God-given."

Capitan wrapped his muscular arms around his new protégé and gave him a hearty embrace. Bimbi, despite himself, burst into tears.

Carmen looked on, ruefully.

CHAPTER FIVE

STEN walked up and looked at the sign. He hated that sign.

**Brooklyn Heights Station
Transit Express, Manhattan Island
all passengers please have working permits
or security I.D.'s ready at inspection gate**

Sten spat. Then he made sure that the belt he had fastened to his trenchcoat was secure and as tight as possible. As he descended into the subway station, he could see U.S. Transit Police at the inspection gate up ahead, checking people as they passed through the turnstiles. There was a long line. The transit police were keen on lines—especially here, in the New York area, with all its ghettoes. They took particular pleasure in telling people when and where they could travel.

They were punks, these cops, Sten thought. Nothing more than serfs armed with guns, yeah...

The line began to move along at a steady pace. Sten counted how many officers there were.

Five.

"Please have working permit or security I.D. ready," one officer announced over a loudspeaker. "This is the gate for the express line into Manhattan."

Dumbo, Sten thought. Of course it's the express into Manhattan. If it was a train to Brooklyn or Queens, then there wouldn't be any need for a permit; there wouldn't be any transit police. These goons were always on the state-sponsored lines; they were put there to guard all the vital routes into the affluent areas.

One of the officers caught sight of Sten and looked him over. The *karateka* was next on line. He withdrew his I.D., then quickly made sure that his trenchcoat was nice and snug. During morning rush hour the chances of his being searched were slim. As for everything else, it had all been arranged. Sten had phoned the offices of three different media masters, giving them Mantis's address and the exact time that he intended to arrive and issue a challenge. A challenge in front of cameras, Sten knew, would be difficult to ignore, even for someone as powerful as Mantis. It was, in fact, the same tactic Mantis had used on Tanaka, the former champion. Yes, he was going to use Mantis's tactics and, if need be, he thought, tugging at his trenchcoat, *Tanaka's weapons.* He arrived at the inspection gate.

"I.D. or working permit."

Sten handed the first officer his I.D. As he looked it over a second transit official, the one who had momentarily stared at Sten, began to look warily at the *karateka*'s trenchcoat. He motioned to the first officer, signaling something with his thumb. The first officer handed the I.D. back to Sten.

"That's all set," he said. He pointed at Sten's coat. "You got something inside there, pal?"

"No," Sten said, "should I?"

"We're gonna have to take a look."

The second officer stepped forward, followed by the other official. But before either could lay a hand on Sten, the *karateka* exploded with a powerful punch that landed in the second officer's ribs, cracking them loudly. He fell back against his companion, who was lifted off his feet.

Sten quickly jumped over the railing as three other officers began to draw their guns. A whistle went off and Sten began to run and duck, zig-zagging through the maze of people.

"Get him."

Another alarm. The three officers continued to pursue but soon found themselves in alien territory, closed in. They were in the heart of a mob consisting of serfs and Untouchables.

"This ain't cool," one said.

"Right," a member of the crowd added. "So get your asses back to the inspection gate."

The three officers began to back up, their guns ready. No fugitive was worth this sort of trouble.

"Wire Manhattan," the chief officer said. "Tell 'em to be on the lookout for a big dude, blond, Caucasian, wearing a trenchcoat. Tell 'em to watch out, I think he's armed."

The chief officer looked out over the crowd again.

"Damn, I know he's in there somewhere...."

By this time Sten had made his way to the central platform. The express had already arrived and people had begun to board. Sten found a seat quickly and began to catch his breath. He looked inside his trenchcoat. Two pairs of nunchakas—the finest Sten owned—were tucked securely within. He heard a voice over the loudspeaker system:

"Your attention. There is a fugitive aboard this train. We repeat: There is a fugitive aboard this train. He has just assaulted and injured two officers of the United States Transit Police...."

On the train, the announcement was greeted by a round of applause. Sten laughed. It was just like the old days, and he was dripping with sweat.

"This is a federal offense. This man is aboard your train. Please help and cooperate. The fugitive is Caucasian, blond, very well built, over six

feet and wearing a trenchcoat. Proceed with caution. He is probably armed.
Transit police will be waiting in Manhattan to help, should you be able
to identify him. . . ."

There was more laughter in the car as the train started to move;
then applause. Everyone looked over at Sten. They knew it was
him. As the loudspeaker again started to bellow, a member of the
Zed Advesta cult stood up and removed a sawed-off shotgun from
his long winter robe. The Zed Advesta was a black mystic cult,
based in part on the old Zoroastrian faith, and its members wor-
shiped fire. This man appeared to be one of their warrior priests.

"All defenders of freedom shall be saluted."

He aimed his weapon at the loudspeaker and fired. It exploded
instantly, spewing sparks and fragments onto the passengers. As
the people cringed in terror, the fire priest abruptly backed off.
He approached Sten and motioned for him to follow.

"Trust me," the fire priest said.

"Why . . . ?"

"Because I am one crazy God-fearin' nigger who could blow
you in half, right this here and now."

The fire priest lowered his sawed-off shotgun and motioned
for Sten to move into the next car. Sten complied. As they entered
the next car they could hear the loudspeaker once again. The fire
priest approached the speaker box and raised his weapon.

"Shit . . . !" someone yelled, and the passengers began to duck.
The priest fired again, shattering the speaker and sending sparks
jumping all over the car. As the people fled hurriedly into the
other cars, the fire priest laughed heartily and held out his arms
in worship. There was smoke everywhere.

"God save us!" someone wailed.

"God will save you. Just worship his fire."

Choking, Sten staggered back and tried to make sense of what
was happening. That crazy Zed A had just shot off another round,
Sten thought. He looked at the weapon. Remington 701, four
barrels—and the last two he's saved for me.

"We're alone now," the strange man said. He lowered his shotgun and pointed a finger at Sten. "Say, baby—tell me. Is you a sacrifice?"

"A sacrifice?"

"No, no—a sacrifice you ain't." The priest seemed lost in thought.

"What do you want with me?" Sten asked.

"What do the demons want with you?" the priest replied.

"Demons?"

"The cops, baby. The 'Armored Men.' They want you, and there ain't no way you gonna be able to slide your way into Manhattan."

"I'll manage it."

"No way, baby. Right now they're callin' up an army, just for you. They're gonna be waiting right by Grand Central. You did some poor plannin', my man, by takin' on the officers that way, 'less you was prepared to go—I mean to 'sacrifice.'"

"What the hell you mean by sacrifice?" Sten asked.

The fire priest smiled and reloaded his shotgun. "Oh, my man, sacrifice is the thing, don't you see? For the Fire Chief it's the supreme act."

"What—who's that?"

"Never you mind, baby. I'm just talkin' about the Lord. I'm one of his servants."

You're fuckin' nuts, Sten thought.

"And... despite what you're thinking," the fire priest said, "I ain't nuts. I wasn't born to be sacrificed on this planet at the sweet age of thirty-five and to be nuts at the same time, no, no how...."

A strange wave of anxiety shot through Sten, settling finally in the pit of his stomach. He was standing face to face with the Angel of Death and, somehow, he knew he had to get away. Sten began to back off, cautiously unbuttoning his trenchcoat.

One good shot with the nunchakas, he thought, and I can disarm him.

"Saaaay—hold your hand there, baby," the priest said. "Keep it nice and low. I got no reason to kill you."

"That's all I wanted to hear."

"What you got in there?" the fire priest asked, running his free hand along the outside of Sten's coat. "Ah, sticks...?"

"Nunchaks."

"What for?"

"To fight someone."

"Ain't gonna work against the Armored Man. You know that."

"It's a private fight."

The fire priest laughed. There was a sensation of pressure. The train was passing out of the tunnel that ran through the East River. Sten's ears began to pop.

"In no time we're gonna be in Manhattan, the central domino of the Shaitan," the priest said.

"Who—"

"The Devil, baby. The Evil One. Now you listen here—you listen good, my big, baby white boy. My council elected, last night, that I be sacrificed. That means I die, I go—but fightin' the Armored Man. I was plannin' on doin' it Central Park style, but your situation has altered the scene. I want to help you, 'cause I got the feelin', the divine premonition, that *you* are the people, that you got a good score to settle, I mean—with the Armored Man."

"So..."

"So I want you to listen, because I'm sacrificin' out in Grand Central—to help you." The priest looked about, then shifted his gaze back to Sten. "But before I give the directions, understand this good: sacrificin' ain't easy. Talking is one thing, doing is another. When the real moment comes, life and death are the same. We're born dying, we die living, so when the great moment comes to shake the Fire Chief's hand, don't worry about what's around, do and go where you have to. Sacrifice, my man—some of us gotta do it so's that others can learn how to play the game the easy way. Sad fact, too, but that's the way the Fire Chief lays the plans."

There was a sudden burst of light.

The transit express had ascended onto its monorail track above Wall Street, heading nonstop for Grand Central. The fire priest motioned for Sten to move back.

"I'm headin' up to the front cars, you go to the rear. Wait to get off. You'll hear shootin'...when you do, wait some more. Then move out toward the Shuttle. You should be safe then."

The fire priest began to back away. Sten suddenly felt empty inside. He wondered if he should ask him to stay, to speak more. The fire priest smiled, as if he knew all this.

"I'll be meetin' you again, my man, but, next time—in the Sun."

So saying, he tucked his sawed-off Remington into a holster under his robe, bowed to the puzzled *karateka*, then backed away, smiling. Without another word, he exited into the next car.

Sten suddenly found himself doing the same—only, as the fire priest advised, in the opposite direction. As he entered the next car, people began to point him out—not as the former rebel wanted over the loudspeaker system, but rather as a hostage just released.

"Look," Sten could hear. "He's alive!"

"Are you all right?"

"Who is he?"

"Is he crazy?"

"He didn't shoot you or nothin'...?"

Sten felt people touching him, as if he were a person who had just returned from the dead. He continued into the next car, then the next.

The transit continued on its monorail course through the heart of lower Manhattan, shifting eastward after Chelsea toward its one and only stop: Grand Central Station. It was a clear day, and from their elevated position the passengers could get an impressive view of the Hudson on one side, the East River on the other. Because the train's large glass windows refracted the sun like a magnifying glass, Sten found himself sweating unbearably as he finally came to rest in the last car. People began to look at him strangely. He hoped no one would recognize him. After a moment or so he began to listen to the loudspeaker.

"Black male, thirties, dressed in an African robe, armed with shotgun and very dangerous..."

Sten couldn't believe everything that had just happened. The official voice continued:

"Will all passengers please have their I.D. or working permits ready

when the transit pulls into Grand Central. Please cooperate. Officers of the United States Transit Police will be lining the main platform for your security. They will be heavily armed. This is an emergency. Please stay in the train. Do not make any unnecessary movements or gestures. There are two dangerous men aboard this train...."

Great, Sten said to himself. Just great.

"We repeat this message. This is an emergency. Please be on the lookout for two men aboard this train: a large Caucasian, very tall, wearing a trenchcoat; and a black man wearing an African robe. The black man is heavily armed and both men are dangerous. Please try and stand clear of the cars they are in. We repeat, this..."

The system suddenly went dead. There were muffled shouts from the cars up ahead. Sten realized that it was probably the crazy fire priest assaulting the deputy conductor. The train only had two conductors. The transits were all computerized anyway, and the police never rode them between stations for fear of their lives.

Sten watched as the passengers in the last car began to move back. They had recognized him.

"Hey, look," Sten said, "I'm with you...."

"Don't hurt us," an old Hispanic lady said.

"No, don't you see, mama, I'm with you."

Suddenly they heard over the system:

"This is Elijah the shah speakin' to you and this here's now the people's radio station. Ain't no one gonna get hurt. Jes' the Armored Man and me, that's all. We's gonna be doin' a little sacrifice, that's all. So if y'all could oblige me, everyone start workin' their way toward the rear cars. Jes' gonna be a little noise and some smoke. That's all. Jes' move on real quiet and calm, into the rear cars...."

Sten looked out the windows of the car—the windows facing east, toward Grand Central. Atop the old station there appeared the great architectural wings of the monorail depot—"Mercury's Grand Central," the builders had called it. The great concrete wings jutted up into the sky, offending the heavens and piercing the clouds.

The transit drew closer and closer, winding its serpentine path toward the station. Sten could see things clearly now up ahead.

My God.

He could see a steady stream of transit officers forming along the main platform, at least thirty of them, with dogs.... And all for one man—no, two.

Sten began to shake as he never had before. And it wasn't the drugs, he realized. No, it was the particular kind of danger he faced. This was something new, not like the ring.

Mantis...

As the first cars of the train began to rumble into the station, Sten thought of Mantis...and then there was a loud explosion followed by screams and smoke.

Elijah the fire priest shah, standing in the front car, had hurled a grenade. Immediately, the emergency brake was activated and the train came to an abrupt halt. People bounced off the sides like pinballs. The last cars stood precariously out, on the monorail still, overlooking Thirty-fourth Street below.

"Jesus."

"I'm hurt..."

Alarms sounded everywhere. The grenade had torn into the front line of officers, killing three of them and two dogs. Elijah fired off a round at close quarters, dispersing whoever remained. He ducked down and looked at the bloodied bodies of the conductor and his deputy. The deputy had pulled out a gun from the front cabin, forcing Elijah to blast him and the conductor at close range. He peeked through a shattered window and saw a phalanx of officers up ahead, in the front of the station. The train began to move slowly, monitored by the central computer in the station.

In the rear, Sten breathed a sigh of relief as he watched the train pass over Thirty-fourth Street, into the station. Shots rang out again.

"Fire into the front car," had come the orders.

The transit police had begun to open up at a distance with their

Uzi-9s, peppering the front car as it began to roll into the station. Some of the officers took up a position for a flank attack against the train's forward cars.

Elijah had retreated into the third car. He opened fire again, dispersing the advancing flank of transit officers. The train stopped again. The police began to fire tear gas into the first five cars. Suddenly, the doors were monitored to open and a grenade came flying out, bouncing off a girder. Transit officers scattered for cover but did not make it in time. Blood splattered everywhere and a leg fell.

Elijah emerged from the train, holding his shotgun in one hand and a grenade in the other. He had just pulled the pin from the grenade when bullets from the Uzi-9s cut into him. The grenade went off and Elijah's shattered body fell in bits and pieces on the platform.

Sten quickly made his way out of the train as alarms rang everywhere, great brass in a symphony of anarchy. He hustled out with the crowd, trying to remain as inconspicuous as possible. He had discarded his trenchcoat by now, and the nunchakas were secure under his baggy shirt.

Sacrifice, he thought. And what a lesson.

He looked back quickly. There was nothing but smoke—smoke and figures moving in chaos. Wiping the sweat from his brow, he continued flowing with the crowd. In a few minutes media masters began to appear, minicameras in hand, and as they did, Sten thought of the masters *he* had called. He found himself hoping that all the trouble at Grand Central wouldn't alter their course. They have to be there, at Mantis's apartment, Sten thought nervously, if my plans are going to work. They *have* to be watching. Otherwise I'm as good as dead.

The media masters *were* watching, the train station at least, and the twenty-four-hour news channels were quick to focus in on the recent bloodbath. Within minutes, images of the brutal confrontation were being broadcast throughout the area.

As the events flashed on one screen five miles away, a female leopard sat nearby, purring calmly, oblivious to the drama that was being played out before her.

"Interesting..." a strange voice whispered, and a hand reached out to stroke the passive feline. It was the hand of a man, and the man's arm was dressed in camouflage colors. As the hand continued to pet the leopard, the animal's purring increased, reaching a deep steady drone. After a moment or so the drone did not go unaccompanied, because the breathing of the man, inspired by the touch of fur, established a kind of counterpoint. It was a strange sound, the man's breath, but it was steady and the big cat felt quite comfortable with it, so comfortable that the animal began to roll over in total submission.

"Interesting," the strange voice whispered once again, "and very amusing."

CHAPTER SIX

CODE: AIKI. The name had begun to appear more and more, at first in whispers, then in loud cries from the ranks of the military—ranks that soon found themselves on the desertion list, fading into the protective sea of Untouchable communities throughout the country. "Ai" and "Ki," two simple Japanese words that meant something like "spiritual harmony." That, at least, was the best translation Central Intelligence could come up with. As for the movement itself, the authorities had few leads. Unlike so many of the other cult movements that had evolved across the nation, this group, this "Aiki," had proven to be extremely shadowy. As such, it represented the most dangerous threat to the status quo. Promising soldiers had simply walked away from their careers, and no amount of investigation could seem to bring forth either the outline of the cult or its organization.

It's only a matter of time before the infection spreads to the Arena, Abe thought as he switched off his radio and sat back in his seat. A friggin' bloodbath at New Grand Central. That crazy Zed A bunch. Just a short time and they'll be put away, the whole group. But this "Aiki," this Aiki stuff is dangerous. Abe looked down at the portfolio that had just been sent to him. Pacificism— it was like trying to sink claws into jelly when you were trying to fight it. He stopped reading the portfolio and looked up to see Charlie coming through the doorway.

"It's time," Charlie said.

"Time for the 'old sewer' to get cleaned out, right?"

"I didn't say anything."

"Good, don't."

Abe put the portfolio aside and rose from his seat. It was time for the vaporizer and then his weekly massage.

"The bones, they grow old," he told his assistant, straightening his back. "But the internal plumbing—it rots."

He left his office and headed for one of the express elevators.

Cults, cults, always cults, he thought. It's the subtle ones you gotta watch out for—like this Aiki mind cult. They're as deadly as the drugs. The Zed A. If they blow off a few cops, so what? It only turns everyone else against them, because they use violence. Violence is easy to control. It's the peace stuff that's really dangerous. This Aiki shit, damn...

A letter and portfolio had arrived not more than an hour ago from a Central Intelligence office. The letter requested any information concerning the Aiki group, and since Abe had helped break down the old martial arts organizations, he was asked to check into the backgrounds of several Aikido practitioners. Included in the portfolio was information on several "potential leading figures" of Aiki, one of whom Abe knew slightly. But so what? Why should any of this be of concern to him? Because the Arena was his baby? No. Not any more. The Arena was Mantis's baby now. For sure.

The express elevator arrived and Abe was soon speeding toward the basement complex, his mind focusing on something else that had been disturbing him: Sten.

What *about* that big blond baboon? God forbid he should be

connected with that Zed A shootout.... No, that was foolish thinking. But wait—the report said something about *two* men, one white. Abe began to turn over the possibilities in his mind. He was still lost in thought when—a half-minute later—the elevator doors opened.

Abe stepped out of the elevator into a gymnasium that occupied the basement floor of the Palisades Sports Complex. The subterranean vault featured a maze of gyms, pools, saunas, and weight rooms. Everything I need for my "weekly" clean-out, Abe thought. Except that this week my clean-out is filled with business. Filthy business. He made his way through the complex, past young giants pumping iron and rich beauties toning their precious flesh, thinking about business and the portfolio and the information it contained—information about a man who functioned as Abe's weekly biorhythm instructor and fitness consultant. Abe entered the bright-tiled vaporizer room and nodded to the other "over-the-hill" businessmen who were stripping down. The instructor had yet to arrive.

All right, where is he? Abe thought. He'd better show his face.

Just then he heard somebody clap his hands and enter the room. Abe turned.

"Greetings," Capitan said.

Yeah, Abe thought, *greetings*.

Throughout the vapor session Capitan was painfully aware that Abe was watching him, surveying him. It was a surveillance that went far beyond the demands of the normal follow-the-leader workout. As Capitan took regulated breaths and then motioned for his class to do the same, he felt the old-timer sizing him up. Capitan knew it had all been too easy, free-lancing his talents around the posh health clubs of various corporations, hooking his knowledge of anatomy and breath control into the credeer system. It was work that brought the bread home and helped him to support... "other things." Well, now it looked like "other things" might have to be put in abeyance for a while.

The old-timer nodded to him. Capitan hit the switch on his

portable control panel, watching as the hibiscus vapors began to flow into the well at a steady rate, red fumes dancing. He smiled at the class.

"Breathing time," he said.

"So we gotta do this hiba-hooba stuff?" Abe said, grunting.

"Hibiscus, Mr. Goldman," Capitan corrected. "And yes, we always do the hibiscus vapors first."

"It smells," another man said.

"Yes, it's pungent—but it fires up the system. And as for smell, gentlemen," Capitan continued, "the majority of you are so filled with internal putrification that if you were allowed to take an inner whiff of yourselves, you'd keel over."

Someone let out a resounding fart. The vapor-well echoed in response.

"Attack of the nasties..."

Everyone waited for the odor to clear. Capitan folded his arms. "You're only punishing yourselves," he sighed. "I get paid to suffer." He put his finger on the switch and began to raise the volume level, red vapors gushing in now. "Let's start with some deep breathing."

"Why?" Abe asked, his eyes dancing with mischief.

"Because I said so," Capitan said. "I'm the boss here."

Boss, indeed, he thought, noticing the old-timer's sly grin. Yes, the heat's on, in some way. But on me? Why me? Bimbi suddenly came to mind, his new guest....

"So you're gonna teach me?" Bimbi had said as Capitan brought him into the studio.

"Yeah. But how come you know I teach?" Capitan asked cautiously.

"Because my brother told me," Bimbi said. "My brother José, who's dead."

The name José wasn't familiar, which was normal. Monitor Five sent all Aiki followers to either Monitor Eight in Brooklyn, who was Capitan; to Monitor Six in Manhattan; or to Monitor Four in Queens. It was from monitors such as Capitan that followers received advanced instruction in Aiki techniques, after which they were returned to normal civilian life. The names of Aiki disciples were unimportant before they came and especially unimportant after they left. The process was a dispassionate one. For survival's sake, intimacy was not encouraged. José had no doubt already received some training and just needed guidance, but now he was dead, the unfortunate victim of a street fight.

As Capitan looked at Bimbi, he thought he could see some of José's essence passing through his kid brother. He knew, though, that Bimbi was no soldier, that he was not fuel for the movement. Rather, he was someone who needed his own personal touch as an instructor....

José, then Bimbi, and now this Goldman character, staring at me...

Capitan raised the volume on the controls, the vapors rising so fast that they turned the glass-sealed chamber into a virtual steam bath.

"You're gonna kill us..." someone joked.

"Breathe deeply, gentlemen," Capitan instructed them. "The hibiscus opens up the veins—the fun is just beginning."

There were laughs and smiles, but Abe continued to stare at Capitan, a stare that had about it a quality of amusement. Capitan continued to guide the old men through their series of breathing exercises, everyone but Abe whining and then retreating at his commands.

Capitan finally lowered the vapor intake, motioning for everyone to breathe easy. The red fumes faded as all the old-timers broke into a chorus of relaxed sighs. Then Capitan hit another switch and fresh air seeped into the vapor-well. Everyone stretched back, chests rising and falling in steady rhythm. The vapor chamber was the latest Soviet invention aimed at breaking down the body's cholesterol count. A handy tool for the older crowd, Abe thought. He felt his muscles relaxing even as his mind raced over the information he had in the portfolio.

* * *

SECT: AIKI. OTHER KNOWN ALIASES: SHINDO, SHINJITSO. PURPOSE
OF SECT: MIND NEUTRALIZATION. PACIFICATION OF "MIND WAVES."
EMERSION INTO THE "VOID."

FOUNDER: GEIDO HOSHIMA. JAPANESE NATIONAL. BUDDHIST PRIEST.
SHINTO LAYMAN. AIKIDO MASTER EIGHTH DAN GRADE. FURTHER HIS-
TORY UNAVAILABLE.

SECT OPERATIONS: WORLDWIDE. NO KNOWN CENTRAL GROUP
MEETINGS. SECT OPERATES THROUGH "MONITORS," MEN TRAINED IN
MIND NEUTRALIZATION TECHNIQUES. FURTHER INFORMATION UN-
AVAILABLE.

POLITICAL ORIENTATION: PRESENT HISTORY INCOMPLETE. INFOR-
MATION INSUFFICIENT BUT MOVEMENT BELIEVED TO BE DIRECTED
AGAINST THE MILITARY.

INVESTIGATIVE SUGGESTIONS: ALL EARLY DISCIPLES OF HOSHIMA
BELIEVED TO HAVE BEEN DRAWN FROM THE RANKS OF AIKIDO PRAC-
TITIONERS. INVESTIGATE ANY PRESENT PRACTITIONERS WITHIN RE-
GIONAL AREA.

Abe had examined the list of potential suspects in his area.
Capitan's dossier was at the top.

J. CAPITAN, U.S.A., NATIONAL. BORN CITY OF BROOKLYN 3/5/95. B.A.
COLUMBIA UNIVERSITY, PHILOSOPHY. NATIONAL JUDO CHAMPION, 18.
INSTRUCTOR AT AIKIDOKAN, 21-25. APPLIED FOR VISA TO JAPAN 2021.
RETURNED TO STATES 2022. BELIEVED TO HAVE STUDIED WITH GEIDO
HOSHIMA. NOW LIVES: SLOPE ZONE A-15, CITY OF BROOKLYN, DISTRICT
ZONE 3. PRESENT OCCUPATION; BIO-RHYTHM INSTRUCTOR. FURTHER
COMMENTS: INVESTIGATIONS CONCERNING SECT HAVE LINKED DE-
SERTERS WITH A CERTAIN "MONITOR EIGHT" IN BROOKLYN AREA. FUR-
THER INFO INCOMPLETE.

A short but impressive history. And he's smooth, Abe thought.
He could be our man.

Aikidokan, yeah...

Abe remembered the Aikidokan, the great hall out on Long

Island which had been the largest martial arts school in the country. He remembered how the Demo-A operators had been sent in, with orders to suppress its activities. They had deliberately drugged the head *sensei*, Ashi, one of the great practitioners of Aikido but a weak-willed man when it came to vice. Once the *sensei* was removed, the job of mopping up was accomplished easily by Abe's goons. But Capitan. Capitan was long gone and—according to the reports—in Japan. Smooth, Abe thought. Real smooth.

After the session was over and the glass chamber raised over the vapor-well, the masseurs entered. Abe quickly pulled Capitan aside.

"You're my man today," Abe told him.

"Oh...Well, actually, I believe I was scheduled to—"

"I rearranged the schedule," Abe said. "I'm good at that—rearranging things. I'm good with rules, regulations—and making people obey them."

Capitan nodded politely. "I see. You, well...you teach people things."

"Yeah," Abe said, "that's it. I hold class, just like you."

"Do you teach things verbally," Capitan asked, playing along, "or physically?"

"Depends upon the person," Abe replied, waiting for Capitan to prepare the massage table.

Capitan grinned. "I like the oral approach best." He motioned for Abe to climb on to the soft-cushioned table.

"Trouble is," Abe said, hopping up and then grunting, "it usually never works..."

Capitan began to rub his hands over the fleshy back of the old gangster, waiting for Goldman to make his move. When, after a few minutes, the old-timer had said nothing, Capitan settled down. He began to examine the scars on the old man's body—scars that told of a past of violence, of knife wounds and bullet holes. They were not the scars of fights in the ordinary sense, of hand to hand, cheap street punk brawling. Rather, they were the scars of attempted hits—clean hits, but hits that had just missed their mark.

Cumulatively, they told the history of a man who had nine lives. There were two knife wounds near the kidneys, and six wounds from bullets. Two had pierced the shoulder area; two more had entered the left leg; and the last two had chipped away part of Abe's left elbow. An implant concealed the missing piece of limb. Capitan stopped for a moment, slightly awed.

"What's up?"

"Nothing."

"You lookin' at my scars?"

"Can't help but notice. First time I've worked on you."

"Two hits, every part. They always missed—I mean, the right area. You know why they're two each place?"

"No," Capitan said, continuing to massage.

"The Regal automatic. Top notch—a Canadian rifle. Instead of single breech, it had a double. Best precision sniper gun ever made. It was designed for recoil; that's why they made it double breech. You shot and the second bullet went out less than half a second after the first. Only trouble was, with me, they put the gun in the hands of amateurs. They'd aim: bam! bam! But they'd always hit me in a place that'd let me get up and live. That ain't wise for a sniper."

"No," Capitan said.

"Sniper's job is to put you away. It's not hard work. Everyone knows deep down how to put people away. Some people just know better than others."

There was a long silence as Capitan massaged and waited for Abe to continue....

"Take you, for example. I bet you could snuff me out real quick with them fingers of yours and all that kung fu you know."

"Snuff you out?" Capitan said. "Why would I want to do that?"

"I don't know. Why would you want to go pull people outta the army, then brainwash 'em?"

"I wouldn't. Never thought about that."

"But then, it wouldn't be a bad idea, right?"

Capitan just laughed and continued massaging. Abe turned his head and gave another sigh of pleasure.

"Good hands," he said. "Say, tell me, you used to teach Aikido, right?"

"Uh...huh."

"You any good?"

"So so. I'm third dan rank, but that never means anything nowadays."

"You use to play judo. You were a national champ, right?"

"Yup."

There was more silence. Abe sighed again and flexed his left hand. He glanced at it, at the nails.

"I busted up my shoulder to become the champ," Capitan said. "I was never able to compete again."

"Ah, I see. So then you took up Aikido, huh?"

"Right."

"And you studied with a guy named, uh—Hoshima, right?"

"Wrong," Capitan said.

"Wrong?"

"Wrong. Hoshima is a monk. He lives in Japan."

"But you went to Japan."

"Right, and he refused to teach me," Capitan said. He dug his fingers in between Abe's shoulder blades. "Anything else you want to know?"

"Ooh—tough boy, eh?" Abe laughed. "Where'd they teach you *this* technique, Japan?"

"Right. *Shiatsu-Ho.* This is for the sinuses."

"Then why're you diggin' into my shoulders?"

"Because everything's attached."

"Ooh." Abe winced, enjoying the painful technique. "Attached—like people's breath, eh?"

"You learn fast, old-timer."

Abe let out a bizarre laugh. Then he eased into silence as Capitan continued to massage.

That's good for now, Abe thought. I'll hit next when he least expects it. But he moved—his hands—when I mentioned Hoshima. He didn't expect me to be listening to him through his hands.

Yeah, hands. Hands always tell stories.

Abe turned his head and closed his eyes. Capitan shook his head, amused. Cagey old bastard, he thought. He knows everything and he doesn't know shit.

Hoshima...

Capitan's thoughts drifted back—back to Asia, to Japan and his meeting with the man who was to be his true master. Thoughts, drifting back...

Capitan smiled and continued to massage.

He had set out in search of a Zen master in the hope that he could train his mind. He had left Tokyo and all its twenty-first-century glitter and headed for the northern wilds of Hokkaido Island. Over the years more and more monks had migrated there to escape the insanity that was spreading throughout the rest of industrial Japan. Hokkaido was cold, especially in the winter, but there was peace and several new monasteries had been established on the island. Zen Buddhism was flourishing once again—Zen, the great "Reality Sandwich of the Divine," as Capitan had once termed it. It was there on Hokkaido that a true master would appear, of that he was sure.

When he reached Hokkaido with only a backpack slung over his shoulder, Capitan decided to just wander. It was late summer, the weather was getting brisker, but the landscape was divine and he was drawn, almost mysteriously, into the interior, into the mountains, where he began to camp out. A mining crew that he met happened to tell him of an old hermit they had seen living up further in the hills. Rumor had it that he lived in a cave. Capitan decided he would investigate.

But all he succeeded in doing was getting lost. After a freezing night and a morning spent thawing out, Capitan prayed to Fate to show him the way back to more civilized terrain. En route, he happened to come across a path and decided to follow it. As he made his way along he heard scraping sounds. Picking up his pace he came across a series of stepping stones placed in "orderly disarray" as best he could describe it, amidst a sea of pebbles. Everything about the setup was orderly, distinctly man-made, and yet thoroughly in disorder, almost natural. Next, there was a series of plateaus leveled into the side of a steep hill—leading up to a cave. And the stepping stones continued, placed at various intervals through a river of pebbles. The pebbles climbed like a waterfall in reverse up to the next plateau, and Capitan found himself hopping the stones and following as if he were in the middle of a stream. Finally he reached the mouth of the cave. There was a stream of pebbles surrounding it, like a moat, with two stepping stones acting as a bridge. The "moat" ran around the course of the mountain. Capitan heard the scraping again. Rounding the "stream" he finally chanced upon the hermit.

It was a meeting that was to forever change his life. The hermit was raking the pebbles, in a universe of his own. Mesmerized, Capitan stopped and watched. The old hermit had long white hair and beard. Everything was matted. He looked up.

"Nan ja?" he asked. What?

Capitan smiled and said hesitantly, in Japanese: *"Watakshi-wa Amerikanjin des—"*

"Yes, yes. Another American," the old man said in perfect English. "Americans, Americans—everywhere. Even up here now. Why are you here?"

"Oh…" Capitan had been caught off guard by the man's fluency. "I'm here…well, to find…a monastery."

"What would you want with a monastery?" the strange man asked, turning his attention to his garden.

"I want, well…I want to train there."

"Why?"

"Why?"

"That was what *I* asked, not you," the old man said.

"Yes." Capitan smiled, growing confused.

"Well then, tell me why."

"Well, I want to train in a monastery in order to, well…why else?" Capitan asked, shrugging his shoulders. "To train my mind—to gain enlightenment."

"What is that?"

"What is what?"

"This enlightenment you're talking about."

"I don't know," Capitan smiled innocently. "If I had it, I wouldn't be here looking for it."

"What a dolt," the strange man said abruptly, and rake in hand, he started to attend to a far corner of his garden. Capitan smiled. He was not one to be riled easily.

"Well, I suppose I am."

The older gentleman spied Capitan's backpack.

"What is that there?" he asked, "On your backpack, tying your sleeping bag in place?"

"Oh, that. That's my black belt."

"You're a student of the arts and you use your belt to tie your sleeping bag in place?"

The old man's tone was firm and disciplinary, and Capitan was embarrassed. He had lost his clip and had been using the belt very casually as a replacement. He bowed apologetically.

"Excuse me. I am wrong. Please—"

"No apologies, you pig."

"Pig?" Capitan laughed. He was not going to be easily riled.

"Yes. Using your belt like some American rubber band. You're a judoka, no doubt—a judo player?"

"Oh, yes, once upon a time."

"I know that because only a judo player could be so crass as to think of his belt in that way. 'Athlete's mind,' that's what judo people have, an infection like in the foot."

Capitan laughed heartily, unable to restrain himself.

"Now what's so funny?" the old man demanded.

"Well, to be honest, uh...*you*."

"What impertinence!"

"And if you must know, I practice Aikido now, or did, and—"

"Ah," the stranger said, his rake ominously in hand, "then that explains it. Aikidoka, eh?"

"Yes."

"I should have known."

"What?"

"That you were an Aikidoist. I knew from the start that you were dangerous—"

"Dangerous?"

"Do not interrupt me," the old hermit roared. "You've come to kill me, eh?"

"Kill—"

"You don't think that I don't know that all Aikido people are assassins?" The hermit still held the rake firmly in his hand. Capitan found himself trying to reconcile the stranger's humor with his fierce tone and features. He stepped back a bit as the stranger aimed a finger at him. "Aikidoka are clean-cut Ninja, that's all. Nothing more, and nothing less. They pretend to be peaceful; they pretend to step aside. Aikidoka fight with the web. Once having drawn their opponent in, they sting them—" He suddenly lunged his rake at Capitan, who leaped aside quickly—"with a punch or a sneaky jab."

"Which is what you just did to me," Capitan said, cautiously watching as the old-timer circled him with the rake. Capitan slowly followed suit and the two of them described a poetic catlike dance around the rock garden. Capitan watched as the hermit placed his bare feet upon the large cold stones that rose like islands from the pebbly sea, his toes touching instinctively and lodging themselves firmly like the talons of a bird.

Capitan suddenly slipped on a stone.

"Look out," the hermit cried. "You'll ruin my garden!"

"What about my neck?" Capitan said, as he quickly regained his balance.

The old-timer lunged a second time but Capitan leaped out of the way, refusing to counterattack. "You've come here to assassinate, insult me—and destroy my rock garden," the old man roared. "Well, I'm not about to let you get the chance." So saying, he lunged again and again at Capitan, the young man dodging each time, turning in an instant. Finally Capitan attempted to take hold of the rake in order to calm the old man down—but the hermit swiftly withdrew the rake as quickly as he had thrust it.

Capitan was now fully aware that he was up against someone who knew all too well what he was doing. The old codger lunged at him, and using the rake as if it were a spear, forced him backward.

Suddenly, he slipped again on a rock.

"Fool!" the old-timer yelled, "you'll ruin my pebbles. Stay on the rocks."

"But you're trying to kill me," Capitan roared back.

"So what? What if I am? Don't step in the pebbles when I attack you. Stay on the rocks. If you don't stay on them, you'll drown. Pretend the pebbles are water, water, water!"

As he lunged again, Capitan tried to take hold of the rake, but to no avail. With stunning precision, the hermit placed his feet on the stones and pivoted out of the younger man's reach. Capitan moved forward but his feet slid once again on the rocks.

"I told you: don't fall in the stream, you'll drown."

"As if you care," Capitan said. He dodged another lunge of the rake but was unable once again to take hold of it. The old codger smiled.

"I do care. I want to poke you with my rake. So make sure you stay in place."

And he lunged again. Capitan darted back and laughed. "Yes, *sensei.*"

The hermit lowered his rake suddenly. Capitan had just addressed him in Japanese as "teacher."

"What did you just call me?"

"I called you *sensei.*" Capitan smiled hesitantly, giving a slight bow. "You have to be a *sensei,* or something, the way you handle that rake. It's more like you're using a spear."

"Or a staff," the hermit said. For the very first time he asked: "What is your name, where are you from?"

Capitan told him. The old hermit gave a hearty laugh and then folded his arms like a samurai of old.

"My name is Geido Hoshima."

"Hoshima himself?" Capitan declared his honor at meeting such a great Aikido master. For it was only as an Aikido master that he had been, up until that time, known to Capitan. He began to babble excitedly about how much he had heard of the great Hoshima, of his ability to almost "disappear from his foes" and—"gosh, I don't know what else to say."

Hoshima smiled.

"Do you know why I provoked you, then attacked you?" he asked.

Capitan shrugged his shoulders, unsure.

"I provoked you, first, to check your inner nature. I attacked you next, to see if you would counter or whether you would respect my age and merely try to keep me at a distance. You passed both tests well."

Capitan bowed in thanks. "People said that you were dead. Or that you disappeared." Then he asked, hesitantly: "Why did you run away?"

"For the same reason that you are here," Hoshima told him.

There was a sudden nudge.

"You through, or what?" Abe asked.

Capitan came to his senses. He threw a towel over Abe.

"All through," Capitan said.

"You started spacin' there, the last few seconds," the old gangster told him, rising. "Ah, that felt good. I'll put the payment through on your card."

"Great."

"And—"

"Yeah—?" Capitan was ready for the cat-and-mouse to resume again.

"Next week you do the same, after class."

"My pleasure."

"Your pleasure, right. But mine's greater." Abe grinned, throwing a mock punch at Capitan's chin. "'Cause I'm payin'."

Capitan waited in the massage room until Abe left. Another masseur had turned the radio on. There was yet another report about the recent shootout at New Grand Central. Capitan shook his head.

Shootouts, arenas, war games—and now this character is on to me. It's all a lesson. It's all meant to teach me something.

Somehow, Capitan had a feeling that things would get worse before they got better.

CHAPTER SEVEN

STEN exited the transit station as quickly as possible. He descended into Old Grand Central, attempting to lose himself in the waves of frightened faces. More transit police could be seen everywhere, rushing in to answer the calls of alarm.

They've forgotten me, he thought. They're putting all their attention into that shootout. They've forgotten, yeah....

He made his way out, onto the street, into Manhattan, the casino state. Here was a different world, a world of "safe" streets where "decent" people could roam unmolested. Of course, disturbances such as the one that had occurred today would crop up periodically. The Professionals who lived on the island had come to realize that the transits from surrounding ghettoes brought with them certain risks. That was why there were checkpoints at the bridges and tunnels, and why the stations themselves had such tight security. But Manhattan needed serf power to operate. That was the reality of the situation. And if it meant an occasional act of terrorism, well, that was the price that had to be paid.

How *had* the fire priest gotten past the inspection gate? Sten wondered. Armed like that? A black man wearing Afro robes? He stood out much more than I did, and yet they spotted me right from the start. Sten shook his head, thoroughly confused, and continued walking uptown.

I wasn't scared, Sten thought. I'm no coward. What sense would it have made to join that crazy Zed A and start shooting cops? That wasn't fighting for the people. And what did he mean by "sacrifice?" Getting gunned down like that was straight stupidity. And yet he did it for me. He changed his plans because he knew the cops were looking for me. Why, why?

It was all too much for the *karateka* to figure out, to even begin to understand. Distractedly, he hailed a cruise van that was going across town.

All internal transit within Manhattan was now free. That was one of the joys of the city. Residents were taxed for their fares annually; outsiders paid a fee each time they submitted their cre-deer cards at the inspection gates. Motor vehicles operated under tight security, and the era of the "gas horse," when everybody owned a car, was long a thing of the past. Civic vehicles, or "cruise vans," had replaced the bus system. There was never more than a minute's wait for a van, and passengers had only to indicate to the driver where they wanted to get off.

Sten hopped into the van, glancing quickly at the passengers. There were just two, a man and a woman—professionals in suits. Rich people, he thought. Whirlpool brains. As he sat down, his body caked in sweat, the woman inched away.

"What—I smell, sister?"

"You said it," she retorted.

"You would too if you'd just come in on that train," Sten said.

"You were on that train?" the young driver asked.

"What happened?"

"Tell us."

Sten had suddenly become the center of attention.

"Some crazy Afro dude started shootin' the cops," he told them. And then he wondered, how about me? How about the big white guy?

"You saw it?" the woman asked.

"I saw a lot of smoke flying, that's what I saw—and bodies."

"This is the second attack like that in a year," the man said, clutching at his briefcase.

The woman arched her back angrily.

"We pay through our noses to support this new U.S. Transit Police," she said, "and what do they do?"

"They get shot," the driver said, "protecting *you.*"

"How about you?" the man with the briefcase asked defensively.

"He has to live in the ghetto, with the rest of us," Sten said.

"Right on," said the driver.

There was a tense moment of silence.

"Well," the man with the briefcase said, "whether we live here, or in Brooklyn, or wherever, we're all in this together. Crime is crime and we have to fight it—I mean this horrible terrorism that is creeping in from all around, and, well—"

"Yes," the woman added. "We're all in this together and—"

"Don't put me on," the driver said.

"Enough. I'm getting out of here," the woman demanded.

"So am I," added the man. "Stop, please—here."

But the driver continued on a bit.

"Here, *please.*"

"I'm stoppin', asshole."

"What's your hack number?" the woman asked angrily.

"It's in letters," the driver grinned, "spelled f-u-c-k-y-o-u."

Class war, Sten thought. He couldn't help grinning as the two indignant Professionals exited the van. One terrorist attack and already people were showing their true colors. The driver looked back at him excitedly.

"So tell me more," he said.

"What's to tell?" Sten said, checking out the street numbers as they continued to roll uptown on Broadway. "We were, uh... rollin' in on the train and then there was this big boom, and we stopped, and uh... well, that's when the shootin' started."

"But, the reports say the shootin' started in Brooklyn."

"Uh, yeah—right, well."

"You weren't on that train, come off it," the young driver said. "You're just puttin' me on."

"No, I was on it," Sten said, his voice growing irritable, his body longing for a hit.

"If you'd been on it, you would've known about the shootin' in Brooklyn and the other guy, too."

Sten froze.

"What other guy?" he asked.

"Reports said there were two. A white guy was with that nigger. Only he disappeared, the T.P. didn't get him. But they're lookin'."

Sten felt himself growing numb as the driver pulled the van over. Two serfs hopped on, corporate ensigns on their work clothes. As the van moved away from the curb, talk about the shootout immediately resumed. The driver kidded Sten about how he had put everybody on because he smelled and needed a cover-up. The young man held his nose, jokingly, but by now Sten was preoccupied with thoughts of the potential danger that he faced: both from those who might possibly be trailing him and—if the media masters didn't show up—from Mantis himself. Sten's body was aching and he prayed that any relapse or withdrawal he might have be put in abeyance until he had accomplished his mission. He looked out the window. Sixty-seventh Street. Just a bit more to go.

Sten continued in the van uptown to Ninety-sixth Street. Signs of a relapse had passed, and as he headed past the infamous Columbia Towers, bastion of Professionalism with its maze of elite shops, and continued on toward Riverside Drive, he realized that the mission he had waited so long to accomplish was now almost upon him. For days he had had Mantis's address engraved on his mind. Soon he would be there.

He would tell the media masters his story, how he had been drugged and how he could have otherwise defeated Mantis easily, on his own. He knew what he wanted to say, but he was nervous and the words were not running easily through his mind.

What if Mantis wasn't home?

That part didn't matter. Sten would issue the challenge and state the case of Tanaka, how the Okinawan champ had been forced to grant Mantis a match. Yeah—it would be the same. And the results would be the same, too. Mantis had defeated Tanaka and changed the course of history; Sten would step in next and dispose of Mantis, bringing things back to where they should be.

Five minutes later the big *karateka* stood in front of a large, old apartment building facing the river and the park. Looking up to the top of the building he could see foliage and branches drooping over the side, and ivy seemed to climb not only up but down the length of the building, forming in clusters so tight around each window that the entire structure appeared to be eaten from within by plant life.

Sten checked the time. He was early, but the media masters were never late. He stared up. Mantis's building. No media masters. Things did not look good. He had not counted on this. He thought they would show. They were always hungry for news. Damn—they had to show.

Suddenly a voice was heard, a voice coming from an intercom system.

"You can forget about the press."

The sound had issued from the entrance to Mantis's building. Sten approached the front gate. Through the iron bars he could see an archway leading toward a courtyard. There was an intercom built into the gate. He could hear the whine of surveillance cameras. Suddenly, the voice returned.

"We sent the press home. You go home, too."

Sten arched his back, his brow furrowing. "I want in."

"To see who?" the intercom asked.

"Mantis," Sten replied, without a moment's hesitation. He tightened up in true karate style, ready for action. Laughter burst out over the intercom.

"What a clown..." the voice said, and again there was laughter.

Enraged, Sten pulled at the gate, hoping to pry his way in. *Zap!* A quick burst of electricity shot through the *karateka,* sending him sprawling. Sten found himself on the pavement, unharmed but shaken.

"Like to try it again?" the voice said, and the laughter seemed to be even louder now. Feeling a deep sense of rage and frustration, Sten whipped out his nunchaka and hurled it full force at the gate. The laughter stopped and the gate inched open, ever so slightly.

Sten approached cautiously, picking up his nunchaka. Then he kicked at the gate with his rubber-heeled boots. It creaked back and he slid through. He proceeded with a martial air toward the courtyard. It was a greenhouse really, filled with exotic plants and encased from above by glass. Up above the courtyard—surrounding it—was a broad balcony. The only entry or exit appeared to be from the gateway. Sten did not realize there had to be another entrance until he saw eight men dressed in camouflage uniforms emerge from the dense forest of plants. One of the men, the largest one—a man as big as Sten but with an anvil-shaped face—smiled and folded his arms.

"Well, well—a visitor."

"Should we spray him?" another man asked.

"No," the anvil-face said. "I want you boys to have fun."

He snapped his fingers and the seven other uniformed men whipped out clubs from their back pockets. They began to surround the *karateka,* slowly and cautiously. Sten made ready with his nunchaka. Suddenly, a man charged, his club held high, and Sten crashed his nunchaka across the attacker's shoulders, sending him crashing into the dirt. As another guard rushed in, Sten dodged and then lashed out with his nunchaka once again. The second man met with the same result. Sten bounced back and prepared for the next assault.

"This guy's good," a third guard said.

"So what?" the anvil-face replied. "It's five to one—get him."

The remaining five guards closed ranks, but this time it was Sten who took the initiative. He broke the attackers' circle, then swung around, dropping one of the guards with a sweep. The remaining four guards rushed him, one jumping Sten from behind, the other three scrambling on top. Sten tried to connect with a good solid punch but found himself unable to do anything but grab hold of an arm. He straightened it. It snapped.

"Jesus."

Another guard rose to his feet and saw an opening. He slammed his club down full force on Sten's head.

Darkness came swiftly....

And then there was light...

And pain. Horrible pain.

Sten was lying on his back, in the courtyard, and there were figures standing around him, but they were all a blur. He could hear voices.

"You know him?"

"Oh yeah, I know him. Chances are he was on that train, too."

"Maybe he had something to do with Elijah changing the schedule, or—"

"Shut up," the other voice said abruptly.

Sten recognized *that* voice.

"Mantis..." he mumbled, trying in vain to raise his head.

"Bring him to."

Sten could see someone kneeling down, drawing closer, holding a vial, and then there was a violent smell, a smell so strong that it was as if someone had jammed a needle into his skull. Everything started to take shape again and Sten was lifted to a sitting position. It took a few more moments for him to gather his senses. Then he could hear strange breathing, half rhythmic, half machine. He looked up to see the right hand of a man, fingers writhing, almost beyond control. Then the face—well tanned, hair blond, eyes green, a green that was inhuman, plantlike...

"Mantis," Sten mumbled again.

"Well, well." The green-eyed ex-commando smiled, circling his prisoner. "Look who we have here. We have that big, blond baboon of a karate man I laid out way back when."

"Laid me out because I was laid out on drugs," Sten said.

"I could have laid you out without them," Mantis said calmly. "The drugs were just routine. The Demo chiefs wanted it that way."

"I came here for a rematch," Sten said.

Mantis nodded coolly. "I assumed that, the moment I saw you. The unfortunate fact of the matter is—I haven't got the time."

"You owe me," Sten said, attempting to rise.

Mantis approached Sten and placed his foot on the *karateka's* chest. He shoved him back, lightly.

"I don't owe you shit."

"Bastard..."

"Spare me the invective." The ex-commando smiled. "How'd you like the search at the Brooklyn inspection gate?"

"*You* told them?"

"No," Mantis corrected. "*You* told them. Indirectly, of course. You contacted the media masters, and they contacted me. Once I furnished the transit police with your description, I expected them to resolve the matter. But you've proven more resourceful than I had anticipated. Who would have guessed that a dumb brute such as yourself could have caused such commotion?"

Sten attempted to rise again, but Mantis motioned for anvil-face to push him back down.

"I have some questions I want to ask you," Mantis said.

"What questions?" Sten asked.

Mantis did not answer immediately. As Sten waited, he took a good look at the man he hated so much. The ex-commando was only five-nine or -ten, not more than a hundred and sixty pounds, and yet all muscle. Sten again asked himself how such a man could grapple with opponents twice his size and throw them about as if they were mere rag dolls. It was amazing—truly amazing.

"Tell me," Mantis said, "while you were on that train did you meet up with a fire priest nigger?"

"What if I did?" Sten asked.

Mantis motioned to anvil-face, who kicked Sten in the head.

"I want an answer," Mantis continued in almost a whisper. "Did you meet up with one of those crazy fire priest niggers on that train?"

Sten stifled a moan. "Yeah, I met him."

"Did you talk to him?"

"What if I did—"

"No games—or my man here will cut you up. Did you talk with him?"

"Yeah."

"And what'd he say?"

"Something about Central Park, and sacrifices. And then he said he'd help me."

"After you beat up those two cops, right?"

"After you squealed on me."

Mantis laughed. "He helped you, because you helped him."

"What do you mean?" Sten asked. "Explain."

"I'll explain certain things. I'll explain this: by scuffling with those cops, you let that nutty coon slip through the inspection gate with his shotgun."

"How'd you know he had a shotgun?" Sten asked.

"Like I said, I'll explain certain things." Mantis stepped back and turned to anvil-face. "It's all clear now," he said. "Our fire priest met Sten and had his mind knocked off center. It happens. But I'm happy with the results."

He looked over at Sten.

"What should we do with him?" anvil-face asked.

"I don't need your sympathy," Sten said.

"Don't worry," Mantis replied, "you're not going to get any." He thought for a moment. Then: "Let him go."

"What—?"

"Because that's exactly what he doesn't want."

Mantis began to back away, and again Sten attempted to rise.

"You *have* to fight me," the *karateka* shouted. "Otherwise you'll never know if you coulda beaten me, fair and square. Do you hear that, Mantis? Huh? Do you hear that?"

Mantis shook his head and walked away. Anvil-face motioned to one of his men.

"Do you hear that?" Sten shouted. "You have to prove to your-self that—"

Sten heard something spray in his direction, and then...his head seemed to turn almost completely around, by itself, with no muscular effort.

Again there was darkness, but for an even longer time.

CHAPTER EIGHT

"**E**VERYTHING'S attached," Bimbi heard Capitan say as they dashed across the street, grocery containers in hand. Behind them a small riot was in progress at Big Food, Inc. "One fanatic starts shooting and everyone else goes crazy."

Bimbi stood and watched as police wagons began to move in on a group of demonstrators.

"What're they protesting?" he asked.

"They got signs," Capitan said. "Read 'em."

"I don't read."

"Oh." Capitan smiled. "Sorry."

"Why? I ain't."

Capitan poked Bimbi.

"Move."

"So what do the signs say?"

"Impolite things—about food prices."

Bimbi looked back to see if a confrontation would take place. Suddenly, bottles started to rain from the windows above Big

Food, Inc. A tear gas canister was lobbed by one of the policemen.
Capitan quickly coaxed Bimbi along.

"Hey, I wanna watch this," Bimbi said.

"Why?"

"Because it's the *people* fightin'."

Capitan sighed. "Those aren't the people. Those are just punks,
looking to stir up trouble. They don't give a damn about food
prices. They *steal* everything they need. Like I said, if one person
goes crazy, everyone else wants to go crazy, too."

"Yeah, well how come those cops are so eager to get mixed up
in that, but don't do nothin' about findin' Enrique?"

The police had released Tomaso without even pressing him as
to the gangleader's whereabouts.

"Because the cops aren't paid to find guys like Enrique," Capitan
said. "A company like Big Food is owned by important people in
Manhattan. *That's* what the cops are paid to protect."

"Then what the hell are we supposed to do to get justice?" Bimbi
said. Capitan quickly pulled him aside as an armored paddy wagon
whipped around the street en route to the now distant chaos.

"What're we supposed to do?" Capitan asked.

"Yeah, *do!*"

"Easy. Develop strategy."

"Strategy?"

"You got it."

"How do you do that?" Bimbi asked.

"You discipline yourself."

Capitan suddenly spotted more patrol cars up ahead. But they
weren't moving, they were parked, zoning off the area.

"Those guys look like they're havin' a bad day."

He pointed Bimbi to a side alley. Before Bimbi knew it they
were back out on another main strip, but further across town.

"Hey, how'd you do that? Get us over here so fast?" he asked.

"Simple—strategy. I know the area, I can cover turf real fast."

"Yeah, we just went zip-zip-zip."

Capitan nodded. Then: "Damn..."

Up ahead there were more patrol cars zoning off the area.

"Them cops look like they're fixin' to crack heads," Bimbi said.

"I wouldn't be surprised. That fire priest killed a lot of their pals today. Let's move."

Back they went into the maze of alleys, Capitan pointing the way.

"In any case," Capitan continued, "economics, boxing, life—it all boils down to strategy."

Back home now, he was unloading the container of groceries. He pulled out a package of chocolate cookies—Capitan had a thing for sweets—and began to read the ingredients listed on the package. Carmen eyed him critically.

"Oh, this is no food at all."

"So then why'd you buy it?" Carmen asked, snatching it away.

"Hey, that cost over twenty credits," Capitan said.

"You should have thought of that before you decided to bring it home." Carmen pretended to hide the cookies. Capitan smiled and resumed unloading the groceries. Bimbi suddenly whacked him.

"Hey? What's with *you?*" Capitan said.

The young Hispanic went into a playful fighting stance.

"I want you to teach me some strategy."

Capitan smiled. "The major starategy...is...this...." He turned and held up a cluster of bananas. Slowly, he raised them higher and higher over Bimbi's face. Without even noticing it, Bimbi began leaning back too far. He lost his balance and crashed against the sink.

"Hey! What happened?"

"Strategy," Capitan said. "Balance, equilibrium."

"I got balance," Bimbi said. "Watch..."

He raised his arms and did a lightning fast lotus sweep kick across them. "Great, huh?"

"That was rehearsed balance," Capitan said. "I'm talking about everyday balance."

"Well, how do you get that?"

"Through the greatest strategy of them all—training."

"Yeah, but I still know a lot of stuff," Bimbi said.

"You don't know anything, yet. If you're going to train with me, then you'd better—"

Capitan paused.

"What?"

"Well, this is pretty old, but...ah, what the hell. Look at it this way: you want a glass of water?"

"No," Bimbi said.

"Just pretend you want a glass of water."

"Why should I pretend I want one if I ain't thirsty?"

Capitan filled a glass with some bean milk.

"That's milk."

"I know it is."

"I thought you said I wanted water."

"Shut up," Capitan said, smiling. He pointed at the glass. "That's your brain."

"My brain don't look like that," Bimbi said. He picked up the glass.

"Just pretend that's your brain, your mind, okay?"

"Okay."

"Now. This faucet here, the water—this represents the stream of consciousness, of thinking. You want to fill your brain with it."

"I do?"

"Yeah. Go ahead."

"I can't." Bimbi giggled.

"Why not?"

"Because there's milk in the glass."

"Right. And you know what that milk represents? It stands for all the stupid and violent thoughts you've put into your head. You can't put wisdom or knowledge into a head that's already filled and committed to ignorance."

"Who says I'm ignorant?"

"I do," Capitan said. "Look, if you want to train with me, then you're going to have to empty your head."

"You want me to be stupid?"

"No. Open."

Realizing that Carmen had gone up to the loft, Capitan quickly pulled out a pack of synthetic cupcakes. He stuffed one abruptly into Bimbi's mouth, then his own. Bimbi began to wash it down with milk.

"Bad news, drinkin' your brains," Capitan said.

Bimbi choked with laughter, his mouth dripping open.

"Even worse news, spitting them on the floor."

"Shit."

"What a mess."

Later that afternoon Bimbi finished telling Capitan all he knew about his brother: about his missions and medals and the full details concerning his death. And then he showed Capitan the credeer card.

José would have been the twentieth recruit sent to Capitan by Monitor Five. Once a war games participant learned the Aiki "technique" from an odd-numbered monitor, he was encouraged to go AWOL and make his way to an even-numbered monitor on the outside. Capitan was an even-numbered monitor: Number Eight. It was the even-numbered monitors' job to ease the deserters' transition into civilian life—to check up on the student and make sure his technique was still effective. It was the odd-numbered monitors who actually taught the technique. They always operated inside the military.

Monitors. An appropriate word, Capitan thought, thinking back to his training. A better word than "monk," or "deacon."

"For, after all," Hoshima had once told him, "let us dispense with all this religious pomp. I am here to teach you about how to control the stream of consciousness. That is not the job of a priest but of a monitor."

And so the phrase was coined. *Monitor.*

Capitan knew that there were three monitors operating within the New York area. But he had never met them, he had never seen them and, what's more, he did not even know who they were—neither they nor the infamous Monitor Five.

"Odds go to the people. Evens go to the soldiers," Hoshima had said.

"Then how're we to know one another?" Capitan asked.

"You're not. There'll be no need to know one another. Just teach to others what I have taught you. That is all that is necessary for now."

Capitan remembered how perplexed he had been

"If the monitors are not to know one another, if they are not to meet, how can we contact or eventually get to—"

"I have told you what I have told you," Hoshima said. "We are not a church; we have nothing to do with religion. You are to return to New York and wait there. Everything will unfold as it should."

The shamanlike hermit took a stick and began to make weird symbols in the dirt. Capitan had never seen the symbols before; they were not Japanese *kanji;* they belonged to no alphabet that he knew.

$$---- \quad \text{o} \quad ---- \quad \text{o}$$
$$---- \quad \text{o} \quad ---- \quad +$$

"What does this mean?" Capitan asked.

"Absolutely—nothing," Hoshima said, smiling. "But it is to be your code name, your symbol. You are to make a sign with these symbols and hang it outside your home. That is all."

"But—"

"Enough!"

Capitan had obeyed Hoshima's orders. And so it was that he now found himself talking not to a member of the Aiki movement but to a young Hispanic who had come to him for guidance. Monitor Five had no idea that Bimbi would get hold of that card...

Monitor Five. He seems to know me, Capitan thought, but I sure as hell don't know him.

He wondered if they would ever meet.

Capitan turned and gave Bimbi a light whack.

"What are you doing?" Capitan asked.

"Lookin' at them mats over there on the floor," Bimbi said eagerly, his body a live wire. "So when're you gonna teach me?"

"My boy," Capitan said. "It's not a matter of when I'm going to teach you. It's more a case of what I am going to teach you."

"Teach me how to fight."

"First—I'm gonna teach you how to lose."

"What?"

"Come here."

Capitan guided Bimbi over to the tatami mats that lined the floor of the academy. Then, raising his arms so that they formed a kind of hoop, he did a full front roll on the mat, springing quickly to his feet. He motioned to Carmen, who was standing nearby. She did the same. Capitan did it again in slow motion in order to give Bimbi a clearer picture.

"You see, all things operate in a circle, including your body when it takes a fall."

"Why should I take a fall?"

"You may have to if you get into a fight."

"I ain't goin' down," Bimbi said. "I ain't losin'."

"You shouldn't equate going down with losing. Sometimes it's the best bet—to take a fall. Now, you try."

"Me?"

"Right."

"On that?" Bimbi asked, pointing at the mat.

"In Japan they used to do it on wood floors. Go on."

Bimbi hesitated a moment, then attempted to duplicate what he had just seen. Instead of rolling forward, though, he rolled violently on his side.

"Ow! That hurt."

"That's because you didn't do it right," Capitan told him. "When you roll, you have to think 'forward,' not 'sideways.'" He stepped back and motioned to Bimbi. "Now, try it again."

Bimbi managed to do better the second time, but his shoulders ached as he stood up.

"Good, that was much better."

"It still hurt."

"It will for a while, until your body gets used to it. It's part of the 'Way.'"

"What 'Way'?" Bimbi asked.

"The Way of Training: pain."

"Oh…"

"Come on, let's roll."

Capitan rolled continuously around the mats. Bimbi looked at Carmen and shook his head. Carmen joined Capitan, and the two of them spun about like tops, springing swiftly to their feet and then going down again. Bimbi laughed and tried not to get dizzy as he watched. Suddenly, Capitan came up behind Bimbi and gave him a quick shove. The young Hispanic rolled over, this time almost instinctively, and sprang back to his feet.

"Hey, that was cheatin'," he said.

Carmen came up swiftly behind him and did the same, the light shove sending him across the mat once again.

"Come on."

"Quit complaining," Capitan said. "Just roll."

"Why?"

"Because it's the only way to learn," Carmen shouted.

This went on for an hour, the light rolling, the sudden shoves, Bimbi's body growing progressively sore, every muscle in his back seemingly stretched to the limit.

"I need a hit," he told Capitan as the class drew to a close.

Capitan kneeled on the mat, ignoring Bimbi's comment.

"Kneel down," he said. Carmen showed Bimbi how.

"Good. Now we just sit for a moment," Capitan said.

"Why?"

"You're full of questions, aren't you."

"Yeah," Bimbi said, finding the *zazen* position unbearable after only a few seconds. He was sweating.

And he was thinking about an emoveer hit. Any kind. One of the four—it didn't matter. The emoveers could change your mood…

"We sit," Capitan told his new student, "to collect ourselves, our thoughts."

Capitan caught Carmen's glance. He could sense disapproval in her eyes. Obviously she felt it was too early yet to school Bimbi in Aiki technique.

"I'm...I'm hurtin'," Bimbi said.

I know, Capitan thought. In your heart, that's where you're hurting; that's where the drugs get you in the end. His thoughts drifted back for a moment to his own brother, Eladio. Eladio had died an addict; he had died on the street. But it was sodac that did it—a relapse during a fight. One big blur and his brother had found himself gutted open with a flashing knife, the Ninja fight-gurus' favorite weapon. It was because of what happened to Eladio that Capitan had always favored the old ways of getting high: some beer, a little wine. They could change you, but they weren't synthetically arranged to make you relapse half-blind in the middle of the day when your life might hang in the balance. Capitan watched.

"I wanna go to the arcade," Bimbi said, beginning to rise.

"Sit down."

Bimbi was ready for tears. "I can't see," he said.

"Tough. You stay seated and finish this class."

There was silence for a moment, broken finally by Bimbi, who began to weep. Capitan clapped his hands.

"Bow," he said.

Bimbi struggled to complete the gesture, then began to vomit....

A strong pungent odor. Capitan winced as he watched Carmen pour what remained of the herb potion into a container. Bimbi had taken the rest, and it had knocked him out immediately. Carmen herself had been slightly addicted before she came to Capitan, but she was well versed in herbs and had cured herself with them. Herbs and willpower, Capitan thought proudly. He tugged playfully at her long hair.

"*Bruja mia*," he whispered, "my witch woman."

How strange she was, still, after these last two years of living and sharing together. She had arrived from out west somewhere with only a bag of clothes and a spirit that could conquer the world. Half cowboy Anglo, half Chicano, she had brownish-red hair that seemed to change shades with the passing of each season. It hung thick and long down to a pair of graceful hips that could not betray her Latin past. How strange, he thought, that he had found her amping away on sodac and watching Sport Arena with a pair of hoods from the Bay Ridge Wing Chun Clan. He had been drinking in the bar there when his eyes caught her tall buxom profile. He had watched with mounting anger as the two hoods slowly started to put their hands on her. And he had prepared to come to her aid, like a knight in shining armor, when suddenly there was a scream and one hood went rolling over, his arm spouting blood. In a second the other punk was pressed face first against the wall with a straight-edged razor at his throat. Carmen's own face flushed angrily, a cross between Geronimo and Annie Oakley, ready to open his jugular at the slightest move.

She had come to Brooklyn looking for adventure. Adventure! As if there was anything worthwhile or inviting about the eastern cities of the twenty-first century. Let alone about the west. A tight network of transit security fragmented the country, making it likely that a person would live out his life and die in the same area where he was born. Regionalism was as much a reality now as it had been when the continent was settled, some five hundred years before. And yet Carmen had managed to cross the country and end up there, in a bar in Bay Ridge.

Capitan's thoughts returned to the present. As Carmen nuzzled against him, he pulled her playfully to his lap. Their lips met. He laughed.

"What's so funny?" she asked.

"Oh, nothing. I was just thinking about that first time we met."

He would never have dared lay a hand on her then, not after what he had just seen. He had approached her gently, telling the Wing Chun hoods to beat it and informing her that it was safer elsewhere.

"Where?" she asked defiantly. "At *your* place?"

Capitan had looked down at the floor. When he looked up, their eyes met and something seemed to connect.

She had stayed at his place for the first few weeks as just a friend, then as a student, the way Capitan wanted it and the way that circumstances seemed to work out. The love came naturally, not forced. And she told him many things...

She had betrayed the confidence of an old lover, a biker chieftain out in New Mexico who had beaten her. He had been cruel, and so she turned him over to his enemies. She had a strange thing about revenge, Carmen did—a quality that Capitan tried hard to remove, an emotion that he had discovered in himself when Eladio died. He faced the same thing now with Bimbi.

"What *about* that first time we met?" Carmen asked, running her hands playfully through his hair.

"You were so sure of yourself," Capitan said.

"I was a junkie."

"You cured yourself."

"You expect him to do the same?" she asked, nodding toward Bimbi, who slept soundly on a futon under their loft.

"No. He's a different case. Something that will take time."

Time, Capitan thought. And lots of it. Time and Providence.

The training continued, and as it continued so did the relapses and the vomiting and the herbs as a cure. Throughout, Capitan made sure that messages were sent to Bimbi's mother. He made sure, too, that Bimbi did not try to return home. Things were still not safe and the authorities might be watching because of José's desertion. It was better that Bimbi stay with Capitan: one less mouth for Señora Arguayo to feed, a healthier environment for Bimbi, and less awareness of the connection between José and Capitan.

Connections... investigations... Goldman...

Aiki. All we are is a popular peace concept, Capitan told himself. Central Intelligence has questioned us before. But now Goldman was asking questions about Hoshima. What did it mean? Was

Goldman connected to Central Intelligence somehow? Were they contemplating a crackdown? Capitan found himself wondering why the government didn't focus on the real cults—like the Zed Advesta.

The Zed A had maintained temples in all the major cities for years, offered services to foster children, ran soup kitchens for the poor, then suddenly it was being blamed for a series of terrorist incidents. A fire priest had held up a bank in Chicago, then blew it up, with himself inside. Another fire priest had attacked the White House, proclaiming himself "Messiah against the Triumvirate." He was immediately gunned down. Then there was this latest incident at Grand Central. Strange, Capitan thought, that none of the fire priests had been taken alive. The Zed A's leader, Big Sun, had disavowed all three incidents, claiming that the actions of the fanatics were not endorsed by the movement itself. Maybe the authorities believed him. How else to explain why the government wasn't making an effort to break the cult up.

Capitan knew that the key to maintaining the secrecy of any underground organization was in creating a vaporous, almost invisible structure. Hoshima had taught him that. That was exactly the reason he had not said too much to Bimbi and why he had held back on his Aiki training. So far he had only taught him *ukemi,* the art of falling. He knew that Bimbi was growing impatient, but it had taken almost a week to ease him away from the drugs....

Capitan looked over with satisfaction now at the young Hispanic rolling back and forth on the mats. He clapped his hands abruptly, motioning for him to stop.

"No good?" Bimbi asked, sweating from head to toe.

"No, great, but I'd like to show you something new."

"You mean something besides falling?"

"Right," Capitan said. "Something called technique. But remember: technique will not make a bit of difference unless you perfect *this,*" he said, pointing to his head, "along with it."

It was an old rap, but the best rap—always the best rap for young punks trying to find themselves.

"Yeah, so? I know some technique," Bimbi said.

"You know nothing," Capitan said.

"So what's to know? High block, low block, side block."

"Those are blocks. I don't teach blocks."

"You don't?" Bimbi said, surprised.

"No. You fought me. Did I use high block, low block, side block?"

"Uh...I don't remember," Bimbi said.

"All I did was step out of the way," Capitan told him. "That's all I teach, really."

"What kinda fightin's that?" the young Hispanic asked.

"The best kind. The kind that keeps you alive. Come here."

As Bimbi drew closer, Capitan put his finger on his own chin.

"So what's your problem?" Bimbi said.

"Hit me."

"I don't wanna hit ya."

"Go on, don't be timid," Capitan said. "Take a good poke."

"Shit..." Bimbi grunted, then suddenly let go with a rapid lead from his left. Capitan quickly side-stepped, shoving Bimbi and sending him rolling across the mat.

"See," Capitan said. "I just turned your own energy against you. Had we been on cement, and had you lacked the knowledge of how to fall, you would have busted your shoulder."

"Hey..."

"It's all beginning to make sense now, right?"

"Yeah."

"Get up."

Capitan motioned for Bimbi to approach again.

"There are two basic movements that you need to defend yourself. You pivot like I just did, or you—" Capitan stepped back and motioned for Bimbi to strike. As the boy lashed out, Capitan entered with a lightning quick motion and seized his arm, pinning him to the mat with it.

"Owwww!"

"Or you enter past your opponent's defenses."

Capitan pulled Bimbi to his feet.

"You make it sound simple."

"It is—a lot simpler and a lot less energy than trying to tense up your body and smack someone. After all," Capitan added, "what's in a punch?"

"I don't know," Bimbi said, making sure his arm was in one piece, "You tell me."

"A lot of negative aggression. But that's beside the point. Any attack has an inner and outer limit. At those points the attack is the weakest. The idea is to avoid the point of impact."

"What's that?" Bimbi asked.

"That's your fist, puddin' head."

Capitan stepped back and smiled at Bimbi.

"Not again?"

"Sure. How do you expect to learn?"

"But this stuff's not natural," Bimbi said.

"It will become natural," Capitan replied, "but in order for that to happen, the same movements have to be repeated thousands of times."

Bimbi looked doubtful. "But—"

Capitan cut him off. "Thousands of times," he said again. "So start counting…"

The training session continued for another hour, and by its conclusion, Capitan was rubbing his shoulder tenderly, reflecting on how depressing it was to grow old.

"What's the matter, Pops?" Bimbi asked. "You hurtin'?"

Capitan settled into a kitchen chair and looked over at Carmen. She was busy preparing dinner but had time to smile back and blow him a kiss. Bimbi went over and took a peek at the meal.

"Shit. More of that Jap seaweed crap."

"You ain't paying for it, are you?" Carmen asked.

"No."

"Then shut up. And what did you expect, steak?"

"Shit, yeah. That's what all them rich folk eat, ain't it?"

"They have the credit, they can eat what they want," Capitan said, massaging his shoulder.

"That's because they're takin' from *us*," Bimbi said, "and come the *revolution*, man, we're gonna take back."

Capitan stopped massaging his shoulder and looked firmly at Bimbi. "That's not your concern," he said.

"What? Sure it is. I'm willin' to fight."

"Against tanks?"

"Why not?"

Capitan shook his head and continued to massage his aching shoulder. Bimbi moved in on him excitedly.

"I mean, isn't that what all this training is for?" he asked, confusion showing on his face. "It's to fight, man—to wipe out the people who killed my brother, and the cops and—"

Capitan slapped Bimbi across the cheek. He pointed a finger at his student, who backed away, shocked.

"You train with me, you don't talk that way."

"Why'd you hit me, man?"

"I didn't hit you," Capitan replied. "I woke you up."

Fighting back tears, Bimbi retreated to the far corner of the room. Capitan returned stoically to massaging his shoulder.

Dinner was eaten in silence that night, Capitan and Carmen watching as Bimbi poked halfheartedly at his food. Capitan wondered why the young Hispanic couldn't just forgive and forget. José's death certainly hadn't helped things, but Bimbi's anger wasn't reducible to just that. No, it was much more than that. Capitan sensed that Bimbi's anger had accrued gradually over the years—that it was the residue of a thousand different disappointments.

Reflecting on the boy's hostility, Capitan thought of his own upbringing—of the gruesome recessions, and growing taxes, and the credit system that had slowly but surely shackled everyone. For the Untouchables like himself, it had been particularly bad. With very few "real" jobs to select from, most of the Untouchables had ended up either in the army or slaving away for the "Work Force," a government-sponsored organization that made sure the masses would get fed—but just so much. It was, Capitan thought to himself, a resource allocation system that kept people constantly on edge, had them constantly ready to fight. The government wanted everyone to be like a bull in a pen, ready to serve the war games should their numbers be called. And sooner or later, every Untouchable's number was called.

Capitan looked over at Bimbi. "You're still mad, because I slapped you."

"No..."

"Sure you are. You're not eating."

"I—I just don't know why you slapped me, man. I wasn't sayin' nothin' wrong."

"You were talking violence," Capitan told him. "You were acting the way you behave on the street. If you want to walk around looking for a fight, you'll get one. That's how your brother got shot."

"He was shot by scum," Bimbi said.

"All right. He was shot by scum. So you want to go after him, become scum too, right?"

"I want revenge," Bimbi said.

There was a long moment of silence. Capitan gave Carmen a look.

"You want revenge?" Carmen asked Bimbi.

"Yeah!"

"Okay," Capitan said. "Then here's your lesson. Take out your revenge, right now, but on that trash can over there in the corner."

Bimbi hesitated.

"Go on," Capitan said, "pretend it's that guy Enrique who shot your brother. Hit it."

"No..."

"*Hit it,*" Carmen yelled.

Bimbi suddenly exploded. With a lightning quick pivot, he swung around and clipped the trash can with his left leg.

"Mother," he cried as he attacked again, kicking the trash can over and over. It *was* Enrique. He *was* kicking Enrique. He was kicking his filthy head in. Over and over. Over and over, kicking it. The can was splitting apart now, and there was garbage raining all over the kitchen. Bimbi stopped, exhausted. He looked over at his teacher.

"There," Capitan said, calmly continuing with his dinner, "are you happy you let it out?"

"Yeah..."

"Now," Capitan said. "Clean up after yourself."

Panting heavily, Bimbi looked about, surveying the mess he had just made. Capitan hurled a broom at him.

"Balance, my boy. Learn the lesson."

CHAPTER NINE

AFTER Sten lost consciousness he was taken by Mantis's men to his dojo in Brooklyn, and dumped outside in the gutter. When he came to, his humiliation was so complete that he locked himself inside, not wanting to see anyone. It was more than the humiliation, though. Having crossed Abe, Sten knew it was only a matter of time before the old-timer sent someone to kill him. It was a price he knew he'd have to pay; he had failed in his mission and if he was going to die, he wanted to make peace with the "Great Way" as best he could. That meant going through all the withdrawals and fasting. If he was going to die, he was going to die clean.

And so he began to train, to train for the end—to be ready. Local grocers who remembered his former glory gave him food; some old students who kept up a degree of loyalty bolstered his pride and made him feel that his life had not been an entire waste. Sten, was, after all, samurai—at least in his own mind. Whether a samurai failed or not in his mission meant little; it was how the

samurai died that counted. As as he waited and began to train
with weights, he felt a tinge of the old self again, of a spirit marked
by strength.

A week passed, but there was no sign or call from Abe.

He's letting me stew for a while, Sten thought. In my own juices.

In fact, Abe was letting him do just that, because shortly after
Sten's futile attack on Mantis's inner sanctum he received a visit
that, had he still some hair left on his head, would have left it
standing.

He was attending a training session of the Arena Farm League
at the Sports Camp Center, just a few minutes away from the
Palisades Complex. Abe had been called in to select candidates
for the major leagues, and as he sat in the bleachers under the
solar tent, watching the trainees finish their warmup, Charlie came
scurrying nervously down the aisle.

"Somebody here—to see you."

Abe looked up. "So quit shaking and send him down."

"All right," Charlie said, hurrying off.

Abe shook his head and watched as the warmup concluded and
training weapons were handed out. Group A received long daggers, two each; Group B, the spears. The weapons were blunted,
traditional adaptations of the old gladiatorial blades. It gave one
side an infighting advantage, the other exterior range. After the
first bout the weapons would be switched, and after that the contestants would be rotated and the process repeated. This would
go on until most of the contestants dropped from exhaustion. The
objective was to promote instincts for survival. It was a format
that Abe himself had designed.

"Mr. Goldman."

Abe looked around. It was the anvil-face, Al Harris, Mantis's
top lieutenant. Al was a former commando who had served with
Mantis in the war games. He had come up on charges several
times for torturing prisoners.

Abe smiled calmly as the big man positioned himself in the aisle
directly behind him, a little gift-wrapped box wedged under his
arm.

"Mr. Harris," Abe said. "Have a seat."

"Thanks, I will."

There was a momentary pause as Abe inched forward, slightly threatened by Al's ominous torso behind him.

"So, what can I do for you?" Abe asked.

"We had a visitor the other day, a guy who works for your office."

Abe went pale.

"A guy named Sten Johnson," Al continued. "He busted up a few of our men."

"So you think I sent him?" Abe asked, not taking his eyes away from the game.

"One never knows," Al said, stroking his chin. "He works for you. He got our address through you."

"Maybe," Abe said. "So you killed him, I hope."

"You're not even saying you're sorry, Goldman."

"I'm sorry," Abe said.

Al's large hands continued to play with the little box. "No, we didn't kill him," he said. "That would have made it too easy for you."

Abe nodded, then focused his attention on one very adept trainee using a spear. He pointed at him. "That guy in red there, he's good. Uses the spear like a rope. Swings his opponent around on it." He waited for Al to reply, then added: "You know, Mantis busted Sten up once back in the old days. He's through now, a junkie."

"That doesn't explain why he works for your office."

"No, it doesn't, does it? You have me there. I'll deal with him."

"Do with him what you like," Al said. "Mantis isn't really interested in punishment. He's interested in information."

"Oh..." Abe leaned his head back, not shifting his eyes from the trainee who had succeeded in whirling his opponent on the edge of his spear right into the wall, knocking him out. "What kind of information?"

"The kind you can supply."

"If I can do anything—"

"Oh you *can*, Mr. Goldman," Al said, leaning his large torso closer. "You *can*."

His breath was rasping, labored. Abe leaned forward, then turned around. "You always sit in back of people?"

Al pointed a finger at him. "You're in no position to be a wiseass."

Abe pointed a finger back. "And I'm too old to be played with. Okay, I'm sorry, I'll deal with Sten—now what the fuck can I do for you?"

Al clenched his fists menacingly. Then he smiled and leaned back in his seat.

"Information. Since Mantis was discharged, he's been refused access to Pentagon files, tapes, information, the works."

"And he thinks I can get access?"

Abe turned and refocused his attention on the training session. The weapons were being switched now.

"Right," Al said. "If you want. You're U-2 and U-2 has ins. That's what we want you to do, get an in."

"Get an in *where?*"

"Enlistment files on foreign advisors."

"You're askin' for the moon," Abe told him.

"No, we're asking for a favor so we can forget about that guy Sten, plain and simple." Al inched the gift-wrapped box forward right next to Abe.

Abe glanced at it cautiously. He chewed on his cigar, then brought his eyes back to the ring, watching as the adept trainee made short work of a new opponent with daggers.

"That guy *is* good. Knocked another guy out with the hilt of his blade."

"They're chopped beef," Al said. "Hamburger meat."

"Hamburger meat's expensive now," Abe said. "These guys aren't."

Al nodded. "So...?"

"So what am I supposed to find out?" Abe asked.

"We wanna know if certain Japanese nationals, officers, are working as advisors in this country."

"What're their names?"

"Never mind their names. Their names are unimportant. We just wanna see the files of *all* of them, got that?"

"I'll try."

"You'll do more than that."

"Cut the heavy breathing," Abe said, lighting up his cigar. "I'm too old for that. Anything else?"

"Yeah. You know those Zed A boys, those crazy blacks running around, shooting people..."

"What about them?"

"We wanna know if you have any of their drop-outs fighting in the minor leagues."

"Files are one thing, rumors are another."

"We trust your judgment," Al replied, inching the box a little closer to Abe. He pointed at it as he rose. "This gift here is just to show that we have no, well...hard feelings."

Abe smirked. "What's in it?"

"Oh, that's a surprise, old man. A big surprise."

"Tell your boss Sten will be dealt with."

Al merely nodded. On the way out he pinched Charlie's nose for the fun of it. Charlie ran down to Abe. He glanced at the gift-wrapped box that Abe had placed in his lap.

"Watch it," Charlie said. "It could explode."

"I doubt it," Abe said, taking the cigar from his mouth. He opened the box slowly, peeling the wrapping away first. He realized that any gift from Mantis would prove bizarre and demented, probably full of "wild life."

"Good God!"

Charlie stumbled backward.

Abe sprang to his feet as a black widow spider emerged from the box. His heart pounded madly. How had Mantis known that he had a mortal fear of spiders? He quickly crushed the arachnid under his shoe.

"Some gift," Charlie said.

"I want Sten found, and quick," Abe said. His voice shook as he spoke. "Then I want him watched. If he makes any moves, anywhere, have him stopped."

"Kill him?"

"No, just stop him. Drug him, spray him, just stop him. Otherwise just leave him be. And contact U-2 Central for me, *now*."

As Charlie scrambled up the aisle, Abe lifted his foot and looked at the squashed spider. It was typical Mantis humor. Mantis's place was said to be crawling with insects and wild animals. Abe knew that the prank wasn't meant to be taken lightly, though. His office had slipped up and now there was a price to pay; he wanted to pay it as fast as possible and then deal with Sten on his own time, his own terms.

Pentagon files, Zed A terrorists. God forbid he thinks I'm gonna be his new contact, Abe thought. No, I'll give him the info he asked for today, but that's it. If I gotta run to the far end of Antarctica to get some peace—that's it....

While Abe pulled strings and waited for the information Mantis needed, he kept a close watch on Sten. Abe was still not sure what he wanted to do with the ex-fighter, but he knew he didn't want to kill him. Not that he didn't deserve it, Abe thought to himself. He had snuffed out better in his day. It was just that there was this nagging thought in the back of his head, eating away at him, saying that he was going to need him. For what, he wasn't sure....

When the information finally arrived, Abe gave it a thorough going over. He examined the dossier on Japanese military advisors presently operating within the country. There was nothing new or exciting about what he found; just a lot of bureaucratic mumbo-jumbo and blunt photographs of mean-looking Mongols with shaved heads. Yeah, he thought, glancing through them slowly, they all do look alike. Except...except for this one.

Abe came across a photo unlike the rest, of an officer named Jigoro Ibari. Although close shaven like the others, the officer clearly stood out, his face more tranquil, deeper in feeling. Abe studied it more closely, then dismissed it and closed the file.

None of my business, he thought. But *this* is. He grabbed the other file Al had requested—the one concerning former Zed Advesta members who had defected to the Arena. There was only one man profiled in the report, a Kalil Oman. Abe studied the case history:

KALIL OMAN, BORN CHICAGO 1998. SERVED ARMED FORCES 2016-20. CULT MEMBER ZED ADVESTA 2021-2029. FORMERLY MEMBER OF INNER CIRCLE. WITHDRAWAL ATTRIBUTED TO POLITICAL-ECONOMIC FACTORS. ENTERED MINOR ARENA LEAGUE 2029. W'S: 20, L'S: 7. WINNER, GARDEN STATE CUP.

Maybe this would make Mantis happy. Maybe not. Abe couldn't imagine what the ex-commando had in mind. The fact that this Kalil Oman was once a member of Zed A did not seem terribly important.

He buzzed Charlie.

"Call this number," he said. "Ask for Al. Tell him we might have what he wants. I'm goin' down for my class."

"What about Sten?"

"What about him? I want him to wait more. You got the boys watching him, right?"

Charlie nodded. Abe smiled and gave his flabby young assistant a quick rap in the belly.

"Workouts, you oughta try 'em."

"So tell me," Abe said between sighs, his back melting under Capitan's rubdown. "You still teach the arts down in Brooklyn, right?"

"Not formally, of course. That's against the law. But occasionally, I'll instruct a friend."

"I heard you were real good. Back when all them karate mags were the rage, I remember seein' your face in there with...uh, what was his name, uh..."

"Ashi," Capitan said.

"Yeah, right, Ashi. Poor guy. Drank too much. Drank himself to death."

Abe smiled as he felt the angry pressure of Capitan's hands.

Capitan quickly calmed himself. Ashi was a sore issue. Capitan's old *sensei* had not died from booze and drugs but from poison—poison slipped into Ashi's food by members of Demo-A.

"Somethin' wrong?" Abe asked.

"No."

"So, what were we talking about? Oh, I remember. We were talkin' about you, how good you are."

Capitan just continued to massage. Abe turned his head and sighed.

"You ever heard of an Aikido master by the name of, uh, Ibari?"

Capitan thought a moment.

"No."

"Tell the truth."

"I am, what's up?"

"Oh, nothin'. Maybe he wasn't no Aikido master. But maybe he studied with Hoshima, you know, that guy Hoshima who you say you don't know."

Abe waited for Capitan's hands to show some sign. But Capitan betrayed nothing. If it's going to be cat and mouse, old-timer, he thought, then I'm going to start going feline. He started to rub very slowly, calmly. Abe waited, then began to grow irritable.

"So, tell me one thing."

"Shoot."

"How come, with all your skill, you never came to me, tried to get into the Arena? Can you tell me that?"

"Oh, that's simple. The Arena is, uh...immoral."

"You don't say."

"Very, very immoral. And guys like you who promote it are going to go to—hell."

Abe burst into a long peal of laughter.

"Hey, I like that," Abe said. "To hell. Very good. You're probably right. But hell, they don't want me there. The Devil sent word, 'no room.'"

"'Thou shalt not kill,'" Capitan said as he began to rub down Abe's legs.

"Ahhh. So killing's bad, eh?"

"I think so."

"Hmm, well that's certainly something to ponder." Abe moved his head over to the other side. He thought to himself, Now I know what I've been saving Sten for....

There was a long period of silence as Capitan massaged Abe, both men waiting for the next move to be initiated. Abe glanced at his watch.

"You good at sword fightin'?" he asked finally.

"Not bad."

"I mean with them Japanese blades."

"Uh, we use wooden swords—bokkens."

"But, if you had to use a steel blade, you could—"

"Steel blades kill."

"Ah, right," Abe said. "Thou shalt not..."

"Thou shalt not..." Capitan replied.

Abe grinned and closed his eyes. His thoughts drifted to Sten— Sten the big baboon who was waiting to die. Then he glanced up at Capitan out of the corner of his eye. He wondered if the former Aikido champ practiced what he preached.

Abe's men were parked in a car just across the street from Sten's dojo. They were so involved in eating fast food that they didn't even see their boss approach. He rapped angrily on the hood.

"Am I botherin' you?" he asked.

"We're eatin'," Abe's head man, Billy, said.

"Oh, well excuse me."

"He's in there, don't worry."

"How do you *know?*" Abe asked. "You're both in here stuffin' your faces."

"We know 'cause he came out," Eddie said. Abe looked over and snatched a sushi roll from him.

"Hey, buy your own."

"Shut up. What's this, more fast Jap food?"

"It's good for you."

"Whatever happened to hamburgers?"

"That's what I'd like to know," Billy said. "Hamburgers and Bar-B-Qs. My mother told me about 'em."

"So what happened when he came out?" Abe asked, examining the insides of the sushi roll.

"We got outta the car and threatened to spray him if he didn't go back inside. So he got stubborn, came at us."

Billy bit casually into a piece of onion-flavored kelp.

"And then what?" Abe asked.

"We sprayed him," Eddie said.

"You hurt him?"

"No..."

"We don't think so."

"I'll kill you guys—"

"It was either him or us, and so we sprayed him," Billy said firmly.

"Then what happened?" Abe asked, looking toward the dojo.

"He fell back, coughin'...and went back inside."

"And we ain't seen him come out since."

"How long ago was this?" Abe asked.

"'Bout three hours ago," said Billy. "Look, he's been cooped up in there for almost a week. He's goin' nuts."

"We're goin' nuts, watchin' him," Eddie said.

Abe shook his head and grabbed a piece of Eddie's onion-kelp. "Stay here."

"You goin' in alone?"

"I'm better off without you," Abe said, biting into the kelp. "Judas priest, what is this?"

"Samurai Delight," Eddie said.

Abe threw the kelp at him. "Like I said, stay here."

Abe walked up the steps to Sten's old dojo. All the shades were drawn. The door was open. Abe entered the main room and looked around. The dojo was very dusty, showing distinct signs of abandonment. Yet everything was tidy, in order. A large emblem of the Rising Sun, painted boldly on a wall, faced the training area, and trophies stood proudly on the shelves lining the room. There were photos, too: photos of Sten in his prime and with his victorious students—photos that revealed a career of devotion and service to the community, a career that Abe had snuffed out viciously during the Demo-A days.

I'm to blame for all this, Abe thought to himself. And then suddenly he knew why he had always protected Sten, why he had always looked the other way when the *karateka* screwed up. Somewhere, deep inside him, there was a feeling of responsibility, a feeling of guilt.

Abe slipped past the training area, down a hall. There was a dressing room, then the studio area where Sten lived. The blonde giant was on his bed, arms covering his eyes.

"I knew you were there," Sten said. "So, why don't you just shoot me and get it over with."

"Shooting's too good for you," Abe replied, looking around the studio area. Again, dust everywhere but everything in order. Clean filth, organized depravity. He looked at Sten. "You thought that was real clever, that game you pulled on Mantis—and on an I.D. that *I* issued to you, huh?"

"I don't wanna be your errand boy no more," Sten said, not looking up.

"Don't worry. You were fired a week ago."

"So. Let's get it over with."

"Screw you and your candy-assed martyrdom," Abe said, sitting down. "Did you ever think of the trouble that I got into because of that?"

"You afraid?"

"I don't want any trouble with Mantis."

Sten sat up and rubbed at his eyes. They were still swollen from the spray. He pointed a finger at Abe and said, "Don't worry about Mantis. I'll handle him."

"Man, you're a real jerk, aren't you? Can't I get it through to you, Mantis is a nut. He's sick."

"Yeah, and I want him."

"You want revenge and revenge is sweet. But Mantis' *job* is puttin' people away. He's an expert at it. I'm surprised he didn't kill you when you showed up at his place."

"He did what he did to shame me. He knew I had no fear of death."

"Well, death is exactly what you're going to get if you keep messin' with him. *The guy is evil.*"

"That," Sten said, "is why I want him. He stands for everything that the people hate about the government. He thinks people exist to be used, to be stepped on. But he's even worse than the government 'cause what he does, he does for his own personal pleasure. For him, it's all kicks."

Abe shook his head. Sten was always bringing the discussion back to the government and the people. Did he think that by killing Mantis the system would change?

"Listen," Abe said, "can't you see that everyone is in their place because they wanna be there? You're always gonna have rich people, you're always gonna have poor people. You got rich folk in the army now, and in the games, because they're bored being rich. And you got poor people makin' it and becoming chieftains. That's the way it is."

"The army bosses put Mantis in the Arena."

"The *people* put Mantis in the Arena," Abe said. "That's what I'm tryin' to tell you and what you should already know. He doesn't represent anyone now. He's the game. He's the free agent."

In fact, he was an institution. Abe remembered how, shortly after Mantis's victory over Tanaka, Mantis had been called before both the U-1 and U-2 boards to account for the charges of hypocrisy he had publicly leveled against the International Arena League and its sponsors. He recalled how Mantis had sat there, thoroughly calm and confident, his eyes flashing an intense green. His anvil-faced bodyguard, Al Harris, sat by his side, the two of them highly amused by the whole affair.

"Look, I helped you gentlemen clear the way for this game," Mantis told them. "And now I'm taking the game over. Only I'm changing the rules. No more just wounding an opponent, so that he'll die outside the arena. That's over. From now on, if you fight, you either win or die. I've got the people behind me; you heard them in the stadium. And I'm going to give them a say in what goes down. If they want, they can give the thumbs up sign. Otherwise, the man on the canvas dies."

At first Abe didn't know what to make of this new character. He had dealt with him personally during the Demo-A days, but that was before the accident, before Mantis had been hit by, as rumor had it, a neutron grenade. Back then Mantis had always been straight business, committed to few words, a commando and an assassin who asked few questions, gave no quarter, and expected none in return.

But during that meeting he saw a different man. The accident, or something, had altered him. He had a certain aura that made everyone in his presence cower. In the ensuing weeks and months, as the camouflage-dressed killer took on one opponent after another, regardless of their size, and finished them off, even Arena officials such as Abe began to realize that they had created a kind of monster.

And this big hulk of a puppy here, Abe thought, as he watched Sten curl some free weights—this guy's just a dessert for Mantis.

"You see?" Sten said. "I'm gettin' it back. Been doin' it all week—the curls and presses. The old strength, it's still there."

But his mind, it wanders now, Abe realized. That's what the pills do to you, like a car breaking down. How can I tell you that, kid—that some of your plugs are gone.

"What is it you really want?" Abe asked.

"I wanna chance to show my spirit again."

"What you want is revenge," Abe said.

Sten smirked. "Can you blame me?"

"No," Abe replied. "I can't blame you. You were a part of something that had to be knocked off. You were in the way. But what's done is done. The Arena's the thing, the dojos and stuff are gone."

"So what's left?" Sten asked. "This fuckin' system's pushed everyone into a corner, man. Maybe I ain't the best one for the job, but the people have to have a champion—a champion who will at least try to stand up to the system."

"The people don't *want* a champion, kid. They just wanna watch other people die."

"I could change all that," Sten said.

"By killing Mantis?"

"You got it."

Abe laughed. Perhaps now it was time. He had been saving Sten, after all.

"You don't want Mantis...now."

"Why do you say that?"

Abe leaned closer. "Mantis," he said, "was just a tool to help dispose of you. You never meant nothin' personal to him. What you want is the guy that set you up."

Sten's face went pale. "What do you mean?" he asked.

"I'm talking about one of the street coordinators from the demo squads. The government had you on top of its list, but it needed to probe into your character first. The street coordinators were the guys who assembled the pertinent information."

"Information?"

"Yeah, information. The demo squads wanted to know everything. The street coordinator's job was to give them more of an inside picture: how you dressed, what time you got up—and most important of all, what your weaknesses were. In your case, the street coordinator found only one—a taste for the ladies."

"So who was this coordinator?" Sten asked.

Abe paused, took a puff on his cigar. "Ever heard of a guy named Capitan?"

Sten thought for a moment, his mind going back, recollecting. "Yeah, Aikido man. Stick fighter, too. I remember him. But we never really met. How could he get information about me?"

"Through crossover students. Guys who study a little of this, a little of that. You had them, right?"

Sten looked down at the floor. "I had thousands of students back then."

"Well, it was Capitan's job to collect information about targeted people in his sector—Brooklyn. He planted some of his people in your dojo and they all came back with the same report: get him a lady friend who'll do what we want her to do."

Sten's eyes showed a flash of anger as he remembered the female Demo-A agent who had addicted him to sodac plus.

"Why're you telling me all this?" he asked.

"Because we have mutual interests now, and because I wanna give you a shot at the guy who really fucked you over."

Sten shook his head. "This guy Capitan. I don't know him—but he was real *budo,* man. A true martial artist. That much I remember. You expect me to believe he'd betray his own kind?"

"For the right price, sure."

Sten considered this for a moment. Abe took another puff on his cigar.

"Everyone has a price," Abe said. "Capitan had his. But as I recall, Capitan's price wasn't too steep. He was easily bought off. I remember him laughing when Mantis floored you."

Sten gritted his teeth. "Are you putting me on?"

"Why would I wanna do that?"

"You expect me to believe all this?"

"I expect you to find out for yourself," Abe said.

Sten took up the dumbbells again and began curling angrily. "So why did you say we have mutual interests? What's that all about?"

"Capitan fucked you over. Now he's fucking C.I. over."

"What's he doing?"

"That's none of your business. The reason I'm letting you slide for what you did is simple. You're needed. Central Intelligence wants someone to put the scare into this character."

Sten smiled. "So I've been elected, huh?"

Abe nodded. "It's a favor you owe me *and* yourself."

Sten did a slow, protracted curl with the dumbbell. "I thought I was fired," he said.

"You are. This job'll be off the card. My card at least. But you'll get paid for it."

Sten looked warily at Abe. "I don't know..."

Abe rose slowly, taking out a small piece of paper. He threw it on the floor. "That's Capitan's address."

Sten glanced at it. "And if I accept?" he asked "What do you want me—"

"To do?"

"Yeah."

Abe shrugged. "Oh, rough him up. Scare him. But keep him in one piece. All this is assuming you can take him, of course."

"I can take him," Sten said.

"Good," Abe said.

"*If* I take the job," the *karateka* added.

The old gangster looked at Sten, his face a strange blend of resolution and amusement.

"You'll take the job," he said.

He turned to go.

"There's just one other thing," Sten said.

"What?"

"You gonna call off those two 'turkeys' out there?"

Abe smiled and nodded. "'Turkey,' right..." He took a final puff on his cigar and then strode out of the room.

Sten sat thinking for the longest time, staring at the address on the floor. J. Capitan. He remembered Capitan's reputation as a martial artist. It was a good one. So why would he want to screw me? Sten thought. Was Abe right, after all? Did everybody have a price? Well, there was only one way to find out. He would have to confront Capitan. And maybe they *would* fight, after all. It would be a true *budo*-style duel. Why not?

But then again, why? Sten wasn't certain. He knew only that he was tired of being Abe's stooge, his errand boy.

He looked over then at the *makiwara*, the punching board, and approached it, thinking back to all of the past betrayal and pain. Measuring the distance to the board, he swung his fist in a wide arc and almost knocked it off the wall. Again and again he slammed his fist into the board, over and over, until his knuckles began to bleed.

Yeah, the spirit was back in him, just like the old days. There was blood on his hands, that was the sign.

CHAPTER TEN

THAT same night Capitan and Carmen sat before the hearth, both pairs of legs crossed, in lotus posture. Capitan had lit a small fire, and now Bimbi approached in fascination, because he had never seen a fireplace before. Fireplaces were antique, a thing of the past. He pointed at the thick log that was being consumed by the flames.

"Is that real wood?" he asked.

"No," Capitan answered, still retaining his position. "It's synthetic."

"But at one time they used real wood, right?" Bimbi asked.

"Yes. When there was real wood available."

"Ain't no wood in Brooklyn," Bimbi said.

"There's no more wood anywhere," Carmen added.

"How about Alaska?"

"What about it?"

"There's wood up there, right?"

"The Japanese and the Chinese own it now. And it's expensive."

"How'd they get it?"

"It's a long story," Capitan said, "one that doesn't concern us right now. What concerns us right now is silence."

"What do you mean?" Bimbi asked.

"He means shut up," Carmen said.

Bimbi stopped talking and, for a long time, shifted his attention between the fire and the statuelike postures of Capitan and Carmen. Finally he decided to imitate them both and, crossing his legs, found that the lotus posture was quite easy for him since his limbs were young and loose. He straightened his back and positioned his hands as Capitan and Carmen were doing, left hand atop the right, forming a circle. He sat there, closed his eyes, and smiled.

And Capitan smiled with him, watching him out of the corner of his eye. He felt his mind wandering, then, his thoughts drifting back to Hokkaido...to Hoshima....

Hoshima's first and primary rule was "to sit."

"There are a thousand and one books and libraries dedicated to the truth," he told Capitan, as he brought him for the first time into his cave. "But they all mean nothing in the end. Words are fuel, they're food—for your brain. But words are not truth. 'Sitting' is the Truth."

Capitan looked about the cave, noting its Spartan design: bearskins as a bed, an oil lamp, a zabuton cushion, a washbasin, soap, a straight-edged razor—and three books; but they were in Japanese and Capitan could not read them. He hefted the volumes and examined them.

"There, you see," Hoshima said, shaking his matted head and grabbing the washbasin. "No sooner do I tell you about words than you pick up books."

"They are a weakness," Capitan said. "Which books are these?"

"If you were a crazy hermit like me, which three books would you possess?" Hoshima let Capitan think for a few minutes while he went out with the washbasin. Finally he returned and looked at Capitan. "Well?"

"Oh,...the Bible, *Leaves of Grass,* Shakespeare."

"What a dolt," Hoshima said, examining the straight-edged razor.

"You asked me, I told you."

"Those books there," Hoshima said, pointing at them with the razor, "are *The Doctrine of the Mean, The Gita,* and my favorite, *Hawaii.*"

"*Hawaii?*"

"Yes, a very old novel by an author named James Michener. I shall lend it to you some time."

Hoshima motioned for Capitan to follow him back out into the late summer sun. They walked over to some gas canisters that the hermit used to store water. He emptied one canister into the basin, then set the basin up on a tripod, over a flame-heater.

"We'll let that boil. In the meantime, I'm going to sit."

He drew himself into a lotus position, resting his buttocks on a rock. Capitan followed suit, not far away. Feeling uncomfortable at first, he gradually eased into the posture and, despite feeling a bit of pain in the legs, found it very rooting, very settling to the nerves. Several minutes passed. Then he heard Hoshima say:

"Sitting is in itself the Truth. The mind can produce all the visions and cartoons it wants but it really means nothing in the end. Truth does not find a secure home in the head, but in the belly. By sitting like the great Buddha, we invite the Truth to settle into us, we give it a home—no more, no less. And what more could be desired?"

Hoshima rose and watched as the water boiled in the basin. He turned to Capitan.

"That is the basis of my teaching. You are through now. You are thoroughly enlightened and are ready to return to your people to be crucified."

"Crucified?" Capitan said.

"Yes. You may do that, or you may help lather me down. I am going to shave."

"Shit..."

Capitan looked over at Bimbi, who was cursing and stretching out his legs. Briefly, Capitan let his thoughts drift back to Hoshima, remembering how he had taken the straight-edged razor and shaved the master down until he was totally bald and beardless, like a monk.

He glanced back at Bimbi. The young Hispanic was again alternating his attention between the fire and themselves. Capitan closed his eyes and smiled.

Unable to bear the silence any longer, Bimbi finally nudged Carmen.

"Hey..."

"What?"

"What are you thinking about?" he asked.

"I am trying to think about nothing," she told him.

"How can you think about nothing?"

"By not thinking," Carmen said.

"Come off it," Bimbi said. "Why would you want to think about just nothing?"

"Because there's nothing to really think about."

"I don't get it."

"I didn't think you would."

"You gotta think about something," Bimbi said.

"Like what?"

"I don't know. How about food?"

"Your stomach'll think about it for you."

"I bet. Look, how can you not think about nothing?"

"With great difficulty," Carmen said. She began to giggle.

Capitan suddenly broke his posture. "Enough of this," he said. "What she means is that the mind enters a peaceful, tranquil state. It doesn't move. But forget that for now." He pointed at the log, burning away slowly, then said, "Fire."

"No kidding," Bimbi said.

"Don't be smart. Now, watch it burn. Watch it eat through the wood."

"That ain't wood."

"All right, it's chemicals. But my point is the same. The fire penetrates it. It doesn't have to force its way through; it penetrates, works its way around, then through."

"Is this some kind of chemistry lesson?"

"In a manner of speaking," Capitan said. "The fire works by Aiki."

He watched as Carmen started and shook her head. He motioned for her to be calm. I know what I'm doing, he thought. I'm using a term, not a technique.

"What's that, Ai—ki?"

"It's a Japanese word," Carmen said. Her eyes were focused on Capitan.

"What does it mean?"

"It means to shut up and listen," Carmen said.

"No."

"What it means," Capitan said, "is that you should tune yourself in to everything around you. That doesn't necessarily mean with just your ears, either. A cobra, for example, hears with its eyes."

"Really?"

"Sure. A dog actually sees with his nose. Hearing, seeing—these are terms that apply to the same thing: the ability to sense things out. Aiki means to sense things out harmoniously."

"I don't get it."

"I don't expect you to at first," Capitan said, his thoughts drifting back again to Hoshima. He remembered how, after he had shaved the hermit, they had sat there on the hillside, looking out on the valleys of Hokkaido.

"What I can teach you," Hoshima had said, "is not my own invention, really. It is more a synthesis: of yoga, Zen, Aikido, karate—everything. But the essential thing is sitting. Sitting is our true nature. Our true Buddha nature. The mind finds peace in the lotus posture—grounds itself—and once the mind is grounded it has time to unite with the breath which is the expression of the true Godhead.

"Our minds are no different than anything else on this planet, my friend. They are controlled by gravity. The body is like a spaceship, the mind like an astronaut. The astronaut needs gravity to function because, lacking it, he will float away. Just as the astronaut wears leaden boots to approximate gravity, so too does the mind create ethics to pinion itself to reality. Both can be weighty and cumbersome, but without them nothing can be achieved. These ethics I speak of—moderation, love, antiviolence—they can best be welded into a single term: 'Aiki.' My art is 'Shin-Do, the Way of the Mind,' but it is the term 'Aiki' that is the secret. It is the secret you shall always need as you are persecuted, beaten, flogged, crucified, and laughed at by those cruel others with their monkeylike minds." Hoshima rubbed his domelike skull and smiled.

The past faded, then, and Capitan returned his attention to Bimbi, who shook his head.

"I don't get it, this Aiki stuff," he said.

"It's really quite simple," Capitan replied. "Aiki's the glue that holds everything together, everything in the Universe."

"Where do you find it?" Bimbi asked.

"Everywhere. In everything and everyone."

"In me?"

"Of course. Only you can't touch it. It's like a spirit or a—a ghost. The Holy Ghost."

"Shit..."

"And if you meddle with this glue, fool with it, life will get sticky for you."

"Is that what I've been doing?" Bimbi asked.

"You want revenge, Bimbi. Revenge is sticky and sweet. If you mess with the glue, you're gonna get stuck."

"I knew you had a Bible rap ready for me," the young Hispanic said, his eyes showing bitterness. "I knew you was leadin' up to something."

Capitan took Bimbi's arm. "Bimbi, everybody in this world is attached to one another by this Aiki. And whether you like it or not, that guy who killed your brother is a part of you."

"Oh yeah?" Bimbi said. "Well, I still wanna kill him."

"Then you'll kill a part of yourself, don't you see?" The fire in the hearth had begun to die out. Capitan put his hand on Bimbi's shoulder. "Always strive to do the highest thing you can. Forgive the man who killed your brother."

"I can't."

"You can," Capitan said. "You have it within yourself. We all have it within ourselves to forgive. If you want others to forgive you, then you have to forgive others. It's a simple law. Think on it."

"I'm thinkin', and I don't need anyone to forgive me," Bimbi said.

He looked away angrily. The fire had died. Capitan rose and motioned for Carmen to meet him up in the loft. He wanted Bimbi to think, to question this fever he had for revenge. It was the kind of fever that broke tragically with action. Senseless violent action.

Vengeance is Mine, thus spake the Lord.

Capitan remembered that proverb. Providence with its strange fingers of fate had taught him that lesson.

Eladio...

When his brother had died, Capitan had been forced to come to terms with that demon known as revenge. He was a lot younger then, like Bimbi. A gang of Ninja punks had cut down his brother— not just one, but a whole gang. And Capitan wanted them all. He was stung senseless by hate. Yet he had waited. He had bided his time because of the gang's numbers, making plans to wreak vengeance on them all simultaneously.

It was simple. They held services at their dojo. Friday night was the big one. No women there, either. Just warriors. And Capitan was ready. Two Molotov cocktails through the windows and it would be over. He could cut down any survivors as they made their way out.

Yes, Friday night. Those hoodlum punk bastards, man—they would all be his...

Capitan laid back in the loft, staring at Carmen's strong back as she undressed. He ran his finger down her spine playfully, but it tickled and she whacked his hand away. He rolled over. Bimbi was down below, still sitting before the hearth, brooding, consumed by that evil worm, revenge.

Vengeance is Mine, thus spake the Lord.

Capitan remembered how he had positioned himself on a fire escape right next to the warehouse where the Ninja gang had their dojo. From here he could easily hop across and hurl the Molotovs down through an old skylight; or he could use one, move back, and then hurl the second as the survivors attempted to escape. But he was going to wait until they were all assembled. There were fifteen of them, the fifteen who had killed his brother— his brother, who was a junkie and a thief, whose passing was really a blessing. Still, Capitan thought at the time, I have to kill them. I have to teach them my revenge. He wanted them all, and he was going to wait. And then suddenly he realized, as he looked about more carefully, that somebody else seemed to be waiting, too.

A patrol car, just down the alley.

The police seemed to be calculating something because the Ninja fight-guru, Black Tony, came outside at one point to consult them. Capitan watched as the consultation turned to pleading. Tony was pulled suddenly into the car and four officers emerged, holding rifles fitted with tear gas canisters. A paddy wagon pulled onto the scene, then another patrol car. The police opened up on the warehouse, forcing those inside to stagger out, choking and coughing. The cops knocked them on their knees and handcuffed them, then loaded them into the paddy wagon.

Capitan was to learn later that Tony and his men had been sent to the Jersey Tombs, the great prison from which few people ever returned. Tony and his punks had tried to doublecross the cops on a drug deal. One never did that....

Vengeance. Capitan had been spared the crime of taking innocent lives, leaving his own soul clean. But how could he make Bimbi see that revenge only soiled the hands—Bimbi, who was still hooked on drugs and walked around in a cloud.

Capitan wondered if it was wise to continue to train Bimbi. In some ways he was making it easier for the young man to seek revenge. The thought troubled him.

He felt Carmen poking him in the back. He smiled and rolled over, cupping his hand under one of her large breasts.

"Nice, uh?"

"Exquisite."

She grabbed him gently by the testicles and grinned.

"Up here, I'm the big *sensei*," she said.

"That means," Capitan said, "that you have to teach *me*."

"Okay..."

"So, uh...what's my first lesson?"

"Plus, with minus—equals," she said, drawing him closer, her long legs winding around Capitan and coaxing him on top of her.

"Ah, I think I can learn that one fast," Capitan said.

As the loft began to creak, Bimbi rolled over in his sleeping bag down below on the tatami floor. He grinned. Perhaps—after all—there were some things sweeter than revenge.

CHAPTER ELEVEN

STEN arrived early the next morning, bare-chested and barefoot, his white *gi* pants shining in the sun. From his black belt hung two nunchakas. As he strutted down the alley that led to Capitan's studio, three winos who had camped there for the night scurried out of his way. Sten scoffed at them and looked at the strange sign hanging in front of the studio door. He pointed at it.

"This where that guy Capitan lives?" he asked.

The winos kept their distance and began to shake their heads.

"Uh, no."

"Well, could be."

"Yeah, maybe."

"Fools," Sten said. "Away with you." He went up to the stairs, tried to spy through the windows, then pounded firmly on the door. "Open up."

Inside, Bimbi was the first to spring to his feet. He scooted over to the door and looked through the peephole.

Capitan was still quite drowsy. "Who is it?"

"Some big dude wearin' a black belt."

"Great. Just great." Capitan eased back onto the futon and groped for his yoga pants.

"C'mon," Sten shouted. "Open up. I know you're in there."

"Hey," Bimbi said, "this dude looks mean."

Capitan glanced at the clock: 7:05. "Anyone who would get up at this hour has to be mean."

Capitan quickly made his way down the ladder and across the studio. With Carmen following close behind, he approached the door. The pounding continued.

"Let's go. Open up."

Capitan peered through the peephole. There was Sten, his arms folded like Sitting Bull, the nunchakas hanging menacingly from his belt.

Capitan stepped back. "Hmmmm."

Bimbi turned to him. "You want me to take care of him?" he asked.

"You're gonna take care of *that?*" Capitan said.

"Yeah, sure."

"Take a look again."

Bimbi looked through the peephole: Sten was still there, his muscular arms folded, the classic portrait of the western samurai.

"Come on," Sten shouted. "I know you're in there, I know you're looking at me."

"Pardon me," Capitan yelled, "but it *is* seven in the morning. Why don't you come back a little later when I'm awake?"

Sten responded by pounding again on the door.

Carmen shook her head. "What an ass."

Capitan abruptly opened the door.

"Ahaaa—!" Sten said.

The two warriors stood face to face. Capitan smiled winningly. "And *who* are *you?*" he asked.

"I am Sten, a great warrior."

"Well, I certainly don't doubt that, but, well—like I said, it *is* seven in the morning and—"

"I have come here to fight you," Sten said.

"Right this moment?"

Sten grunted in affirmation.

"What an ass," Carmen said again.

Sten's eyes narrowed into menacing slits. He took a step forward. Capitan smiled diplomatically.

"Look, you're not being fair. It's really quite early and I have a...well, kind of a dislocated shoulder and—"

Sten opened up suddenly with a palm hand into Capitan's chest, sending the former Aikido champ somersaulting back onto the mats. Bimbi quickly pounced on Sten, only to be abruptly knocked off. Carmen was next. The young beauty dashed behind Sten and attempted to pull him back, off balance, but he quickly broke her grip with his superior weight and focused once again on Capitan, who had sprung to his feet. Carmen ran toward the weapons rack and drew a wooden sword. Sten retorted with a sudden flourish from one of his nunchakas. Everyone froze, ready for a fight. Capitan, regaining his senses, motioned for Carmen to back off. He faced Sten.

"All right bro, what's up?"

"I've come here to fight you."

"Why?"

"Because you betrayed me," Sten said.

"Betrayed you?" Capitan furrowed his brow. "I don't even know you."

"That's not what Abe Goldman says."

"Abe Goldman?"

"So you *do* know him." Sten moved further into the room, circling, ready for an attack.

"Yeah," Capitan replied, circling cautiously the opposite way. "But I don't know you. Goldman says I know you?"

"Goldman says you betrayed me, informed on me."

"Who the hell to?"

"To the demo squads. They wanted information on me and you gave it to them."

"This is crazy," Capitan said.

"Goldman said you'd deny it."

"Right," Capitan said, "because I don't know you and—"

"Cut the talking," Sten said. "I told you. I'm here to fight."

"Why should I fight you?" Capitan asked, almost amused, circling.

"It don't much matter. I'm going to hurt you anyway. But you may as well give your friends here a show." He nodded toward Carmen and Bimbi.

"Well, if that's the case, you'll let me pick the weapons."

"I have my weapon here," Sten said, his nunchakas ready.

"But I have the right to pick," Capitan told him. "That is tradition. You have challenged me by coming to my space."

Sten gave no answer; his eyes were on all three, ready.

"Those nunchakas are for killing, not for points. What other weapons are you versed in?"

"I know all the weapons of the great Zen warriors," Sten said proudly. "Tonfas, sais, the spear..."

"How about the jo?" Capitan asked, taking a thin wooden staff from his weapon rack with caution, not turning his back on Sten.

"I am a great master with the jo," Sten boasted. "And what will you use?"

Not the Aiki sword, Capitan thought. I need room to move here, and the Filipino fighting sticks are the best bet.

"Arnis sticks."

Capitan lifted two rattan sticks from the rack. They were not more than two feet each in length. "Jo against two sticks, how about that?"

"Yes. Yes."

"Then you've got yourself a duel," Capitan told him. He hurled the jo at Sten. The *karateka* caught it and threw his nunchakas aside. Carmen motioned for Bimbi to stay calm as they watched the two contestants stretch and examine their weapons. Finally Capitan approached Sten. "Since you challenge me, it is my right, too, to specify the conditions."

"Quick, let's hear them," Sten said.

"Three points decides the winner. No more, no less. And then we become friends and brothers. We sit calmly and talk all this out."

"Yes! Yes!" Sten cried, preparing to attack with the jo. "And now—defend yourself!"

The first point came almost immediately. Sten lunged madly with the jo but Capitan quickly side-stepped, snapping swiftly with his sticks at Sten's wrists and elbows. The *karateka* was thoroughly disarmed.

"Look, why don't we just make it one point and end it here?"

Sten wiped the perspiration from his forehead. He seized his jo again, and swung angrily at the retreating Capitan. Both warriors danced around each other for a few minutes, wooden weapons clacking in broken rhythm as each attempted to score. Sten persisted in charging, in using his superior size and force to corner Capitan, but the former Aikido champion dashed in and out, using his speed to wear Sten down.

Capitan was impressed. Despite this big brute's wild behavior, he was obviously a credited student of the arts.

Sten lunged suddenly, trapping Capitan against the wall. He tried to lock the *karateka*'s jo with his two rattan sticks but Sten hurled him aside, swiftly jamming the end of the jo into Capitan's side.

"Aha! One to one. You are out of shape, my fellow warrior."

Capitan nodded, collecting himself. He quickly dashed in, striking at Sten's wrists again and scoring. Sten recoiled but was unharmed.

"Two to one."

Sten flushed angrily and began to swing the jo in broader and broader arcs while Capitan danced back, looking for an opening. Just as the *karateka* had completed a swing, Capitan saw his chance. He rushed in, knocking Sten off balance and pushing him to the floor. As the larger man groped desperately for his jo Capitan snapped at his hand with a stick. "Number three."

Sten rose to his feet, seething.

"Samurai!" Capitan quickly shouted. "Are you samurai?"

"I am," Sten said, noticeably swelling his chest.

"Then remember," Capitan said. "A pledge is a pledge."

Sten nodded humbly, recalling his oath. He extended his hand to Capitan, who took it in his grasp.

"Ouch!" Capitan yelled. He wondered in what blacksmith's shop that grip had been forged.

Bimbi's mouth remained open as Sten finished guzzling another can of beer. He swallowed the last drop and crushed the can abruptly in his hand. The four were sitting at the kitchen table now, drinking. Sten and Capitan had just finished clearing the air.

"That cagey bastard," Sten said, referring to Abe. "He sicked me on you like a dog."

"Yes, but the question is why." Capitan thought back to the questions Goldman had asked about Hoshima and his own involvement in the martial arts. He looked at Sten. "Demo quads, eh?"

"Uh-huh. The drugs came first. Then they sent Mantis in to finish me off."

"*You* fought Mantis?" Bimbi said.

"In the old days, before he competed in the Arena, yeah. That was before he was a commando even." Sten went on to explain how he had acquired Mantis's address. He told them all, proudly, about his ill-fated visit, leaving a few details out.

Bimbi hung on every word. "So you wanna fight him again?"

Sten suddenly turned serious. "Yeah, I wanna fight him. I wanna fight him bad. But it ain't only for me. Mantis stands for something bad, and I kind of feel like, well...if things are ever going to be right again, he's got to be stopped."

"Stay away from him," Capitan warned. "You walk into Mantis's space, you're walking into heavy karma. I'm not just talking about fighting, either."

Sten shook his head. "I ain't afraid of him. I'm going to get my rematch, you can be sure of that. But this time it will be in the Arena."

Bimbi stared excitedly at Sten. "You're gonna fight him at the games? To the death?"

"Yeah."

"He'll turn you down," Capitan said.

"Not if I challenge him publicly, the way he did with Tanaka. I've already decided to do it at his next fight, when he faces Savinien."

Capitan started. "Savinien? Hercules Savinien?"

"That's him."

"You know him?" Carmen asked.

"Yeah. I learned arnis with him in Manila. We studied under the same master. I haven't seen him since, but he's big in European Sport Arena. A savate man, kick-boxer. The best. He can be arrogant, though."

"Well," Sten said, "the night of the fight, I intend to be there in a front row seat. Somehow, I'll get the cameras on me and then I'll denounce Mantis—before the people."

"The people won't care," Capitan said. "All they want is blood."

"The people hate Mantis," Sten said.

"They *love* to hate him," Capitan replied. "There's a difference."

Bimbi sipped at his beer, his stomach already bloated. "Hey, bro, you think you could get us tickets?"

"We don't want tickets," Carmen said.

"Yes, we do," Bimbi said excitedly.

Sten laughed. "Now it's my turn to set the conditions." He folded his arms and looked at Capitan. "You won the match, fair and square. So now I owe you something. A gift. And you have to accept it."

"What is it?" Capitan's mind flitted distractedly between Goldman and Savinien and the unsettling effect Sten was having on young Bimbi. "I'll accept any gift so long as it doesn't hurt anyone. So long as it doesn't lead to violence."

"You make it sound like my gift's a bomb," Sten said.

"Well, I don't know you that well," Capitan said. "In any case, you don't owe me anything."

"Oh, yes I do," Sten said. "So the gift is this: front row seats at the Mantis-Savinien fight. For all four of us. I have connections."

"Wow!" Bimbi said.

"We're not going," Carmen said.

"Maybe *you're* not," Bimbi said.

"And neither are you," Carmen replied.

"I've been there before," Bimbi protested. "But never in front row seats."

"Forget it," Capitan said.

Sten ripped the top off another beer. "But you agreed."

"I didn't do anything of the kind."

"Come on," Bimbi said, "why can't we go? I could study other techniques there."

"There are no real techniques in the Arena," Capitan told him. "Just the spirit of death."

Sten waved his hand dismissively. "Come on—go. You could even visit your old friend Savinien. I could get you into the dressing room before the fight."

Capitan looked up, interested. Savinien. It would be nice to see him again.

"Hypocrites," Bimbi said. "You especially," he added, pointing a finger at Carmen. "Didn't you used to pop sodac, watch this stuff?"

"Yeah, once," Carmen told him. "Same as you. But front row seats are gruesome."

"No they aren't," Sten said. "That's where you really get to see the art of it."

"Art?" Carmen said. "Ha!"

As the two began quarreling, Capitan reflected back on the history of the Arena, starting with the era of the demo squads. Those had been bad times. He was lucky to have survived. Originally, the demo squads had been created with two objectives in mind. First, the squads were to destroy the confidence and morale of any combat sport that offered a clean-minded philosophy. Second, they were to see to it that the sport devolved under the leadership of street punks into mere cultism—a kind of war religion. The demo squads maintained a legitimate front, worked ostensibly according to the rules, but they had covert means of advancing their aims. Drugs, seduction, poison—all were used to undermine the existing sport organizations.

Boxing was the only sport to offer more than token resistance. There the toughest breed could be found. But the Demo-A agents were smart. They overloaded boxing with cumbersome rules— overloaded it until it became a farce. And once the sport was viewed as such, it became relatively easy to add to it the antics and showmanship of "professional wrestling," creating finally a hybrid sport known as Arena.

The early Arena contests permitted fisticuffs and grappling only, but as the sport slowly evolved and its popularity grew, the use of blunt weaponry became legitimized.

At some point new types of demo squads, with new sets of instructions, were dispatched. Under their influence, Arena contestants witnessed the slow, methodical removal of all safety rules. Protective gear was discarded and the use of lethal weapons received government sanction. The stage was thus set for the ascendancy of Mantis.

The Tokyo Coliseum...Capitan remembered watching the fight, one of the few times he had ever tuned in. He remembered how, just before the fight began, the green-eyed commando, dressed in his traditional camouflage uniform, had held up his sai daggers for all to see.

As the pit-cameras flashed his image across the globe, Capitan, watching at home, thought he could see in Mantis's eyes a quality of rapture. Mantis was there, standing in the pit, for all to see. And yet, he was not there. He was somewhere else—above it all— looking down on his subjects.

Tanaka, the champion from Okinawa, entered then, looking supremely confident. He had killed every opponent he had faced— all by "accident," of course—and it was clear to everyone that he intended Mantis to suffer a similar fate.

Looking back on it, Capitan wasn't sure why he picked Mantis to win—maybe it was that quality he saw in his eyes—but something told him that on that night the Okinawan's victory skein would finally come to an end. As it turned out, Capitan's premonition was correct, though Mantis did take his time playing with his opponent. The ex-commando's icy calm incited the Okinawan to rush in repeatedly with his nunchakas, but each time Mantis side-stepped him so swiftly that he literally seemed to disappear. Tanaka crashed again and again against the wall surrounding the fight pit, hearing the hoots and jeers of the crowd grow louder and louder with each ignominious thud. Driven to exasperation, the giant Okinawan finally charged his opponent like a bull, swinging his nunchakas in a broad arc. Once more Mantis side-stepped him, but this time he caught him in the side with one of his sais. The fans sat stunned as Tanaka staggered backward and examined his wound: deliberate and light, the mark of a true killer. Undaunted, Tanaka charged again. It was a charge that would make history because this time Mantis spun around like a top, meeting the Okinawan head-on with his dagger. Tanaka toppled over like a log, his belly spurting blood.

It should have ended there...at that moment....

But Mantis had a treat.

The medics rushed in, only to be chased away by a quick flourish of the ex-commando's remaining sai. Amused by Mantis's gesture, the crowd decided to back him, hurling missiles, bottles, trinkets, and garbage down into the pit. "*Mantis! Maaaantis!*" It gained in intensity until the entire coliseum was intoning the new champion's name.

Mantis smiled. He walked over to Tanaka, writhing on the canvas. With a light shove of his foot he pushed the giant over, onto his back. Then he stood over him, placed his foot on his chest, and waved his free sai over his head—an open gesture to the crowd.

"*Thumbs up or thumbs down?*" he asked, his deep-throated voice instantly quieting the fans. "Thumbs up or thumbs down?" he repeated. And then he asked in Japanese: "*Nani-Ga Hoshi Des-Ka? Hai? Ie?*" He motioned next with his unarmed hand, matching words with action: thumbs up, or thumbs down?

"This is something new," a commentator said.

"No," Capitan remembered hearing another commentator add, "this is something very *old.*"

Cameras were turned on the faces of the Tokyo fans. Their expressions shifted from shock to perplexity to amusement to pleasure. As if directed by a master puppeteer, fifty thousand fans simultaneously gesticulated the reply: *thumbs down.*

Mantis smiled and abruptly plunged the sai dagger into Tanaka's throat....

Afterward Mantis was taken into custody and charged with murder. The Tokyo fans responded with a series of riots that left about twenty people dead. When he was finally permitted to appear before the TV cameras the new Arena champion claimed that he was innocent and accused the Sport Arena's sponsors of hypocrisy. He pointed out that he had simply done outright what contestants had been doing all along; that he was, in fact, only an instrument of the people's will. It was the Arena's fans who had passed judgment on Tanaka.

"Are the people murderers?" he asked the press. "The government has declared that Sport Arena is a sport for the people. Then why shouldn't it be the people who decide the outcome of each fight?"

It was irrefutable logic—logic that won for Mantis the support of millions of Arena fans around the globe. And in the face of such support, the government had no choice but to acquiesce. Overnight the Arena was transformed into a true gladiatorial spectacle, the pit in which the matches were fought became known as "The Death Ring," and Mantis, Sport Arena's most charismatic champion yet, presided over it all like a dark and powerful god. Through Mantis's macabre displays of showmanship, the people's lust for blood was deepened, made more addictive, until finally it became almost a tangible thing—a force that Mantis could concentrate in himself and use for his own ends.

As Mantis arrogated to himself more and more power, it became inevitable that he would eventually turn his back on the people—

declare his independence from them altogether. This he did a few months later in a series of matches that had him spitefully reversing all of the fans' decisions, regardless of whether they had asked him to spare his opponent or finish him off. Too late now to punish him for his actions—"killing" had become, after all, part of the Arena status quo—the people were thus reduced to being humiliated by the very champion they, through their staunch support, had installed.

Capitan's reverie was broken suddenly by the strident voices of Bimbi and Carmen. Their disagreement over the advisability of attending the upcoming Arena contest had escalated into a full-scale shouting match.

"You're not going," Carmen said. "And that's it."

"Who are you to stop me?" Bimbi said. "I'll go anywhere I want. I'm a free man—"

"Quiet," Capitan said, "both of you." He looked over at Sten. "Maybe it would be good for the boy to see it up close after all. Illusions can be dangerous."

Carmen muttered something under her breath.

Sten beamed. "Good, then it's settled." He crushed another beer can in his hand.

"This will lead to no good," Carmen said.

"It will lead to where it has to," Capitan told her.

"I repeat, it will lead to no good."

Carmen did not look at him but got up from the table and walked into the other room. Bimbi turned and hugged Capitan. Capitan said nothing. He watched as Sten downed yet another beer.

CHAPTER TWELVE

KALIL Oman was a family man. He had three wives and many mouths to feed. When he left the Zed Advesta cult with his caravan of offspring he knew that the only way to provide for them was to fight, so he entered the minor Arena leagues and tried as best he could. There were no thoughts of glory, just survival.

Fortunately, Kalil did more than survive. He rose quickly, gaining the status of a minor champion, and as a consequence the credits poured in. There were still not enough, though, to support a man with a virtual tribe greeting him at the doorstep. Thus, when Kalil learned that an additional 100,000 credits had been added to his bank account by a person who was apparently one of the big promoters of the major league, along with an invitation for an interview, he was more than ready to comply with any demands that might be made of him. Entering the Palisades Complex that fine afternoon, Kalil was unaware that he was becoming involved in something totally unrelated to Sport Arena, that he was about to become the latest figure in a campaign of terrorism that had already shaken the country....

His appointment was for 2:30, room 495. Arriving early, he seated himself in the reception area and waited to be summoned. There were only a few pieces of furniture in the room and nothing at all to read. As he looked around for something to focus on, he saw a large, anvil-faced man suddenly emerge from an adjoining office. The man smiled as he caught sight of him.

"You Oman?" Al Harris asked, opening up a file he was carrying.

"That's me."

Al seated himself behind a white reception desk. "You used to be a Zed A, right?"

"Look, what is this?"

"You're not being paid to ask questions," Al said. "Besides, we have every right to ask you these things. That Zed A has been responsible for a lot of violence in the past few months. If we move you on to the major leagues, we wanna make sure you have no connections with them. Is that clear?"

"Sure...of course." Kalil began to relax. This was just routine, something everybody had to go through.

"Now. We want to know something about the group's activities while you were with them."

"Like what?"

"Just relax and let *me* ask the questions. First: tell me something about the group's foster home service."

"That was our main thing," Kalil said, slightly puzzled. "A lot of sisters were hangin' around without men to help raise the kids, so we set up a permanent Day Care to help out."

"Just black kids?"

"Black kids, white kids, yellows, greens, pinks. It was our policy to take in everybody. Basically, though, it was just blacks, yeah."

"Very good," Al said. "Second: how close were you to Big Sun, the head man?"

"I was one of his bodyguards," Oman said.

"Then you were *very* close to him. He relied on you."

"Like I said, I was a bodyguard. That meant I was entrusted with the safety of his life." Kalil didn't like where the man's questions were heading. "What are you, C.I. or something? What is this—"

"Like I said, I'll ask the questions."

"I still deserve—"

"Mr. Oman," Al said, "our office just deposited 100,000 credits into your bank account. That gives us the right to ask anything we want. If you don't like it, we can simply arrange to have the deposit withdrawn. That is in our power. Now, which will it be?"

One hundred thousand credits bought a lot of patience. Kalil smiled. "Okay, shoot. Ask away."

Al looked down at the file. "Now, tell me why you left the group."

"I wanted my own life. The Zed Advesta runs on a communal basis. I wanted to be my own man—think for myself."

"You left with hard feelings, then?"

"I was labeled a defector. Yeah, you might say that."

"Do they hate you?"

"They don't hate me, no. I'm a...lost sheep, kinda."

"They'd take you back, then?"

"You *are* C.I., aren't you?"

"Mr. Oman, answer my question. Would they or wouldn't they take you back?"

"Yeah, they'd take me back probably."

"Without a lot of questioning?"

"Hardly. But I have no intention of going back."

"Deep down you don't," Al said, running his large hand down the edge of the file and then tapping it with his fingers. "But, if our office were to pay you an additional hundred thousand credits or so..."

Kalil rose to his feet. "Look, a low-down fighter and killer I may be—but I ain't no lousy traitor."

"Mr. Oman, calm down, do calm down. We were not suggesting that you betray anyone. Just that you, well...'examine,' and I use that word in quotes, the possibility of returning to your old flock."

"And—?"

"And once having done that, gaining an audience with Big Sun, so that you can press home our interests. It's all very simple, really."

"You make it sound simple," Kalil said, not about to be fooled.

"It is simple, Mr. Oman. It's as simple as feeding three wives and fifteen children." Al leaned back in his seat and folded his arms, a wide grin on his face.

"You white bastard," Kalil said.

"Now, now. That's no way to treat the hand that's going to feed you. And we are going to feed you well."

"I haven't agreed."

"*Yet.* You haven't agreed yet."

There was a long pause as Al waited for Kalil to cool off, to collect his thoughts.

"What do you want me to do?"

"We want you to go back, pretend that you've seen the error of your ways. Then, when even Big Sun is convinced of your sincerity, we want you to open up discussions about a certain child."

"A child?" Kalil did not know whether to be amused or shocked.

"That's what I said. A child. A white boy. He should have been brought to the community by a Japanese fellow. This is a picture of him."

Al pulled a photo out of the portfolio and handed it to Kalil. The fighter looked closely at it. It was a photo of a Japanese officer. There was something about him—a certain quality. Kalil couldn't put his finger on it. He handed it back to the anvil-faced man.

"What's his name?"

"Even if I told you, you wouldn't recognize it. Now, the Zed Advesta has foster centers in five different areas, right?"

"One in New York, two in L.A., one in Chicago. We also have a farm in Kentucky," Kalil said. "But look, even if they do believe I want to come back, you think they're gonna start givin' me info about some white kid with a samurai stepfather?"

"They will, if you hand them this."

Al handed Kalil a blank credeer card.

"There's nothin' on it," Kalil said.

"Wrong," Al said. He withdrew a penlight from his vest pocket and shined the neon end on the card. "Look again."

Kalil saw some strange symbols:

$$---- \text{ o } ---- \text{ o}$$
$$---- \text{ o } ---- +$$

"So?"

"So just hand it to your old guru. Tell him that Monitor Five says hello. Tell him that he wants to know about the boy. Tell him that, in exchange, he'll provide information about these terrorists who are blacklisting his group."

Kalil glared. "You know who these terrorists are?"

"Never mind what we know. We're paying you two hundred grand to just drop in and ask some questions."

"I don't get it."

"You're not supposed to."

"You guys are C.I., aren't ya?"

"You'll find out soon enough," Al said. "Any questions?"

"Yeah. Why me?"

"They know your face. They don't know my face. Somebody's gotta go in there and arrange things. Any more questions?"

"Yeah. You guys never wanted me for no major league, did ya?"

Al smiled. "Could you make two hundred grand fighting, and in one week?"

Kalil slowly shook his head.

Al rose to his feet and handed him the photo of the Japanese officer. "When you mention Monitor Five, flash this picture around. I can assure you that it will get Big Sun's attention. We expect you back here by Monday. Okay?"

Kalil hesitated. "Yeah...sure."

Al ushered Kalil to the door. "Monday, same time."

"Right, same time," Kalil said. He tucked the photo in his pocket and walked out, listening as the door closed abruptly behind him. I'm being raped, he thought. I'm letting these guys rape me.

Then he remembered the two hundred grand and it didn't seem so bad.

The first thing Capitan did when he arrived at the Palisade Complex's basement gymnasium that day was to cancel his vapo-rhythm class and leave word with Charlie. If at all possible, Mr. Goldman was to meet him for his massage session an hour before the scheduled time.

When Abe arrived, Capitan approached him, feigning an air of nervousness and trepidation.

"What's the big idea of sending that ape to get me?" Capitan asked.

Abe started undressing. "Who? Sten?"

"That's him."

"Sten paid you a visit?"

"He did more than that, he almost knocked down my door. If I hadn't had such a strong bolt on it he would have."

"I thought you were a big warrior?"

"I never had to fight a brute like *that*."

Capitan hoped the act was working.

"All right, look, calm down."

"Why'd you send him after me?"

"Who says I did?"

"He did."

"Did I?"

Capitan did his best to appear exasperated. "Goldman, I want some answers."

"I want some answers, too," Abe said. He stood there, bare-chested, feeling stronger than ever. "You've been playin' games with me."

"I've told you all I know."

"You're lyin'."

"That man's a killer."

"He is, eh?" Abe laughed. This was going to be easier than he thought. He took the cigar from his mouth and examined it. "Look, square with me, okay?"

"About what?"

"About this Aiki stuff. I mean it. Sten's my dog. I can sic him on you again if I want."

"I've told you—"

"You've told me shit, Capitan. Now tell me good: what's up with your group?"

There was a long pause as Capitan pretended to collect himself, to calm down. He was, in fact, a bit nervous. He knew he was going out on a limb by doing this.

But the limb's secure, Capitan told himself. Now I know why Hoshima set things up the way he did. He turned to Abe.

"All right, I studied with Hoshima."

"Good. That's just what I wanted to know. Now, what did you study exactly?"

"The art of Shindo. It means the Way of the Mind, the Heart."

"It's a religion?" Abe asked, lighting his cigar.

"It's a way. A discipline. There are no gods or preaching."

"And what do you do?"

"We train the mind."

"To do what?"

"To level itself out. To contact its Essence."

"Essence?" Abe said. "What Essence?"

"The Essence in all of us. The Buddhists call it Big Mind, the Hindus call it Atman."

"I thought you said this wasn't a religion?"

"It isn't."

"It is if you're contacting something."

"But that something that we're contacting, it's not something you talk to or really pray to."

"Then what is it?" Abe asked, his irritation showing.

"It's in you and me, but we're not it."

The old gangster rose, his eyes fixed in a cold stare. "Don't play around with me."

"I'm not, I swear to you," Capitan said, his tone obsequious, servile. "Any meditation school or book on the subject will bear me out. We use a posture to center the mind, and then we use different sounds to tranquilize it."

"Like hypnosis?" Abe asked eagerly.

"That's it. That's exactly it."

Abe leaned back, satisfied so far.

"What's the Aiki part?"

"That's the state you arrive at when you get, uh—get hypnotized. It's our code."

"So how does it all fit into the plan—Hoshima's plan?"

"Hoshima has disappeared."

"Don't lie—"

"I swear to you," Capitan said, and this time he was in earnest. Hoshima had suddenly vanished after Capitan left Japan. There was no longer any word from him, no letters, and the only Aiki followers contacting Capitan were soldiers who had never heard the name in the first place. Though there was a possibility that Hoshima had some reason for not contacting him, Capitan had become convinced that the master was dead (that is, until recent events suggested otherwise). He opened his hands to Abe. "I swear to you."

"Back to him later. What's the group's plan?"

"To teach the mind to neutralize itself. Our main objective is to reach the military. Soldiers. Once they learn the way, the path, they usually desert. But my job as a civilian is not to teach them."

"What is it then?"

"To brush them up, make sure their technique is working. Then they go on to civilian life, but I don't know anything after that."

"I'll bet."

"I swear to you," Capitan said. "I'm just a functionary, a contact. The deserters come to me, then move on. I don't even know who the head man is, who's teaching them all this."

What was amusing, Capitan thought to himself, was that all of this was true.

"I need to know more than you're telling me," Abe said.

"Look," Capitan said, "be good to me, and if I find out anything else, I'll contact you. I don't want trouble. That big brute of yours is bad enough. I don't want the C.I. knocking at my door next."

Abe's eyes bored into Capitan. He was trying to decide whether to believe him. Apparently satisfied, he picked up his shirt and put it on.

Capitan watched silently as the old gangster walked to the door. When he reached the threshold, he turned and said, "You haven't told me half of what I want to know."

"I *have*."

"Don't argue. You get the rest of your song put together and get back to me by tomorrow, or Sten'll stop by again."

"But you agreed—"

"I agreed to nothing," Abe said. "Tomorrow I want a list of everyone working in your operation in the New York area."

"But—"

Abe walked out and slammed the door behind him, leaving Capitan alone. He waited for a few minutes, letting the humor of it all well up inside him. Then Capitan burst into laughter.

Abe was not laughing, however, as he ascended in an express elevator toward his office. He was in dead earnest. He had had his fill over the last two weeks of C.I. files, troublesome employees, and bizarre demands from Mantis. Now the tide appeared to be turning. If he played the cards right, he might be able to rid himself of these headaches once and for all.

Back behind his office desk, Abe took out the Aiki file and buzzed Charlie.

"What's up, boss?"

"Work, that's what."

"What happened to your workout?"

"The instructor needed a wet nurse," Abe said. "Now, I'm gonna dictate a letter to you, and then you're gonna send the letter to the following C.I. coordinates, all right?"

Charlie nodded.

Abe wore a smile on his face as he dictated the letter. Mantis has his candy, he thought. Sten gave me back some of mine. Now this C.I. officer, whoever he is, is gonna get some dessert to keep him happy, too.

Carmen rolled over, turning her back on Capitan as he climbed into the loft.

"You're crazy," she said.

"All right, I'm crazy."

"I don't understand you any more," she said.

"I know it's not easy."

"You went and told that gangster everything. You've helped deserters. That's an anti-Fed rap. You could be sent to the D.C. Tombs for that. And this guy, Sten. You've agreed to go to the Coliseum with him, to a place you've always hated—a place that symbolizes everything you've preached against. And what about Bimbi? You were trying to train him and now you're exposing him to all that bloodshed. I...I just don't know where you're coming from any more...."

"Listen to me. Ever since Bimbi came here things have been speeding up. First, Goldman starts questioning me, then this guy Sten shows up—"

"Coincidence."

"No. One thing's just leading into another. That's something Hoshima taught me. Whether people are connected or not, doesn't matter. Circumstance, fate—it seems to roll over people in waves. I'm convinced that, after waiting these past four years, Hoshima is finally going to contact me. The days of sitting back are over. I have to take action—"

"By telling everything to Goldman and going to the Arena?"

"Yes."

"I think you're confused."

"You're right. I *am* confused. That's why I'm taking chances—chances I've thought over as best I can. As far as the anti-Fed rap is concerned, if C.I. had wanted to send me to the Tombs, they could have done it three years ago when I started with this Shindo business. Some of the deserters back then who came to me were agents, checking me out. The government has been on to us all along. No, if they want anyone, it's not me. They may want the odd-numbered Monitors, like number Five. It's Monitors like him who select the students and teach them the technique. But I'm not even sure that C.I. wants them."

"If they don't want anyone," Carmen said, "then why is that guy, Goldman, questioning and threatening you?"

"I'm not sure. Listen, I know I'm taking a gamble here but the whole idea is to get him to report me—"

"You're crazy, *crazy.*"

"Because—and listen to me, listen good—Goldman thinks he's working with the C.I. or something. But I don't think he is at all. I think that Monitor Five is trying to contact me. I think it's Monitor Five who's posing as a C.I. officer. He's just getting Goldman to do the work for him."

"That sounds really crazy. If this Monitor Five wants to contact you, then why doesn't he just do it himself?"

"That's the thing I have to find out, that I don't know. Apparently he's playing it safe, or something."

"And so, in the meantime, you're going to go out on a limb for him." Tears were forming in Carmen's eyes.

"For me the limb is secure."

"That's what you assume."

"That's what I'm hoping."

There was a long silence. Carmen refused to look at Capitan. He tried running his hands through her hair, but she pushed him away.

"And what about this guy, Sten?" she said finally.

"That's a personal thing. That old shyster gangster was trying to muscle me, so now I'm gonna play around with him."

"By going to the Arena?"

"Sten wants to make waves. I want to see Goldman's face when he does."

Carmen flashed a tight, ironic smile. "You hypocrite," she said. "You've sat around and preached like some guru about kindness and compassion and now...now you want revenge."

"No, I want Goldman off my back, and I'm going to use Sten to do it."

"It's still revenge," Carmen insisted.

"No, it's common sense. I played the mouse today so that tomorrow I can turn things around and be the cat. If I don't show up—if I don't use Sten to my advantage—then Goldman will be after me all the way. I'm asking you to understand this."

"I don't."

"Please try," he said, moving closer to embrace her.

She slid out from under his arms, turning her back on him once again.

"I have been your student and lover, and for two years I have seen you in one way," she said, crying softly. "Now I'm confused and I don't know what to think—how to look at you. Give me time to understand."

Capitan could think of nothing else to say. He just sat there, staring at Carmen's strong back, and let his thoughts drift off... to Hoshima.

"The world is a snake," the master told him during one of their last sessions together, "a snake that sheds its skin. The skin is the world order—its institutions, governments, and centers of learning. When the skin grows old, shows signs of decay, then it must be abandoned. We are nearing such a time now. The snake is growing sluggish, it feels ill, its hide is worn and it is preparing to shake it off. It is a natural process, one that is often painful. The snake needs food and nourishment to complete the task. My art of Shindo is food for the snake. That food is slowly digested and becomes part of the new skin, the new layer that will throw off the old one. The food must be given first to the muscle tissues, the tissues that do the fighting, the work. The muscle tissues are the warriors. That is why I have taught my art only to fighters such as yourself. Each of you is a separate cell, functioning on its own, yet a part of the snake. When the time nears to shed the old skin, all the cells will unite and begin to work as one. It is, as I've said, a natural process, one that never fails...."

One that never fails. Capitan hoped Hoshima was right. He was not one to question his teacher, but keeping everything so secret, preventing the monitors from knowing each other—it was a course of action that left room for doubt. No teacher, after all, was free from error. Capitan smiled. What was it Hoshima used to say about doubt?

"Doubt is a great source of antigravity," Hoshima had told him. "It uproots the mind. When we sit we are creating soil for the mind to grow in. A firm gravitational base. Doubt can uproot you. Try and sit and doubt at the same time. Either you will conquer doubt or doubt will conquer you. So do not doubt...."

All right, Capitan thought. I won't doubt. And I'm sitting; he realized that he had gone into his meditation posture without even being aware of it. I'll conquer doubt. I'll believe that Monitor Five is posing as a C.I. officer, that he is using Goldman to make contact with me. I'll believe that everything is going to work out just fine.

Capitan knew that he was either being very wise or very foolish.

CHAPTER THIRTEEN

THE Brooklyn Coliseum, home of Sport Arena for the greater New York area. It rose ominously over the old Flatbush region, dominating the otherwise dull and lifeless skyline. A series of race riots had conveniently leveled the area in Flatbush a few years prior, making the area suitable for construction of a stadium. The locals quickly labeled the ten-story edifice the "Bowl of Death." For eight years now it had stood, a piece of ancient Rome married to space-age design and welded fast into a decaying twenty-first century urban landscape. From the very first day the Coliseum opened, the fans had flocked to it. Young, old, rich and poor crowded the circular porticos, popping emoveer pills and setting up a cacophonous babble as, many levels below, the contestants girded themselves for battle.

Tonight was no different. In fact, tonight was something of an occasion, for Mantis was fighting again—Mantis the Grand Master who hadn't been seen publicly in over a year. Although the prospects of a close match were slim—the fighter from France was not expected to pose much of a challenge—it didn't matter in the end. Mantis was Mantis—the man everyone loved to hate. No matter how abbreviated the fight, the crowds knew the champion would make it interesting. Thumbs up or thumbs down—the younger fans gave the signal to one another as they queued up with everyone else to pass through the security scanners. The bets began to flow, sodac pills and emoveers passing hands as a sign of credit. Capitan watched it all and shook his head.

"This is madness," he said.

"You ain't seen half of it," Sten said.

Bimbi poked his teacher. "You mean you ain't ever been here?"

"No."

"Why not?"

"Why?"

"'Cause, well...this is where it happens."

Capitan said nothing. He looked over at Sten, wondering if he could be depended on. I need him now, he thought. I need him and somehow I feel he's going to need me.

"You're sure you can get me in, down to see Savinien?" he asked.

"No problem," Sten assured him. "I know half the crew in this place."

They made their way under the scanners, one of a series of monitoring devices that checked for concealed weapons. Bimbi pushed forward, next to Capitan.

"How come Carmen stayed home? What's her problem?"

Capitan looked at his student reproachfully.

Bimbi smiled. "Oh, sorry."

Carmen hadn't spoken to Capitan since the night before, since the argument in the loft. And Capitan hadn't tried to break the ice. He had decided to let things just take their natural course. He was too confused by his own actions to do otherwise.

They were passing now through the gates, into the first floor portico. The credeer machines could be seen up ahead, their colored lights flashing as information was fed back to the security officers. Sten passed his credeer card in front of the screen. There was a green flash.

"Deduct three," Sten told the machine. There was a white flash and the machine replied, "Pass." Bimbi watched the whole process in awe. He turned around to ask a question of Capitan and noticed three punks attempting to slink past the screen. A blue light flashed suddenly and the punks were rooted to the spot, their bodies frozen.

"Hey, look at that," Bimbi said, watching as the punks grimaced and officers moved down to arrest them.

"Yeah, that's a new feature," Sten told him. "The machine now has the capability to freeze the nervous system. Used to be the cops would have to run after everybody. Not anymore."

"What happens if you can't pay, if your card is down?"

"They let you through. Then they deduct when you do make some credits. Everybody's gotta make credits sooner or later."

"I bet the fighters get paid well."

"You gotta start at the bottom, though."

"How do you mean?"

"The minor leagues first."

"Yeah. Is it hard to get in?"

"It's hard to stay alive."

Capitan closed his eyes. My God, he thought, what have I done, bringing him here? The kid's got a brain like a monkey. I'm just throwing him back into the jungle again by exposing him to all of this. He watched Bimbi's head bob excitedly over the crowd as he spotted a concession stand.

"Kelp fries! Get me some kelp fries," he shouted. He turned to Capitan. "You ain't sayin' nothin'."

"What do you want me to say?" he asked.

"Be excited. This is the Arena."

"Yeah..." Capitan turned to Sten. "So?"

"Let's put this monkey on line. I'll take you across."

"You guys ain't gonna leave me?" Bimbi said.

"Just stand on line there," Sten replied. "We'll be back."

Capitan handed Bimbi his credeer card.

Bimbi smiled. "I'll go easy."

But Capitan wasn't listening. He was looking at Sten.

Sten gave him the okay sign. "I'll get you down there, don't worry."

"I believe you."

"Then why're you staring like that?" Sten asked.

"I want to know what you're up to."

"I told you. I'm gonna pull off a big surprise after the fight."

"What if Mantis loses?"

"He won't. That friend of yours from France doesn't have a chance. He's a Frog that's gonna croak. Ha! Get it?"

"Yeah." Capitan's mind was racing as they moved at a steady pace toward a neon sign that read: Circus Gate #2. "And Goldman, will he be here?"

"He's at every fight. He'll be sitting one row in front of us."

Capitan smiled.

They were standing in front of Circus Gate #2. Sten inserted his card in the security slot and the door slid open. They passed into a dark corridor that led in a circular direction toward a series of elevators.

"The elevator will take us below," Sten said. "That's where they keep the animals—in cages, of course. Only thing this place hasn't got is some Christians."

Give it time, Capitan thought.

The doors opened then, Capitan registering surprise as they entered a glass elevator. It headed slowly down a shaft that was designed to look out onto the lower floors of the Coliseum. The first floor was a maze of cages, housing lions, tigers, bears, wolves and even elephants. Their separate sounds blended into a bizarre symphony that reverberated in Capitan's skull, then faded as the elevator passed downward.

Sten could see that Capitan was uncomfortable.

"Wild, eh? They keep the animals there so that the noise will be heard up above. It fires up the spectators."

"Christ..."

"Ah, it's okay. Animals like that ain't got no place any more. Might as well give 'em a home here, feed 'em."

Some home...

The elevator passed a giant training area next, similar to a gym but filled with a series of bizarre contraptions that were evidently intended to simulate martial arts movements. The entire floor appeared empty, unlit.

"This is where they work 'em into shape," Sten said.

The elevator passed to the next floor, which was closed off.

"This is where they've put the surveillance cameras. It's a big maze of wires and machines. I never go here."

The next floor was a subterranean paradise, filled with whirlpools, gardens, and open steam baths.

"It's a pleasure garden. You know how, back in ancient times, they used to treat the gladiators real good? Well, they do it here, too. The real champs never use it, though. Just the up-and-coming."

The elevator passed on, down to the last floor, which was closed off as well. Sten inserted his card again and the glass door opened.

"This is it, end of the line. Here's where the dressing rooms are and the Waiting Station."

"The Waiting Station?"

"Boy, you don't know anything. The Waiting Station is where the challengers and champions face each other—stare each other down before the fight." He pointed down a large corridor that ran from the outer portico toward an inner, central chamber. "The Waiting Station's down there. All the corridors lead into it. It's like a wheel. We're standin' on the rim, the corridors are the spokes."

"So the Waiting Station is the hub?"

"Right. In the center of the station is the central lift, or elevator. That's what takes you up, into the arena. If you wanna fight, then you gotta go to the Waiting Station. There's usually a ten minute wait or so before the lift is activated. During that time your opponent has the opportunity to psych you out."

"Very clever."

"Ain't no other coliseum has a setup like this one. Not the Emperor's in Tokyo, not the La Grande in Paris, not the Big Circus in London. No, Brooklyn's got the big baby." Up ahead, Sten saw two security guards blocking the entrance to a corridor.

"Johnson, how's it going?"

"Good."

"Word has it you got fired," one of the guards said.

"Word has it, but that ain't official."

"We'll close our eyes. What's up?"

"I wanna get my friend in to see the Frenchman."

"Sorry. No way. It's too close to the fight."

"C'mon, do me a favor."

"You gonna pay us off?" the head guard said, lighting a cigarette.

"Go fuck yourself."

"Is that Frog expecting him?"

"Tell him Capitan is here," Capitan said. "He'll see me."

The head of security stepped into a tiny glass booth and made a phone call. He had a brief exchange with the person on the other end of the line, then popped his head out and said, "Name a street in Manila."

"Luzon twenty, number five."

The guard nodded and returned to the booth. A second later he stepped out and pointed at Capitan. "Okay. But just you."

Sten patted Capitan on the back. "You remember where our seats are?"

Capitan nodded. He watched Sten walk away, then followed the guard down the corridor just beyond the booth.

"Easy to get lost here," the guard said.

"I believe it."

It was not long before they stood in front of a dressing room. Capitan could feel cameras scanning him. The guard hit some keys on the security panel, then a voice boomed over a speaker. "Aha! *Mon vieu! Quelle surprise!*"

The doors slid open to reveal Savinien. He was sitting on the edge of the dressing table, his manager and crew around him. He waved the guard away and motioned for Capitan to enter.

"*Mon vieu, mon vieu*—long time no see, eh?"

Capitan came closer and embraced the Frenchman. Savinien stood back and looked him over.

"Ah, but you have lost some weight, no? And you look pale."

"I live in New York," Capitan said.

"Yes, no more sunny times like the old days in Manila. What have you been doing all these years?"

As Capitan talked he looked approvingly at Savinien. The Frenchman had not changed much: still tall and slim, still perfectly toned and fit. His trademark long black hair had not grayed in the slightest; it still fell in beautiful curls around a face that was stunning and arrogant. Capitan remembered that, years ago, Savinien had been billed as the great "Don Juan of Sport Arena." The moniker seemed to fit even now.

"We two fought many bouts together," Savinien told his attendants. "I, of course, won all of them handily."

Capitan smiled. The training and the friendship had lasted but a few months, but both warriors had never forgotten each other. Capitan had watched Savinien's career blossom slowly as an Arena fighter. And now...

"I always knew you'd end up here," Capitan said.

The Frenchman nodded. "After I left Manila, I returned to France. There I took on all the scum of Marseilles with my savate art. I had begun to tire of it when I saw my chance to gain real fame in the Arena. I used both my savate boxing and my stick fighting to become champion of Paris, the king of La Grande. Then I hopped the channel and took on every one of those Anglais dogs at the 'Big Circus.' In Europe, I am the master. But, as you know, the Arena council says that I must defeat this Mantis dog to become 'Grand Master.' That is the reason I am here."

"Do you have any idea who you're taking on?" Capitan asked.

"I have no fear of him, or his iron blades."

"The man's weapon is the sai. Unless you're going to use something other than sticks, you don't stand a chance."

"That's why I've changed my sticks," Savinien said. He motioned to an attendant, who brought over a leather case. "These are my own invention, just for Mantis." He opened the case and took out two iron rods, the same length as arnis sticks—about two feet— only thinner. He handed one to Capitan. "What do you think?"

Capitan waved it about in his hand. "Nice."

"And light, very light." The Frenchman suddenly lashed out at Capitan, who quickly blocked the oncoming stick. Savinien's manager looked on in concern.

"*Ne peur pas, mon bête,*" Savinien said, "my friend here is fast, and always ready."

"They're light, but not light enough," Capitan said.

"*Il a raison,*" the manager said. "*C'est juste comme j'ai dit—prend le baton.*"

Savinien waved his manager away.

"He wants me to use the spear," Savinien said to Capitan. "The minute there might be danger, it's 'use the spear.'"

"You were good with the spear."

"I am better with these," Savinien said, his smile fading.

"Listen to me, old friend. Mantis is a great infighter."

"And so am I."

"Granted, but you're new with these rods and Mantis is a veteran with his sais. That makes a difference. If you commit yourself to close fighting he's liable to have an edge. A spear could keep him at bay. You could make it your game. You—"

"Enough..."

"*Écoute bien,*" the manager added. "*Le baton serai ton coupe—*"

"Enough!" Savinien looked at Capitan with suspicion. "What kind of a visit *is* this?"

"One of concern. For you, old friend—for your safety."

Savinien threw Capitan a mock punch. The Frenchman was hot-headed, but never one to stay angry for long.

"Listen to me. I will move too fast for that pig, see? I have studied his style. He does not kick much, he rarely uses his feet. I will pick him apart with my legs of fire, and then I will dance around him, keeping him confused.... But wait, here you are—the best opponent I ever faced. I must make use of you."

He motioned to his attendants. They handed him two pairs of rattan sticks. Savinien grinned as he handed a pair to Capitan.

"You don't—"

"Of course. I want to see if you are as fast as the old days. You must attack me with everything you have."

"Really—"

"As a friend—my friend. Please."

"Very well..."

"After all," Savinien said, as Capitan began to take off his sweater, "you have been sent here, to me—by God, to make me ready."

Capitan thought to himself, if you're not ready by now, you'll never be. He smiled at the Frenchman.

"Go on—attack," Savinien said. "I'll block all moves." Capitan hesitated for a moment, then slowly started to strike. The manager looked on in concern as the Frenchman quickly parried each blow. Savinien laughed madly. "Come on, faster."

Capitan lashed out in a series of lightning quick moves. Each time Savinien parried Capitan's blow, laughing madly as he did.

Bimbi sat next to Sten in the choicest of front row seats, not more than thirty feet from the Arena pit. A few feet away stood a gaggle of VIPs and media masters, all come to see if the French fighter would pose a challenge for Mantis.

"I'm really here," Bimbi mumbled, half to himself. He looked at the Arena once again, at the walls, and at the thousand and one video cameras covering it from every angle, feeding back to the central screens that hung like space-age chandeliers in front of each ring of seats. He tried to imagine himself in the Arena pit, fighting against some future champion, but could not visualize the scene.

Sten looked down, searching for Abe. He had not yet arrived. The *karateka* eased back in his seat and fingered his program nervously.

"That who's fighting?" Bimbi asked, pointing at the scoreboard.

"Right," Sten said, finally glancing at it. "Hey, we got the Ozark Twins facin' the Minnesota Maulers. Big dudes..."

"Heavyweights?" Bimbi asked.

"Heavy heavyweights."

Sten folded his program in half. He glanced down once more at Abe's seat. Still empty. The green lights began flashing throughout the Coliseum, which meant the games were about to begin. Bimbi turned and watched as a rather haughty-looking Professional sat down next to him. The man opened his schedule and gave the young Hispanic an arrogant look. Bimbi waited and then returned the gesture. The man looked away.

"Well, *excuse* me," Bimbi said under his breath.

The crowd began to hoot as the central lift ascended, rising higher and higher until its bottom reached a point even with the floor of the pit. The cylinder rotated, the doors opened, and a muzzled grizzly bear emerged, its leash held tightly by two trainers.

"A bear?" Bimbi said, looking at Sten.

"You got it."

The cylindrical lift rotated shut and then descended back down into the bowels of the arena as the two trainers guided the bear into a corner. All around Bimbi, camera crews conducted last-minute checks of their equipment.

"This is great," Bimbi said. He watched as the lift rose once again and a large brute of a man, bigger than Sten, emerged from the cylinder.

In a matter of minutes the fight was on, the screens showing the action up close as the bearded giant engaged the bear in a wrestling match. As Bimbi watched eagerly, Sten looked down at regular intervals to check Abe's seat. Finally, the old gangster arrived with Charlie and his eyes caught Sten's. Sten gave him the protest sign with his fist. Amused, Abe blew him a kiss and then sat down.

"Come on, Bulbo!"

Bimbi watched fascinated as the bear turned the giant man over, onto his back. The young Hispanic glanced over at the Professional, who was looking at his program. Bimbi poked him.

"Hey, bro—" he asked, pointing at the program, "what's that say?"

"What, can't you read?" the man asked.

"No."

"You never went to school?"

"School? What school?"

The man shook his head. "It describes what you're looking at right now: 'Hurricane Smith, former Olympic champion, fights Bulbo, the Crusher Bear.' Unremarkable, but amusing…"

Bimbi took a long look at the Professional as he fanned himself haughtily with his program. Bimbi poked him gently again.

"Say…"

"What *now?*"

"Are you some kinda fruit or something?"

"*Agghhh!*" The crowd rose to its feet as the bear collapsed on top of Hurricane Smith, crushing his ribs. The wrestler writhed in pain as shouts and catcalls fell on him, and then the medics rushed out from the Coliseum's emergency wings. Bulbo's trainers waved their arms proudly and began to lead their champion beast back to the opposite corner. Bimbi yelled and hooted, then looked about.

"Say, where's Capitan? He's missing all this."

At that moment Capitan was very busy striking blows left and right at Savinien, who was drenched in sweat. After a minute the dough-faced manager interposed himself between the two.

"*Assez! Assez. Il faut que tu as quelque chose pour Mantis!*"

Savinien gave his manager a quick rap with a stick and smiled at Capitan. "He always steps in."

"He's right, though," Capitan said, looking at the manager's wounded face. "You should save your energy."

"I have lots of energy."

The manager mumbled something at the attendants. Savinien opened up with some vindictives of his own.

"And maybe when we get back to France, I find myself a new manager," Savinien threatened.

"*D'accord—si tu vive,*" the older man said.

Some crew, Capitan thought.

A security monitor flashed. There was a report over the intercom: "Ten minutes to Waiting Station, thank you."

"Right," Savinien said. "Soon comes the good part, when I face Mantis before the fight. But look—I have you with me now."

He turned and slapped Capitan on the back. Capitan grew pale, realizing he should never have agreed to even set foot in the Coliseum, that he should have listened to Carmen. Damn it.... He stepped back and forced a smile. "I must leave—"

"Oh no." Savinien said. "You are going with me."

"But the rules..."

Savinien laughed. "What rules? There are no rules in this sport, you know that." He turned to his manager and attendants and rattled off in French. "I tell them you come, too—that I am the king here, I give the orders. Ah," he said suddenly. "*Je dois pisse.*"

As he walked down around a bank of lockers to a urinal, the pudgy manager approached Capitan.

"Monsieur, he will not listen to me, I have no power over him except to set his schedule. I am a manager who is no boss. You must tell him to use his spear instead. Perhaps to you he will listen."

"Ricard, go to hell!" The shout had emanated from the john.

Savinien came out, his aura large, active. The manager inched away as the Frenchman came over and slapped both hands onto Capitan's arms.

"You come with me to the Waiting Station. You help to give me strength."

Strength, sure, Capitan thought to himself as he gave a resigned nod of agreement. Lots of strength. But strength never won a fight on its own....

The security monitor reported in again: "Eight minutes to Waiting Station, thank you."

Savinien made ready, his attendants rushing around him as the cries from the arena seemed to penetrate and echo even down here. Up above, a great fight was going on, Bimbi watching mesmerized as the Ozark Twins fought a tag team battle with the Minnesota Maulers.

"Big mothers..."

The Ozark Twins were using clubs with spikes driven into them, plus tough oxhide shields. The Maulers were simply wielding giant broad axes. They swung them now angrily, driving the opposing giants back against the walls. Finally the fighters began to pair off, disdainfully rejecting the tag team format. The crowd hooted and howled as the screens flashed the fights close up, cameras switching back and forth between the separate battles. Suddenly an Ozark twin lost his footing and fell back. He took refuge under his oxhide shield as his Mauler opponent stood over him with his ax and rained down savage blows.

"Hey, this is even meaner than when I saw it a few years ago," Bimbi said.

"Yeah. No foolin' around now," Sten told him. "These guys mean business."

The crowds went wild as the Mauler swung his ax in a last mighty arc, crashing it through the Ozark's shield and digging it abruptly into the fallen man's skull. The fans continued to howl as the Mauler backed off and watched the blood spurt in a jet from the Ozark's forehead.

"Great, eh?" Sten said, cracking his knuckles.

Slightly nauseated, Bimbi watched as the other Mauler traded blows with the remaining Ozark. Seeing that his twin had fallen, the giant began to pound madly at his enemy. The first Mauler rushed over, his ax ready, and fell upon the Ozark giant from the side. In a matter of seconds the battle was over and the crowd began to throw down debris. As both Ozark twins lay dead, their blood absorbed by the heavy canvas, the Maulers from Minnesota paraded about, one of them bending down to collect the many pills that had been thrown to them in tribute. Meanwhile, hundreds of cameras whirred, recording it all on film.

"Well, that's that," Sten said, glancing down at Abe again. The old gangster was refusing to look back. He was having Charlie do it for him.

Charlie turned to his boss. "You think he's up to something?"

"Could be. I'd like to know who that Spic is that's with him."

"There's an empty seat between 'em, too."

"Yeah, I noticed." Abe looked up at the screen, watching as it began to play old clips of Mantis and his most famous fights. The crowd immediately began to chant "Mantis, Mantis..." in slow steady rhythm. Abe glanced at his watch. "Any second now they'll be entering the Waiting Station...."

"Mantis...! Mantis...!" The chant began to build in intensity as clips of the great fighter's career flashed across the screen. It was a collage of slaughter: victims run through with swords, stabbed with sais, pummeled into unconsciousness by Mantis's pistonlike fists.

Bimbi looked about anxiously. "Where the hell's Capitan?"

Why am I here, Capitan asked himself as he humbly made his way down the corridor alongside Savinien. The Waiting Station was clearly visible up ahead.

A cameraman suddenly dashed in front of them. They were on television. Savinien gave his old friend a hug. "You are here with me—for luck."

They emerged from the darkened corridor and entered the Waiting Station. Cameramen and reporters were everywhere. Capitan quickly spotted the central lift, thinking it looked more like an electric chair than an elevator. But there was something else to notice, too, at the far end of the station.

Mantis.

Mantis sat calmly, surrounded by his bodyguards. Al was clearly visible among them. The reporters suddenly rushed in front of Capitan in an attempt to surround Savinien.

"What're your thoughts about the fight?"

"Can you beat him...?"

"How's this place compare...?"

The questions blended into a chaotic wall of sound. Capitan noticed that the cameras were on him now, too.

"What the fuck?" Abe almost swallowed his cigar as he saw Capitan on the video monitor.

"Hey, that's—" Bimbi nearly jumped out of his seat.

Sten raised his eyebrows. "Capitan?"

"Is that the guy—?" Charlie asked.

Suddenly the cameras shifted away from Capitan, focusing again on Savinien. Capitan noticed that there was one lone camera on Mantis and his crew, and that no reporters dared go near. Finally a timid newcomer approached the champion with his microphone.

"Hi, boys," he said. "I'd like to ask a few questions about—"

"Beat it," Mantis said abruptly, his eyes boring into him. The young man laughed nervously, then backed off. Mantis rose as he saw Savinien point his way. The champion approached the challenger with Al at his side. As he drew closer, Mantis began to stare intently, past Savinien—at Capitan.

"What're you looking at?" Savinien asked.

"I'm not looking at you," Mantis said. "You're already dead." He pointed to Capitan. "I'm looking at him." He walked over to Capitan. "I've seen your face before."

"Have you?" Capitan replied.

"Yes," Mantis said. "An article—in one of those lollipop karate magazines. An Aikido and judo man. A stick man, too. Right?"

"Guess so."

"I hear you're good."

"After me," Savinien boasted, "he is the best."

"Shut up," Mantis said. Savinien started angrily, but his manager held him back. Mantis smiled and took a step closer toward Capitan as pictures of the scene flashed back to the Coliseum crowd. Abe was flustered because the audio wasn't working. He poked Charlie.

"Damn."

"What?"

"I can't hear. Why don't you read lips?"

Mantis could be seen looking Capitan over, from top to bottom. He smiled. "Fresh meat. How come I've never seen you in the ring before?"

"You remember the old saying?" Capitan said politely. "Thou shalt not kill..."

"Oh, with me you'd have no problem," Mantis said. "All you'd have to do is *be killed*."

There was a slight pause as Capitan looked Mantis over. Somehow he seemed to be so mortal, so full of error, his vision of things a mistake. Capitan shook his head.

"You know," Capitan said. "Somewhere along the line, bro—you done missed the boat."

Mantis flushed, then fixed his eyes on Capitan. For a moment Capitan felt as if the green-clad killer were entering his own body, digging into it. Then he centered himself and returned the stare. Finally Mantis stepped back and pointed. The audio was working now.

"You're mine, pal," Mantis said.

Savinien tried to interpose himself. "Not after *I* get through with you."

Mantis continued to back away. "You're mine," he said again, and then he turned to Savinien. "I already told you, *you're* dead."

"*Cochon!*"

"*Mange.*"

The trainer and his men tugged Savinien back. The lift rotated. It was time for the match.

Abe turned around and stared grimly at Sten. Sten flashed a smile and gave his old boss the finger. Bimbi tugged at Sten's arm.

"Hey, that was somethin', huh?"

"Yeah," Sten said. He was distracted now by his own plans. He watched as Abe turned and whispered to Charlie. The younger man got up and headed for Sten as the crowds began to roar. The lift was rising into the Arena.

"What's up?" Charlie asked Sten as he drew close to him.

"You tell me," Sten said.

"Didn't you go mess up Capitan?"

"No. As a matter of fact, I made friends with him."

The cylindrical lift rotated and Savinien stepped out, waving his iron rods to a mighty hand from the crowd.

"You did what?" Charlie asked.

"I made friends with him. You deaf?"

"Yeah, you deaf?" Bimbi asked.

"I thought...well..."

"You don't get paid to think about me any more," Sten said. "Just tell your boss down there one thing…"

Savinien paraded around the Arena in true Latin style, throwing kisses to the ladies and saluting the box of the Arena League president.

"Tell him," Sten said, "that I ain't his dog. I don't sic people at the snap of a finger."

"You used to."

"Used to is 'used to,' get it?"

The lift rose again, the cylinder rotating, and Mantis stepped out. In his hands he held leather wrist guards and a weapons case. The crowd hooted madly.

"Mantis…! Mantis…! Mantis…!" The roar rose up through the steel rafters of the Coliseum as Charlie made his way back to Abe and told him the news.

"Made friends with him? What the—" He glanced back at the *karateka*. Sten blew the kisses this time.

A bell sounded and Mantis and Savinien approached the president's box. The president, a very gaunt man, read aloud the rules, his voice echoing across the Coliseum.

"You men know the rules. There are no rounds; you cannot leave the arena once committed to the action; you *can* retreat to your corner, but your opponent is permitted to follow if he so chooses. The champion as always has the right to choose the opening means of combat." The president turned to Mantis. "Hands to weapons, or weapons to hands?"

"Hands to weapons," Mantis said.

"You both have thirty seconds to prepare."

Savinien mocked Mantis as the camouflaged killer strode to his corner. The crowd began to count down as the seconds flashed on the video screens.

"Twenty-nine… twenty-eight… twenty-seven…"

"Man—where's Capitan?" Bimbi asked, looking about. "He's going to miss this."

"He probably has to return by one of the side lifts," Sten said. "He'll be here, soon enough."

"Nineteen...eighteen..."

Capitan scooted up the steps quickly, two reporters close on his heels.

"There he is."

"Fifteen...fourteen..."

As he headed for his seat he passed the aisle where Abe sat. Their eyes met. Capitan made no sign, neither did Abe.

"Twelve...eleven..."

Capitan reached his seat. Two reporters moved in on him quickly.

"Why was Mantis..."

"He was pointing at you..."

"Listen," Capitan said quickly. "I don't know anything—"

"But I do," Sten interjected. "This guy trains fighters."

"What?"

"Eight...seven..."

"He's trainin' me to take on Mantis next."

"Is this a hoax?"

"You saw him down there, didn't you?"

"Two...one."

The fight was on. Even the reporters diverted their attention for the moment as Savinien rose from his corner and made the sign of the cross. Mantis smiled and repeated the gesture, only on Savinien. They moved to the center of the arena and began to engage, the Frenchman dancing around as Mantis assumed a casual boxing stance. The reporters began to split their attention between the fight and Capitan and Sten.

"Let's get this straight. He's training you to fight Mantis—"

"Sit down," someone yelled.

"I'm not training—"

"Look," Sten said, cutting Capitan off. "You want the hottest story in this city, you get your ass back here quick after this fight."

"Sit down!" People had begun to scream at the two young reporters. Unruffled, they told Sten they would return, and walked back to the press area.

"What're you doing?" Capitan asked.

"I did you a favor, now you're gonna do me one."

"But—"

The crowd roared as Savinien began to attack, kicking and lashing out with his feet. Mantis merely parried each blow with a quick flash of his hands. There was a second exchange, Savinien kicking, Mantis parrying the Frenchman's feet, and then suddenly the ex-commando opened up with a right jab that sent the Frenchman crashing to the ground.

"Hey, that guy's a good boxer," Bimbi said.

"He's a killer," Capitan replied.

Mantis backed off, giving Savinien time to collect himself. The Frenchman attempted to dance again, only now it was Mantis's turn to make the flashy moves. He began to corner the challenger into a wall and Savinien responded with a roundhouse kick. Mantis quickly caught the outstretched leg and hurled the Frenchman onto his back. Enraged, Savinien sprung quickly to his feet only to meet a well-coiled heel kick from Mantis that sent him crashing back again, this time into the wall. An open knife hand followed next, landing abruptly in the Frenchman's neck, but the blow was deliberately light. Mantis backed away with a smile as Savinien choked and staggered to his feet.

"You disappoint me," the champion said, his right hand writhing in a bizarre fashion, the fingers dancing with a will all their own.

"Mantis…! Mantis…!" The crowd began to chant as Mantis turned and walked back to his corner, leaving Savinien to stumble about and collect his senses. Bimbi turned to his teacher.

"Things don't look so hot for your friend, do they?"

"No. Things look…dim."

They watched as the champion began to fit his wrists with leather guards. After they were in place, Mantis opened his weapons case, pulling out the iron Okinawan daggers that were his trademark. He flourished the sais in a very conservative manner, but the gesture was enough to send the mob into a frenzy. Savinien, meanwhile, was making ready with his iron rods. The challenger was clearly shaken but ready to continue. Both contestants moved toward the center of the arena. Mantis flashed his sais into an inverse position, the blades guarding his wrists....

"Like a praying mantis," Sten said. "That's his rep. He springs from the legs and devours with the claws."

Savinien attacked quickly with his rods. The Frenchman began to dance away for a moment, then once more engaged. Mantis deflected, swiftly flashing his blades out and slicing open a thin area of Savinien's side.

"He's finished," Capitan said.

The Frenchman began to retreat as Mantis beat him back against another wall. Savinien lashed out madly with his new weapons, trying to save himself, but Mantis merely laughed and dodged the blows. Suddenly Mantis leapt in and dug his knee into Savinien's groin, simultaneously digging the inverse blades of his sais into the challenger's back.

"Christ, no..."

The mob went wild as they watched Savinien fall, severely wounded.

"Mantis! Mantis! Mantiiiis!"

The champion raised his blades in triumph. He looked about the Coliseum, awaiting the decision.

"Right, it's your baby," Abe said. He smiled grimly as Savinien struggled to his feet, then collapsed.

Bimbi was watching the crowd now as it came to a unanimous decision: *thumbs down*. He considered, then turned his thumb down, too.

"Sure, why not?"

"Are you crazy?" Capitan said, pulling Bimbi's arm back angrily. "I know he's your friend, but—"

"Even if he wasn't, are you an animal?"

Bimbi grunted apologetically. No, not an animal, Capitan thought. Just a monkey who I've lost, for sure.

Pills and jewelry and odd sorts of paraphernalia began to fall into the arena pit, landing near Mantis and bouncing off Savinien as he crawled toward the wall in an attempt to raise himself. It was *"thumbs down"* everywhere. Mantis continued to parade around the ring, flashing one sai casually, then another. Finally he walked over and began to examine the bleeding Frenchman.

"Mantis...! Mantis...!" The chant rose along with sixty thousand arms, each one declaring: *thumbs down!* Mantis took the opportunity to mock the crowd. Kneeling, he spat on the gifts the fans had thrown him, but the people began to howl and repeated the *thumbs down* gesture. Mantis spat on another gift and threw it out of the arena pit, watching as Savinien attempted to raise himself. Mantis pointed at him and then the crowd. He took his hand and made a defiant *thumbs up* gesture. The people protested, but again the champion made the mercy gesture and swept his arm across the Coliseum. Very gradually, the shouting died down, an eerie silence taking hold. For a brief moment all was still, the only sounds the hum of the video circuits and Savinien's stifled moans. Then, suddenly, and without notice, Mantis raised a sai and hurled it full force into the Frenchman's back. Capitan started violently in his seat as the crowd erupted in a scream. Sten sprang up immediately and shouted, *"Killer!* Killer—for sport!" He rushed down to the edge of the arena pit and pointed at Mantis, shouting once again: "Killer!"

Security police were quick to move in on him, but so, too, were the two reporters Sten had spoken to previously.

"He kills for pleasure," Sten told the reporters.

"Oh, no..." Abe muttered, hiding his eyes and shaking his head. "I wash my hands of him."

Charlie watched as the guards tried to pin the *karateka*. A cameraman was inadvertently clubbed and a wild scuffle ensued.

Bimbi turned to Capitan. "Should we help him?"

"He wants this," Capitan said.

"He does?"

Capitan nodded. He watched as Sten shouted back at the crowd, "Killer! Killer!"

"Let's go, pal," a security officer said as he attempted vainly to get the blond giant in a full nelson.

"We wanna talk with him," the reporters said.

"Fine. In jail."

"Killer!"

Sten pulled loose from four security guards and approached the railing. The champion looked up, aware of a commotion. Sten aimed a finger at Mantis as the security guards got hold of him once again.

"Mantis, you're through. Do you hear me, Mantis? You're through."

Mantis recognized Sten now.

"You again...?"

"Mantis!"

Abe stood up and glared at Capitan as the guards led Sten away. The old-timer's jaws were shut tight, nerves twitching angrily. He mounted the few short steps to Capitan's row of seats and pointed his finger at him. "You'll pay for this," Abe said. "Nobody dupes Abe Goldman and gets away with it. Your ass is mine."

Capitan smiled. "Apparently my ass belongs to someone else now."

"Who?"

"Mantis."

Abe nodded, remembering the scene on the video.

"Yeah. Okay. We'll see."

Capitan watched as Abe headed down the steps and then out of view. He looked down at the arena pit. The lift had descended. Mantis was gone....

Al was there, standing at the Waiting Station, when Mantis stepped off the lift. The champion started to remove his leather wrist guards, then motioned to his lieutenant.

"That guy, did you find out his name?"

"Yeah. Capitan."

"Capitan, eh? Well, isn't that a coincidence." There was a long pause as Mantis finished removing the wrist guards. He examined his right hand. The fingers were normal again. He turned to Al. "I want a full report on him. Everything: where he lives, what he eats, how he breathes. Got it?"

Al nodded with a smile that was no smile.

CHAPTER FOURTEEN

THE two reporters were quick to arrange for Sten's release, which is exactly what the *karateka* wanted. He had seen what the media could do, had watched as Mantis himself used the media masters to his own advantage. Now it was *his* turn to exploit the system...

They entered the detention cell, two new-breed media men dedicated to making any possible kind of trash and garbage into headlines. Sten welcomed them with a heavy handshake.

"Well, Mr. Johnson—we've bailed you out."

"And we want to talk to you. We really do." The reporters had a cameraman with them.

"I'm ready," Sten said. "Start shootin'."

The two reporters questioned Sten for an hour. When they had finished, they had a condensed thirty-minute interview with the *karateka* that could be shipped to the major gossip networks. The news team would have liked to interview the mystery man whom Mantis had pointed at before the fight—such was the curiosity concerning Capitan—but lacking knowledge of his whereabouts, they settled on Sten as the next best thing. Sten did not disappoint....A rapt audience looked on that night as the *karateka* babbled to the TV cameras:

"I was once a world-class karate champion, but I was duped by sponsors of Sport Arena into using drugs."

"Why would they want to do that?" a reporter asked.

"Because they were tryin' to break down all the martial arts. They wanted to create a void that could be filled by the new product they had created—Sport Arena."

"Product?"

"Exactly." Sten went on to tell how he had worked for Abe's office, how he had been trampled by the feet of the "Big Machine," and how Mantis had denied Sten the right to combat because he did not have any standing in the Arena leagues. It was a careful mixture of truth and lies—all calculated to promote maximum public interest.

"You shoulda plugged him," Charlie said as he watched with Abe.

"Can't now. The Media Masters have a ring around him so tight a fly couldn't squeeze past without gettin' photographed."

"This is bad."

"It ain't good," Abe said. He looked over at the telephone, expecting it to ring any minute with either the Arena president or maybe even Mantis himself on the other end of the line.

Mantis would not be calling, though. After watching Sten's interview that night, he sat for a long time, distractedly stroking the female leopard who sat purring in his arms. Al shook his head.

"You're the one who wanted to let him go," the bodyguard said.

"He really wants a fight, doesn't he?"

"You don't plan to —"

"Then so be it," Mantis said, finally deciding on a course of action. "The sooner I shut him up the better. Did you check out that guy, Capitan?"

"Everything's here," Al said, handing him a report.

"I want to pay him an indirect visit," Mantis said. "Is there anything in that report that will help?"

Al thought a moment. "He has a young student..."

"Ah..." Mantis nodded. "That sounds good. Tomorrow, after that Oman fellow gets back, we'll travel to Brooklyn, look around some. In the meantime contact U-1 and tell them that I intend to accept Johnson's challenge. Tell them to waive the point system, too. If they resist, warn them that the consequences will be far more serious if they don't comply."

Al nodded and hurried off. Mantis glanced down, then, at the report on Capitan that had been handed to him, at the top line: "Capitan Alzerras has been identified by some informants as Monitor number Eight."

He thought for a moment. "Yes, why not?"

Also watching Sten's interview with interest that night was Big Sun, head guru of the Zed Advesta, the mystical tribe of blacks who based their faith on the ancient fire worship of the Zoroastrians. Big Sun—his real name was Habib Galan—had at one time been a commando in the army. He had been wounded while carrying out a mission in Mongolia and had been sent for convalescence to an R & R center in Japan. It was during his stay in Japan that he met an extraordinary man who was to become his teacher, launching him on a career of self-styled divinity that had only recently been marred by an inexplicable series of terrorist incidents. Until now, Habib could find no way to account for the attacks by members of his sect. But after listening to the accusations Sten had directed against Mantis, accusations that conjured up unpleasant associations with the past, Habib could sense a pattern beginning to emerge. He remembered a violent incident, a brutal incident that had occurred while he was in Japan, an incident concerning his teacher and two other students like himself. The haunting image of a sword and a smiling, rolling head passed in front of Habib's eyes as he glanced again at the card that had just been handed to him:

```
---- o ---- o
---- o ---- +
```

"He's found me..." Habib mumbled.

"Who, Big Sun?"

Habib's ring of bodyguards stood ready, attentive. The Zed A leader eased back in his ebony throne chair, his large hand toying with the card. He shook his head and turned to one of his men.

"The child named Aquila—is he safe?"

The bodyguard nodded. "We have him under close guard."

"How does Kalil look?" Habib asked.

"Strong, Big Sun. But his eyes, they talk of much sin."

"You searched him?"

"Thoroughly."

"Strip him down and search him again. And put him in robes before you bring him before me."

The bodyguards bowed and left, one man remaining. Ever since the first terrorist incident Habib had insisted on taking extra precautions. He looked now at the guard standing watch on him, wondering if even he could be trusted. What was to prevent him from going mad, too, just like the others. Elijah, Mustaf, and Omar—all had been among his top men before something, or someone, had gotten control of their minds. Habib thought he knew now who that someone might be.

Mantis. Mantis had to be behind it all. This card that Kalil had brought with him—it could be from no one other than Mantis....

Tokyo...Rest and Rehab Center No. 9. Habib watched as the officer across from him examined his right hand, then his fingers. The officer's code name was "Mantis." Habib had seen him before; he had just led the hit in Tibet on the Temple of Kali. Rumor had it that he and an East German officer, a woman, had been struck indirectly by a neutron grenade, and had been brought back to Tokyo for treatment. Since Habib's own unit had launched a diversionary raid into Mongolia, Habib thought it appropriate that he introduce himself to the commando.

The two immediately struck up an interesting friendship. Like Habib, Mantis was well studied in philosophy, and they spoke for many hours about Christianity, Islam, the Buddha and Ahura

Mazda, the Zoroastrian belief in the Supreme as symbolized by fire. Once, Habib remembered, they were carrying on a discussion in the officers' club when Mantis did a headstand before the bar and held it a full ten minutes. The conversation continued. When Mantis resumed a normal standing posture, a Japanese officer applauded him.

"It's good for the body," Mantis said, smiling.

"Ah, but what about the mind?" the Oriental soldier asked.

"What do you mean?" Habib said.

"Exactly what I said. What about the mind? What do you do for it?"

"You mean, meditate?" Mantis asked.

"Yes. What techniques do you use?"

A discussion followed about mind techniques, ranging from hypnosis to mantras. Habib sensed the officer was feeling both him and Mantis out. Then the officer started to talk about the future of the world order and asked where they both thought it was going to go. He asked if their loyalties were really to "Truth," which they seemed to discuss so much, or to profit. Mantis avoided a direct answer, preferring to turn the subject of Truth into a debate. The debate culminated with Mantis turning the tables on the Oriental officer and asking him whether *he* stood for Truth or for profit.

"Oh, for Truth," the officer said.

"You speak with conviction," Mantis said. "That indicates you clearly know this Truth."

The officer nodded.

"Can you show it to us, then?" Habib asked.

"I can show you the way there," the officer said. "Everyone has to journey on their own in the end."

"But you're the guide, right?" Mantis asked.

"I'm the guide to the guide."

"Oh, then guide us to the guide," Mantis said. "And tell us your name."

The Oriental officer smiled. "Call me *sensei*, teacher."

"Not mine," Mantis said in calm defiance.

"No, not yours," the officer said with a smile. "That is quite clear." He looked at Habib. "Tomorrow you will both need a massage." He handed Habib a card, then sauntered away.

That was the card that had led to the first lesson....

And now this—*this card*—all a part of it.

Habib closed his eyes, his posture firm and erect in the ebony chair as his mind began to follow its breath, thoughts drifting back to that first meeting with Hoshima....

Habib went with Mantis to the address on the card the following day. It was in one of the lower dens of Tokyo, a shiatsu parlor bathed in a symphony of noise and abrasive Oriental neon light. Habib joked that he felt like they were explorers in one of those old mid-twentieth-century movies, but Mantis's humorous side was no longer in evidence. The blond commando was deadly serious now, as if girding himself for a long-awaited confrontation.

As if it were yesterday, Habib remembered standing at the dojo's entrance. The shoji screens were open, revealing clean tatami mats, zabuton cushions, a white futon neatly laid out and, farther up, a tokanoma or recess area housing a kakemono, a scroll with *kanji* symbols. Habib pointed at it.

"You speak Japanese. What's it say?"

"Shin-Do," Mantis said. "The Way of the Heart, Mind."

"Which is it?"

"In the East, the heart and mind are supposedly one."

Habib removed his shoes and stepped in as Mantis held his ground, cautiously looking around. Then he followed suit, removing his shoes and crossing the tatami with his bare feet. It was not long before a bald-headed man in his late fifties entered and bowed politely.

"*Konban-wa*," he said. "Good evening."

"*Konban-wa*," Mantis said, bowing stiffly. Habib bowed to the old man with a more polite, servile gesture.

"Please, be seated," the man said. He went over to the tokanoma and lit some incense. Then he returned and sat down in lotus posture. He motioned to both Mantis and Habib.

"Please, straighten your postures," he said. "You Westerners, still to this day after so many decades of marriage between East and West, sit like noodles."

Habib grinned, finding it quite funny. Mantis glared.

"We came here for a massage," Mantis said, "not a Seiza sitting exercise."

"Seiza, the Art of Sitting, is the greatest massage the body can receive."

"What about Shin-Do?" Mantis asked.

"That is the greatest art for the mind. But it begins witl Seiza. My art should really be called Seiza Shin-Do, or perhaps Shin-Do Seiza, or Even Shinseiza-Do. Yes," the strange man said, scratching his bald head, "I like that last one."

"Is this some kind of joke?" Mantis asked.

"No, not at all. I am here looking for students, good students."

"Maybe we're looking for a good teacher."

"I am he," the gentleman said, humbly, but with a humor so fine and subtle that Habib felt he was being lit up inside.

"And who are *you?*" Mantis asked.

"He's funny," Habib said.

"My name is Geido Hoshima. And I am an illuminated master whose mind radiates all enlightenment out to the ten thousand universes of the Buddha Bodies which are central coordinators of the Eighth Quadrant of Life."

Habib burst into laughter, his head touching the mat as his guts opened with good feelings. Mantis rose angrily.

"This is nonsense," he said.

"Oh, but it's funny, brother."

"I'm not laughing."

"No, you are not laughing," Hoshima said, "because you put your ego before harmony and you separate your heart from the rest of the world, saying 'them' second and 'me' first."

Mantis waved him away and turned to Habib. "I'm leaving."

"Because he's scared," Hoshima said, folding his arms.

"No," Mantis said softly. "Because I have rules about hitting old men."

Hoshima let out a little ripple of laughter. "If I even so much as gave you the chance to hit me, without hitting back myself or defending—you still couldn't touch me."

"I think he means business," Habib said, glancing up at Mantis.

"Then I'll take him up on it." The green-eyed commando smiled.

What happened next Habib would never forget, because as Mantis stepped forward to grab Hoshima, the older gentleman magically disappeared. One moment he was there and the next he was a few feet away mumbling a Buddhist mantra and shaking his head.

"Gate, gate, paragate, parasangate—bodhi, svaha!
Gate, gate, paragate, parasangate—bodhi, svaha!
Gate, gate, paragate, parasangate—bodhi, svaha!"

After a few chants he returned to normal composure. Habib and Mantis could not believe their senses.

"I lose a year of my life every time I do that technique," he told them. "So I chant, because it's all 'gone, gone,' but I'm still fulfilled. Now either sit down or leave," he added, motioning to Mantis.

A slow, uneasy grin crossed the commando's face. He gradually settled with perfect posture upon a zabuton cushion, eyes not moving from Hoshima.

And so it began, truly began. Both soldiers applied for extended leave to study with Hoshima.

Hoshima. So many great, good thoughts about Hoshima. How he had taught Habib the art of Shin-Do and how Habib had sat and trained his mind to dive to its source and how he had found that source to be warm, penetrating, like the Sun. The source of all things, the Sun and its fire.

"The Sun. It's like the sun," Habib remembered telling the master one day after his first true realization, his first spark of *kensha* or illumination.

"The Sun, is it?"

"Yes."

Hoshima turned to Mantis. "And have you felt anything?"

"Yes," Mantis said. "I have felt the smell of the food I ate on my breath."

"Excellent," Hoshima said. "Very soon now you will both be thoroughly enlightened beings who will be able to journey on the mana waves of the supreme *sat-chit-ananda* to ice cream galaxies, yes."

Though Mantis laughed, Habib took the jest seriously. He was very concerned with his vision, which he wished to express to his people when he returned to the West. He expressed his concern to Hoshima.

"Is my vision of fire and the sun wrong?"

"No, no—not in the least," the master said. "After all, why do we have Buddhism in one place, and Christianity in another? Because the Truth is so vast and inexplicable that it must be translated in various ways. The mind of Jesus saw the truth in one way, the great Shakyamuni in another. So it goes. *You* see and experience it as the Sun."

"It is the Moon," Mantis said teasingly.

"Full or new moon?" Hoshima asked.

"Gibbous," the commando said. Hoshima waved him aside.

"Now, today I want you to think about ethics. Without ethics all this sitting and meditating is futile. What we are doing is tending the gardens of our mind. You can't tend to the garden without fertilizer and water. That's where the ethics come in."

Hoshima smiled at Mantis. "What are ethics to you?"

"Survival of the fittest," the commando said.

"That, my friend, is a very dim outlook. Very dim, indeed."

"What would you suggest?" Mantis asked. "The meek shall inherit...?"

"That's good for a start, yes. Then we have nonviolence."

"Not a wise choice for a soldier," Habib said.

"For warriors there is only the code of death," Mantis said.

"In the case of righteous wars, yes," Hoshima said. "But in the case of silly little war games like the ones you and your brothers fight your code is a blatant lie."

It was the first in a series of confrontations Mantis was to have with the master, confrontations that led to tragedy, sudden tragedy...the sword flash and the head rolling and the face smiling and...Mantis...

"Big Sun..."

Kalil had been brought in, dressed in clean robes. Habib took a few breaths to collect himself into "Big Sun." A few moments of silence passed as former disciple and former guru stared at one another. Kalil found himself weak, powerless before the mighty man on the ebony throne. Finally Habib rose and walked over to Kalil. He embraced his former follower, and the Arena fighter burst into tears.

"Welcome home," Habib said.

"Oh, Big Sun...I have been sent here to...spy on you, I think."

"I know," Habib said. "That card told all."

"Who sent me? What am I doing?"

"Sit with me. We shall talk."

All that was needed was for a little hole to form in the dike and then the information poured forth in a torrent. Kalil told his old leader everything that had been said to him in the interview, even about the credits that had been given to him. Then he handed Habib the picture of the Japanese officer. Habib just glanced at it and cast it aside.

"Who am I working for? What's the child got to do with all this?"

"I will tell you about the child, in time. But first you must know that Mantis is hiring you to do all this, and that you are in danger."

"Mantis? The grand champion?"

"A devil, my son. Incarnated now in Mantis's flesh. This Japanese officer in the picture and Mantis and I all studied together under the same teacher in Japan. We were all taught many powers of the mind. But Mantis misuses the power—he is to be avoided. Under no circumstances should you contact this person who sent you here. You will be putting your life in danger."

"But I'm expected back," Kalil said. "They'll kill me if I don't return."

"They'll kill you if you do, only very slowly."

"Then what can I do?"

"Return to us," Habib said, his fierce eyes penetrating.

Kalil looked away, trying to gather his strength. The Big Sun was like a human vacuum, capable of sucking you into his aura, diminishing you until you were nothing more than a satellite orbiting his fiery presence. I left because of this, Kalil thought. He wants me back but he's not giving me any two hundred grand. That white bastard may have been mean looking, but I left there free to be my own man. It's the lesser of two evils...damn, I want freedom.

Kalil turned to Habib. "What's the story about the child? Why would Mantis send me to find out about some child? Some *white* child?"

"Because we have the child."

"Whose child is it? Mantis's?"

"Yes, it's his son," Habib said.

"His son. How come you have his son?"

"Because he was brought to us by the Japanese officer who appears in the photo."

"I don't get it."

"We are protecting the boy from his father. Mantis wants to kill his son, so this officer here and I took custody of the boy after his mother died."

"Why in the world would Mantis want to kill his own son?"

"That is not for you to know, either now or in the future. Take my advice: return to us. Do not attempt to go back."

"But, the man, the one I spoke to—he said he'd have information for you about Elijah and all."

"It's very clear now," Habib said. "There's nothing more I need to know. Something I had observed tonight plus this card and the child put it together for me. If you return to the man who sent you here, the same thing will happen to you that happened to

Elijah and Mustaf and Omar. Mantis hypnotized them."

"Hypnotized them?"

"He has that power, even more. He chose them because they were once soldiers, well trained, capable of fighting. You with your experience in the Arena would be attractive to him as well."

Kalil shook his head, finding it all too incredible. "I can't believe—"

"*Believe*," Habib said. "Look into my eyes and *believe*. For your own sake and the sake of your family, *believe me*."

Habib held Kalil's head and made him look directly into his eyes. The Arena fighter fought the stare for a moment, his mind attempting to focus on the 200,000 credits, then he began to drift, into the eyes...the eyes of the Sun. Kalil's mind was swimming now...sinking and then swimming...trying to swim...for the 200 suns....

CHAPTER FIFTEEN

THE sign was gone now. He had taken it down, though he knew it would do little to forestall discovery.

It would take only a matter of hours, Capitan realized after watching the interview with Sten, for the media masters to be at his door. Such was the power and speed with which the masters operated. He was marked now, marked for some special rendezvous with fate....

Carmen had left, walked out. There had been a note:

My dearest,
With all my heart and soul, you have knocked me off center, completely. I am out for a few hours, a few days, to collect myself. I am with you but you drive me mad with what you are doing. I must have some time to think.

Carmen

He read it again, for the umpteenth time. The phone rang.

"It's Sten," Bimbi said.

Capitan did not respond. Instead, he walked over to the phone and hung up the receiver. A few seconds later, the phone rang again. This time Capitan disconnected it from the wall.

"Why'd you do that?" Bimbi asked.

"Why do you think?"

"You mean you ain't gonna train Sten to fight Mantis?"

"Of course not."

Capitan sat in the lotus position and watched as Bimbi paced restlessly back and forth. The boy was obviously agitated.

"You were out. You've been taking drugs again," Capitan said.

"Yeah? Well, so what? You know, I think you're freaked out because that Mantis guy has got your number as a warrior."

Capitan took a long look at his student. "And what's my number, as a warrior?"

"I think you're scared of death."

Capitan smiled. "No. It's not death that scares me, Bimbi. It's the killing. Not the kind that one has to do to protect his family, but the kind that goes on in the ring—cold-blooded killing."

Bimbi shook his head. "What are you talking about? You don't approve of any kind of killing, even if it means protectin' the family. My brother needed protection, but he sure didn't get any from me. And the guy that killed him is still walking around laughing because he didn't have to pay the price. I don't know why I'm wastin' my time studying with you."

"Maybe you are wasting your time," Capitan said finally. He could see that he was getting nowhere with the boy. Bimbi had persisted in taking drugs. He had persisted in nurturing these fantasies of revenge. Capitan wanted to remain silent, but added, "If you choose to think about killing, then you are no longer my student."

Bimbi backed away, hurt. He had not expected Capitan to say that. "Sit, sit—that's all the fuck you ever really do. Ah, I woulda never learned anything from you anyway." He was ready for tears, but wasn't about to let Capitan see them. He stormed out of the house.

And then he wandered the nearby streets, confused, lost, not knowing what to do or where to go. He was so upset that he never noticed the black sedan following him.

Inside the sedan Mantis sat in the back seat with Al, watching. Al pointed out the window.

"That's him. Guy named Bimbi. Street people say his brother was a soldier, got gunned down a while back in a fight. Now this guy wants revenge. He's been studying with Capitan about three weeks now."

A few minutes passed as the car rolled along behind Bimbi.

"Hot-headed Spic, eh? Well, keep on following him."

Bimbi continued down the street unaware of the sedan. Mantis glanced at his watch. "Oman should be back by five," he said.

"*If* he comes back," Al added.

"He'll be back," Mantis said. "Two hundred thousand credits says he'll be back."

"You expect him to have info about the kid?"

"It doesn't matter," Mantis said. "What matters is that our surgeon friend, Dr. Schneider, shows up. I intend to turn Mr. Oman into a real surprise package. Now," he motioned to his driver, "let's get this over with."

The sedan pulled up alongside Bimbi. Al rolled the window down and said: "You..."

Bimbi froze in his tracks.

"What?"

"Come here."

"Why?"

"Just come here."

Bimbi's legs began to weaken, then recoup their strength and flex, ready to run.

"Why?"

"Because," Al said, sticking his ugly face out the window, "there's somebody here that wants to talk with you."

Bimbi took a few steps back.

"You guys ain't cops, are you?"

There was muffled laughter from inside the sedan, laughter that was bizarre enough to prompt Bimbi to panic and run. He headed down the street as fast as he could, but the sedan was quick to follow, skirting across the sidewalks defiantly and then cutting off Bimbi so abruptly that the young Hispanic went somersaulting over the hood. He began to cry in shock. Al stepped out and pulled him into the sedan.

They drove on a ways before Mantis said anything. Bimbi, who sat handcuffed between the champion and Al, fought back tears, not daring to look either way. He began to shake. Al held him by the arm.

"Keep still."

Mantis smiled and pointed at the handcuffs.

"You like those?"

"No..."

"That why you're crying?"

"I'm not crying."

Mantis looked grimly out the window, then motioned to Al. "Take 'em off."

Al unlocked the handcuffs. Mantis looked out the window again as Bimbi rubbed his bruised wrists. "Do you know who I am?" Mantis asked finally.

"Yeah...I know."

"And you want to be a fighter?"

"Says who?"

"Never mind who. You've been training under that guy Capitan, right?"

"Yeah."

"What's he been teaching you?" Mantis asked.

"Stuff..."

"Stuff. Just stuff?"

"Yeah..."

"What kind of stuff?"

"Well, uh...fightin' stuff," Bimbi mumbled, not knowing what to expect.

"What's he call it?" Mantis asked.

"I...I don't know, I—"

"Sure you know."

"I don't, honest. He does a lot of sittin' around and, uh—"

"Does he meditate?" Mantis asked.

"Yeah, lots of that."

"What's he call his meditating?"

"Nothin'. He just sits like a zombie and—"

Mantis motioned to Al. The brute held Bimbi's leg firmly, gently but firmly.

"Think, my little cucaracha. What does he call his meditating?"

Bimbi's mind swam in confusion, then it came to him, the word, it was—"Aiki. He calls it Aiki."

Mantis nodded and smiled. The sedan rolled along. He turned to Bimbi finally. "Aiki, eh?"

"Yeah, that was what I think he called it."

"And what did he say about it?"

"I, I don't remem—"

Mantis motioned to Al again. There was the firm but gentle grip.

"Think, my little cockroach."

"He...said...something about...glue."

"Glue?" Mantis said, amused.

"Yeah, somethin' about glue and, how it holds everything together—this Aiki stuff."

"And what else?"

"Uh, nothing...nothing else."

"Sure there is, think."

"He...said...I'm confused..."

There was the grip again. Bimbi was ready for tears.

"Think and don't cry," Mantis said firmly. "If you cry, then you'll annoy me and I'll hurt you for real. Think."

There was a short pause as Bimbi summoned up the courage to look at Mantis again and speak.

"He said somethin' about the...the Holy Ghost. That this Aiki stuff was like the Holy Ghost, in all of us, and...that..."

"That's enough," Mantis said. He looked over at Al and nodded. "Looks like we found our man." There was a long silence as Mantis looked out the window, his rhythmic breathing echoing gently throughout the sedan. Bimbi could not help but listen to the rise and fall of the breath, and as he did he began to grow lightheaded, as if his mind no longer had roots. He shook his head. Mantis smiled and turned to him. "Why'd you leave his place?"

"Who says I did?"

"You left his place, all pissed off."

"How do you know?"

"Never mind how we know. You left his place, my little friend, because you want revenge against that guy who killed your brother."

"Hey, yeah! How'd you—"

Mantis raised his head to indicate silence. Bimbi obeyed, his mind attentive, loyal—like a dog.

"And that guy Capitan, he doesn't believe in killing, right?"

"No. He sure doesn't."

Mantis motioned to the driver. "Stop the car."

As the sedan pulled over, Mantis motioned to Al, who handed Bimbi a wallet.

"There's a credeer card in there," Mantis told him, "and a security card to get you into Manhattan. My address is in the wallet. If you want to learn the art of revenge, then I'll be waiting there to teach you all about it. Now—" he motioned for Al to open the door, "*get out.*"

Bimbi emerged from the sedan, the daylight blinding him. He watched half-stunned as the sedan rolled away. He stood for a long while, staring at the wallet, wondering what had happened.

Kalil returned to the office where he had been originally interviewed by Al. Big Sun had released him under the condition that he return home with a fellow fire brother, and then head directly with his family for the Zed Advesta farm in Kentucky. Kalil had agreed, but managed to slip his fire brother escort en route. Money was talking to him now, and not even Big Sun's piercing eyes and holy aura were going to deter him from the big bucks. After all, he had been deceived by that big daddy guru before, deceived into working eight hours a day, seven days a week without pay for the greater glory of the Brotherhood. Why should he believe everything Big Sun told him now? Everyone outside the Zed A was always portrayed by the group as either a demon or an angel possessed by demons, and he was not about to be fooled any longer. No, it was time to think smart....

Kalil closed the door abruptly behind him and sat down in the white-walled reception area. Al appeared a minute later.

"Mr. Oman..."

"I'm back."

"I can see that," Al said. "So what have you to tell us? Did you see your old guru?"

"I saw the Big Sun, yeah."

"Very good. You told him we had information concerning the terrorists?"

"I told him everything. I even told him I thought you sent me to spy on him, too." Al smiled his no-smile as Kalil babbled away: "He told me the child was fine, that it is Mantis's son, and that Mantis wants to kill it. He also said that Mantis is the one I'm working for and that he's behind all the terrorism."

"Very, very good. You've been active. He told you Mantis was behind the terrorism?"

"Yeah, he said Mantis hypnotized three of our brothers, hypnotized them to kill." Kalil stopped to catch his breath. He was sweating. The room seemed hot, hotter than usual, like a jungle. "In any case, I don't think he wants to talk."

"Who?"

"The Big Sun."

"Oh, that doesn't matter," Al said. "What matters is that you did your job. We have one more task for you, though..."

"Does it pay?"

"My, we're getting greedy, aren't we?"

"You know, they warned me not to come back here."

"Did they now?" Al said, rising and heading for the office door. He motioned to Kalil.

"What's up?"

"Follow me."

After hesitating a moment, Kalil rose and followed Al into the adjoining room, not knowing what to expect. He entered an office that had been converted into a greenhouse, the broad windows opening up onto a South Jersey landscape of oil tanks and low abandoned buildings. Light flooded the room, momentarily blinding Kalil. As his eyes adjusted, he saw that he was standing before an office desk and that Mantis was seated behind it. There was a terrarium on the desk. Mantis motioned for Kalil to take a seat.

"Relax..." Mantis said.

Kalil inched into his seat as Al showed himself out.

"You know me?" Mantis asked.

"Sure. It's an honor."

"Thank you." Mantis had a pencil in his hand. He pointed out the window, not looking back. "It's ugly, isn't it?"

"I've seen worse," Kalil said.

"Those tanks out there, they're like ant hills. Look out at them and tell me if there isn't a touch of the ant hill in them."

Kalil stared out for a while. "Yeah, I guess so."

"Of course everybody sees things differently," Mantis said. "Some people see life as a war between good and evil. Your old guru, for example. Now, he used to be a close friend of mine. He told you, didn't he?"

Kalil nodded.

"Unfortunately, he's under the illusion—the very medieval illusion—that I am possessed by some demon. In fact, according to him, ninety-nine point nine percent of humanity is possessed by demons, and only he and his chosen flock are destined to see, to reach the—what do you call it?"

"The Fire Chief."

"Yes, that was the term he was working on while we were still friends, back in Japan. He made that vision up, you know. I find it rather shallow, rather worn out—good versus evil, archangels fighting Satan and all. After all," Mantis said, looking at the glass terrarium on his desk, "we *are* living in the twenty-first century."

Kalil shifted nervously in his seat. "Yes," he managed to mumble.

"I'm inclined to prefer *my* personal view of things," Mantis added, poking at something in the terrarium. The he leaned back in his seat and stared at Kalil. There was a long silence.

"What *is* your personal view of things?" Kalil asked finally.

"Well, it all boils down to what I like to call the insectivorous nature of man," Mantis said. There was a sudden buzz on the intercom.

"Dr. Schneider is here," Al said.

"Tell him Mr. Oman will be ready in a moment."

"A doctor? What's up?"

"Oh, nothing. Just a physical. We want to make sure you're in shape for the next job."

"I don't need a physical," Kalil said, starting to grow alarmed.

"It's just routine," Mantis said calmly, poking once again at something in the terrarium. "Tell me, Mr. Oman—have you ever seen one of these?"

He pointed inside the terrarium. Kalil looked hesitantly at Mantis, then leaned closer, trying to locate the object of interest.

"I don't see nothin'."

"That's because you're not accustomed to looking for camouflage," Mantis told him. "Look closer now, and separate green from green."

Kalil looked closer, into the terrarium, his eyes suddenly focusing on something, something moving, something very green....

CHAPTER SIXTEEN

BRIGHTON Beach, Brooklyn.
The boardwalk. Once a well-knit community of elderly Russian
Jews had roamed here, but no longer. In an attempt to appease
the growing number of youth gangs, the city of Brooklyn had
turned the area into a no man's land—a neutral zone. Now the
beaches and the boardwalks were lined with debris; the buildings
were burned out; the sand was littered with garbage; and gulls
roamed the area in such numbers that the entire region had been
dubbed "Gull City."

On this crisp fall afternoon a very well-built Oriental man
watched from the boardwalk as two men climbed atop one of the
lifeguard stations in the distance. The man rubbed his hands and
zipped up his jacket. He was young, in his mid-forties. As Asians
go, he was average height. But to the two punks watching him
from a nearby pinball club, he was tiny, easy prey, an apple ripe
for the picking. They watched as the man stared out across the
beach, toward the men on the lifeguard stand.

"Let's roll him," the first punk said.

"I'll do it. It'll only take one."

"How do you know? That guy's some kinda Chink. Maybe he knows something."

"Like what?" the second hood asked.

"I don't know..."

"Asshole," the second hood mumbled, walking across the board-walk, toward the Oriental. He waited until he was about five feet away, then said abruptly, "Yo, Chinaman—gimme your wallet."

The man turned, and as he did the hood saw that he was not someone to be trifled with. His head was close-shaven, which meant that he was probably a soldier. The stranger gave him a smile and waved his finger in warning. The young hood stopped for a moment, then thought about his pride. He decided to lunge forward. The Oriental pivoted quickly and sent the punk crashing to the ground.

"Shit....*Lou!*"

The hood motioned for his friend to help. They both charged the stranger, but the man spun like a top and sent both punks flying in opposite directions. The other thugs from the pinball hall watched in awe as their two comrades rallied and prepared to charge again. The second punk flashed out his knife. The stranger waved a hand in final warning.

"Use a knife and it will turn against you," he said.

There was a pause as the thugs sized the stranger up. The first hood shook his head and slowly backed away.

"I'm out of this one," he said.

"You're gonna leave me standin'?" the other said, the knife still in his hand.

"You can come with me."

"Shit."

The hood folded up his knife and aimed a defiant finger at the Oriental. "You're lucky, Charlie Chan," he said, walking away. At the same time he was thinking, Shit, *I'm* lucky...

The stranger smiled, then folded his arms and leaned against the railing, looking out across the beach. The hoods were at a safe distance now.

"Just watch it, Charlie Chan," they yelled.

The name's Ibari, the stranger said to himself, thinking back to those westerns he had seen where a cowboy leaned against the bar and introduced himself. Ibari, or Yakahama, or Tung Cheng. I am a man of many aliases. He returned his attention to the men at the lifeguard station and smiled. To some people, I'm even known as Monitor Five.

Sten had just jumped down from the lifeguard station into the sand. From atop the stand, Capitan watched as the *karateka* proceeded to do a series of rapid-fire pushups. Sten had finally contacted Capitan and pleaded with him to agree to a meeting—a secret "rendezvous" as he called it. So now they were at the beach, Sten using exercise to calm his nerves and Capitan meditating on recent events....

Bimbi had walked out...

Carmen had yet to return...

Abe was gunning for him...

And so, maybe, was Mantis...

Capitan broke free from his reverie long enough to notice a few gangs patrolling the beach. Fortunately, there was no cause for alarm. Not with Sten here to sic on them, Capitan thought.

The two men had to meet in places like this now. The media masters had left them with no other choice. They had set up camp outside Capitan's studio and Sten's dojo, hounding each man for stories whenever he emerged. And I have this big baboon here to thank for it all, Capitan thought, as he looked down at Sten again.

"Ninety-nine...a hundred...a hundred 'n one..." Sten continued counting vigorously.

How did I get myself in this mess, Capitan asked himself. Where'd I go wrong? Taking Bimbi in? No, that was my solemn duty. Where then? Was it Goldman? Yes, Goldman was the one who started prying, who stuck Sten on me. It all started with Goldman and whoever put *him* up to it. Was it Monitor Five? If it was, why hadn't he shown his face?

"One forty-eight, one forty-nine—*one fifty!*"

Sten jumped to his feet, his massive physique shining, immune to the cold. He aimed a finger at Capitan.

"I'll tell you one thing, that Mantis guy is no clown."

No, he's no clown, Capitan thought. Sten climbed up the lifeguard station and sat next to Capitan.

"He knows if he opts for weapons, first I'll use the nunchakas. And there's no way he can do shit against 'em with those sais."

"Wrong," Capitan said. "Remember what he did to Tanaka?"

"That's true," Sten muttered, his face dropping.

Oh Christ, Capitan thought, this guy's a lamb up for slaughter. Sten wrapped a hand around a railing post and began to crack it with his brute strength. Well, Capitan thought, how about a ram for the slaughter...?

"Anyway," Sten said, "it's a clear game as far as I'm concerned. Hands. Unarmed combat."

"Why do you say that?"

"Because I'm better with the nunchakas than Tanaka was."

"You don't know that."

"I feel it."

"That's your ego talking," Capitan said. "Tanaka was a decorated officer, a trained killer with the Okinawan Air Cavalry."

"Yeah, and I was number one champ in my day."

"You're not listening to me," Capitan said.

"I'm listenin', I'm just disagreein'."

"Then why'd you call me here? To argue?"

"No," the *karateka* mumbled. He fumbled nervously with his hands.

"You can't be predisposed to think that Mantis will use hands before weapons or weapons before hands. He doesn't really see any distinction between the two, between you or Tanaka or Savinien or ... even me for that matter." Somehow that last part about himself had just blurted out. He sat numb for a second because of it.

"What do you mean?" Sten asked.

"Mantis is beyond technique now, Sten. Did your *sensei* ever teach you about the '*ri*' and the '*Ji*'?"

"Sounds familiar..."

"*Ri* is the Universal, the Absolute. *Ji* is technique. We trained in technique to reach the Absolute. When we fight we apply *ji* hoping to connect with *ri*."

"So what's this got to do with Mantis?"

"Mantis doesn't use *ji* any more. He's plugged in as a fighter with that *ri*, the universal. He's enlightened when it comes to killing. An empty hand or a weapon is the same thing. He just applies it, almost unconsciously. And then he kills with it."

The sun had begun its descent toward the western horizon. The wind held steady, holding the gulls aloft in effortless arcs. Capitan looked away from Sten. He didn't know what the karate man wanted, and he didn't know what to tell him. It was official now. Mantis had agreed to a fight. The Arena League was putting up their usual formal protest, but it wouldn't ride. Mantis was the Arena's fair-haired boy—for the moment. What he wanted, he would get. And it looked like what he wanted was Sten's neck....

"Life is precious," Hoshima had told Capitan once. "Precious, indeed. It is part of man's instinct to cling to life. Even the enlightened cling to life. But it is sinful to cling to personal safety when the life of another is in danger. Since we are all beads wound on the same thread, it is foolish to think that we are safe when the bead right next to us is being crushed."

Fine, Capitan thought. But how do you save that neighboring bead? What weapon do you use? He turned to Sten.

"In any case, Mantis can easily turn any plan or game you use against you. Your karate, no matter how good, just fits into a slot for him to play with. He knows all the arts; you go offense, he'll go defense."

"I understand that," Sten said.

"You do?"

"Yeah."

"Then why have you been arguing with me, about nunchakas and Tanaka and all?"

"Because, that will all fall into place. That's why I asked you to meet me here. I want you to teach me."

"Teach you what?" Capitan asked, confused. "You're a master of your own art, I know mine. What can I teach you in so short a time before this fight?"

"Something that you know. Things that you know."

"Like what?" Capitan asked.

"Knowledge," Sten said.

"Knowledge is something you build up. That you study and gather..."

"All right, Truth then."

"Truth?"

"Yeah. Like the Truth you was talkin' about that Mantis knows."

Capitan remained silent. Sten stared at him intently. The gulls danced and cackled over their heads as the sun offered its last glimmerings.

"I know you know that Truth," Sten said, his face open, like a child's. "Because there's somethin' in you that's special, that I respected right off, even as we was sparrin' around. I just never told you. You've seen something, something that I ain't seen or I don't understand. And it's got nothin' to do with fightin', either."

No, not in the ordinary sense, Capitan thought, remaining silent, staring out at the waves.

"It's because you meditate," Sten continued. "Bimbi told me you meditate. Teach me that, how to meditate. I know a little already. I learned a lot of Zen stuff when I started with karate as a kid. I even know the posture, look—" Sten went into a perfect lotus position, his legs crossed, feet tucked comfortably on opposing thighs. "I used to teach it the other way, on the knees. But I just taught kids how to sit still—I was good at that."

Sten was getting to the crux of things now and Capitan was moved. He stared out at the waves, watching them roll in, one by one or in line, each of them crashing and dying and then being dragged back in by the tide to be reformed again. Here they were, Capitan thought, Sten and himself, two waves—only waves with a will of their own. Sten was the kind that was prepared to crash on the shore. Capitan was a wave that held back, that wanted to stay lost in the sea even if it meant...

No, I can't hide any longer, he thought. And I can't wait for any old master to appear, or for myself to rely on invisible monitors who don't really exist. He turned to Sten.

"I can teach you something, yeah..."

"I *knew* it," Sten said.

"If you're good at sitting, then you already know the game."

The sun had dropped below the horizon, painting the water a darker blue. Monitor Five watched from the boardwalk as Sten embraced Capitan. It was all such a graceful portrait, the Oriental thought. Yes, very graceful. Now, let the next scene play just as gracefully.

The winds picked up down the Hudson as dusk gave way to twilight. On Riverside Drive the trees began to scatter their remaining leaves across the park. The street lights shone gently and the new security stations, positioned at every fourth block, began to buzz their ominous neon chant. Bimbi stared at it all, amazed. He had lived in Brooklyn all his life and had never been in Manhattan. I.D. cards like the one he now held were a priceless item for an Untouchable. He took it all in again, the park and the trees and the leaves, then he looked at the address. He could not read but he knew numbers. And a pedestrian had literally placed him on Riverside Drive. After a few minutes he found his way to Mantis's building. He hesitated, looking at the door.

Why was he here? Mantis was evil, wasn't he? He was evil and Capitan was good. Capitan had always been good to him, and he had never scared him like Mantis. So what was he doing getting mixed up with Mantis? For a moment, Bimbi was confused. But then he remembered José, his dead brother, and Enrique, still alive and cruising, and it all came back to him. He had to avenge his brother, he had to face the street, he had to face the city and the turf and the cops, and Capitan's talking just didn't do it for him, didn't provide any answers. What good was peace and acting nice if everyone out there was ready to rip your head off? He had tried to listen to Capitan, but Capitan was just a dreamer. That's why he had left. That's why he was here. Mantis was no dreamer, no—Mantis knew how to act. He was frightening and all, but he knew his shit. And now he had invited Bimbi here, to become his student....

Having come to a decision, Bimbi rang the buzzer.

Al was waiting to show him in. After passing the greenhouse area where Sten had had his ill-fated visit they entered an elevator, a private elevator with a key that Al flicked on, then off, as he looked at Bimbi and smiled his no-smile. Bimbi felt as if the elevator would take forever to reach wherever it was going, the fearsome, anvil-faced man who had gripped his leg not saying anything, just smiling, smiling but not smiling.

The elevator stopped. Al flicked the key. The doors opened.

"Hey, wow!" Bimbi said.

They walked out onto a gorgeous terrace lined with Japanese cherry trees. The trees were in full bloom. Bimbi looked up and noticed that the entire penthouse area was under a giant plastic dome. It was dark now. The heavens were open, in view.

"There are stars. I can see stars."

Al motioned for Bimbi to move on. A tile path ran down between the two rows of cherry trees, leading to a pagoda-styled penthouse apartment. Bimbi walked along it slowly, wanting to take everything in—the trees, and the path, and the sky. He could see sky. They passed a small garden. Suddenly Bimbi jumped.

"Hey..."

"Don't worry," Al said. "He won't hurt you."

It was a large jade statue of the Buddha. The statue had been slashed from head to toe. Al nudged Bimbi and Bimbi glanced back at the statue as they continued. He wanted to ask about the statue but was afraid. They came up to the door of the penthouse. Al hit a button and the doors slid open. He pushed Bimbi in.

"What about you?" Bimbi asked.

"I'm a big boy. I don't play in there any longer."

He hit the button and the doors closed abruptly, leaving Bimbi alone. He turned...

He was in a giant studio area filled with plants, plants so thick and numerous that he felt as if he were in a jungle. There was another tile path. It wound through the jungle, then out of view. After a moment of hesitation, Bimbi followed it. And he heard sounds. Sounds of creepers and jungle things. Sounds of things *unseen*. He wanted to run out, but had nowhere to go even if he could escape. This was all meant to be, yes—his courage returned to him and as he rounded the next little turn on the jungle path he was in a clearing, the path running up and then ending in the distance at a slightly elevated platform, a dais. But then...

"Holy Mother..." Bimbi began to shake, his courage trickling away as he saw the two giant jade statues of insectlike creatures on either side of the dais. Mantis was seated behind it, bare-chested, deep in meditation, like the Buddha in the garden. Feeling as if he were committing some kind of sacrilege, Bimbi cleared his throat, waiting for a reaction from Mantis. Mantis continued to sit stoically in lotus position, though, eyes closed, his abdominal region pulsating madly in and out, in and out, in unison with his intense breathing.

Bimbi approached the dais slowly. His eyes darted nervously left and right to either side of the lush jungle garden. There were things in there. He could *hear them*. He stopped, his legs shaking. Mantis was still breathing, but there was a different sound—the sound of a cat purring.

Mantis' pet leopard sauntered out onto the path behind Bimbi.

The young Hispanic was aware of a presence, but he didn't care to look behind to see, so he moved on, closer to Mantis and the breathing.

The leopard squatted low on its haunches and began a different purr, deeper than before.

Bimbi fixed his eyes on the path directly before him, not wishing to look directly behind or directly ahead. Yet his eyes could find nothing to focus on that did not fill him with fear.

A python emerged from the jungle and slithered across the path directly in front of Bimbi.

"Christ..." Bimbi froze in his tracks as the python disappeared in the undergrowth. He swung around as if to run and spotted the leopard. "Shit!" He ran forward, not knowing where he was going, and crashed in front of the dais. The leopard was inching closer, slowly, stalking, ready for the kill. Bimbi turned and looked up to Mantis, as if to plead for mercy. But what he saw made his flesh crawl even more. The commando's abdomen was expanding and contracting madly with each breath, each exhalation revealing the silhouette of Mantis' spinal column and solar plexus. Bimbi was terrified. He looked back to see the big cat coming closer, then found himself staring at the jade insect statues with their giant claws, ready to spring, to pounce....

"Christ, save meeeee!"

Mantis' breathing stopped suddenly. The sounds in the jungle died. There was silence everywhere. Mantis smiled and opened his eyes. He looked down at Bimbi.

"If you wander into my house, then you should be prepared to meet my pets."

He rose and put on a camouflage shirt. Then he lit some incense. Bimbi looked back nervously at the leopard.

"There's no need to fear," he added. "My pets are very well trained."

He waved his hand and the leopard lowered its head in obedience. Mantis motioned for Bimbi to get up.

"Come with me. I want to show you something."

Bimbi glanced back quickly at the leopard, then followed Mantis along another tile path into the heart of the garden jungle. Within, a large terrarium sat on a stone table.

"Some place..." Bimbi mumbled.

Mantis raised a finger to get his attention. Then he pointed at something in the glass cage.

"Tell me," he asked, "have you ever seen one of these?"

Bimbi looked into the cage. "I—I don't see nothin'."

"That's because you're not accustomed to looking for camouflage. Now, look closer, and separate green from green."

Bimbi focused on the terrarium again, looking through the maze of little branches. He let out a soft sigh as he spotted a large male praying mantis resting on a branch.

"Hey, that's your animal, right?"

Mantis corrected him. "That is my insect." He smiled and took a small box out of his pocket. Inside the box was a baby snake which Mantis proceeded to dangle over the terrarium. He turned to Bimbi. "You have to stop relating to animals, my friend. You have to start getting into the power of insects instead. The whole world, when you come down to it, is nothing more than just one big, giant ant hill. And out of that hill, you get special creatures like him."

He placed the baby snake within reach. The praying mantis jumped up and began to devour it. Mantis stepped back, his hands closing the box delicately.

"Ant hills, Bimbi. We all end up working like mindless ants in the end. Whether it's for the Pentagon or just pimping in the streets, it's all the same. But every now and then, like I said, you meet a special creature. Watch him, Bimbi...."

Bimbi watched as the insect began to tear away viciously at the head of the reptile, the long claws inching the snake's body into its mouth.

"Powerful. Undefeated. Special. Time breeding the divine insect. You Bimbi—you can be a divine insect. With time, through training, you too can evolve into just such a creature." Mantis rounded the stone table, positioning himself directly across from Bimbi. He smiled as he continued. "But you will never, never evolve into anything above a lowly ant if you waste your time with men who preach about goodness and love. And do you know why, Bimbi? Do you know why you can't evolve if you waste your time with them?"

"No, I—"

"It's because things like goodness or love—the things these men hold dear—these things are lies. Lies, Bimbi. The common man stays the common man, he remains a lowly ant because he limits himself by these terms. He sees opportunities and chances to gain power, but he does not reach for them because they involve methods that are contrary to his belief in goodness and love."

"I see," Bimbi said, his eyes darting nervously between the insect and Mantis.

"Do you?"

"I think so."

"Because it is very essential that you grasp this point if you wish to have me teach you... things," the champion said, glancing into the terrarium again. "Men like Caesar, Genghis Khan—they were great conquerors because they were not burdened by the illusion of goodness and love. They understood the secret, they realized that power is what makes this world go round. Power, just like the power you had as a child when you stepped on ants. Anything that gets in the way of power, Bimbi, is your enemy. That includes your own mother..."

Mantis watched with amusement as the young Hispanic hesitated. The champion drew closer. "Power has many enemies. Do you know what the enemies of power are?"

"No..." Bimbi said, not staring at anything now, his legs frozen.

"Truth is the greatest enemy of power. The Truth that the holy men preach about. Truth is a body. Truth has arms. And those arms are your enemy. You must cut off all those arms, Bimbi, so that you can strike a blow at the body of Truth. And one of those arms, Bimbi, is the arm of forgiveness."

Bimbi looked up, his attention aroused, focused now. Mantis smiled and put his arm around him. "What is the opposite of forgiveness?" he asked.

"Revenge..." the young Hispanic replied, his eyes dark, thinking back.

"You want to train with me, don't you?"

Bimbi nodded, his eyes staring straight ahead, absorbed with the thought of Enrique and the chance to get back at him.

"Then your training shall be inspired by the art of revenge," Mantis said. "The man who killed your brother is like that snake I just fed to my pet a moment ago. You're going to be my pet. And you're going to devour your enemy in just such a way *if* you listen to me."

There was a long pause as Mantis sought the young Hispanic's eyes.

"Look at me."

Bimbi looked up slowly and began to focus on Mantis.

"There is nothing here in my eyes to either fear or love. There is no pain here, no pleasure. There is only Void. Look at this Void, boy."

Bimbi began to feel himself losing touch with his own name. There was only the green, the green of Mantis's eyes. Mantis waved a hand.

A cobra emerged from the garden...

"Submit to this Void," Bimbi could hear Mantis say, "and you will unite with all the primordial powers of the Universe..."

The cobra began to wind its way between them...

"Insect, reptile, mammal, plant, all life forms will unite as one within your heart; you will arise anew, divine, special..."

Mantis raised his hands, the cobra rising in unison with them right before Bimbi's face. Mantis smiled.

"And now—the initiation."

He clapped his hands abruptly. Bimbi awoke to see the cobra before him, bobbing, weaving, ready to strike.

"M-A-M-A!"

There was a hiss from Mantis and the cobra lunged.

CHAPTER SEVENTEEN

CAPITAN found that he could not move...up in bed in the loft...

He was in pain...his back...his spine felt as if it were moving, moving against his will...and it was burning, burning horribly...

Bimbi was there...laughing.

"Too bad, bro...it has to happen this way..."

Capitan felt his spine growing hotter and hotter, like an iron rod, glowing...then suddenly rising...rising up and then out... *out of his body.* His spine was beginning to zoom out of his body just like a rocket...through the crown of his head...and then it fell onto the loft...writhing....

It was a snake...!

Mantis's head! And it was laughing. Laughing and winding toward him...closer!

"No—!"

Capitan awoke in a cold sweat. He shook his head, trying to collect his senses.

A dream...and what an awful one. A real nightmare in the classic sense, because it had happened right here. Jesus...

He tried to recall it all. The spine, then the snake, and Mantis's head. He looked at the clock: 4:56, early. He glanced out the loft window, facing the rear alley. The reporters were there, encamped, on rotating shifts, hand cameras ready for any possible sortie he might care to make. He laid back and closed his eyes.

Bimbi...he had appeared in the dream. Now he was gone and God only knows where, Capitan thought. He glanced at the clock again: 5:06. He was to meet Sten back at "Gull City" at 8:00, because the early morning hours were the best time to bust the media masters' siege line.

The media masters—Lords of the Question Mark. He had had a dream about them once and they all wore suits with a question mark emblazoned on the front. Not that they were all bad. They had just become part of the game like everyone else. They had no choice but to play. And in this case, playing the game meant turning Capitan into the next potential victim, fattening him up for public consumption. The public liked nothing better than to speculate on Mantis's chances of finally being beaten.

"Are you going to train Sten?"

"Would you consider fighting yourself?"

"If Mantis challenged you, would you agree to combat?"

On and on it went, the questions rising and falling like a barrage of arrows every time he went in and out of the studio. So now he had to be quick, he had to escape them in order to meet Sten, whose situation was no better, even worse. At the beach they could be alone. It was a good setting to teach Sten the technique. If he could train him in anything it was the technique. Maybe it wouldn't help. Maybe the drugs had already inflicted too much damage. But he had to try....

They met at the beach, at the same lifeguard station. It was cold but the sun was out, rising triumphantly above the eastern skyline, sending out a chorus of gulls to proclaim its arrival. Sten was already there, and as Capitan climbed up to the top of the lifeguard stand he greeted him with a thermos of coffee.

Capitan remained silent for a while, rubbing his hands to keep warm. Sten had bundled up nicely, as advised. They both stared out at the waves. Capitan thought about Carmen. He put his gloves back on and looked around. The beach was empty. Only one man stood in the distance on the boardwalk. He seemed to be watching them.

Pray God he's not a reporter, Capitan thought. He turned to Sten. "All right," he said. "I learned an art in Japan called Shin-Do. What it does is level the mind. It returns it to its original source. Now, like I said, sitting is half the game. Since it's awkward up here to do the lotus position, just sitting erect will do. It's just as good. By sitting we center the body, and by centering the body we invite the mind to center, too. Man's true nature is to center and to float about. He is constantly doing both, flowing from one state to another. Are you following me?"

Sten nodded, enthused, his posture erect, his eyes closed reverently. "Yeah, go on, go on..."

Capitan smiled and looked back, to the boardwalk. The man was still there.

"By sitting we invite the mind to return to its center of gravity. The mind doesn't like gravity, yet it is happiest when it is grounded. That sounds strange, but it's true. The mind loves to roam, like a child, going wherever it wants, but eventually it grows dissatisfied; it returns to its mother, gravity's center, and falls asleep, contented."

"So, what do I do, to keep it contented?"

"That's what I'm getting at."

Capitan looked back. That man was still there, watching....

"There are two points on the body we aim at. Point A here," he said, indicating the third eye region, center of the forehead, "and point B here," he added, pointing to a region slightly below the navel. "We call them the Relative and the Absolute, respectively. Most of our time is spent in the Relative, point A, since that's where the senses are located. But what we don't realize is that we can function quite nicely if we concentrate on point B, the Absolute area. It's called the Absolute because it is our center of gravity."

"So how do we get there?" Sten asked, his eyes still closed.

"Patience, amigo...."

He looked back, toward the boardwalk. The stranger had not moved. He thought a moment and turned to Sten.

"This true, inner nature—it's everywhere."

"The Void, right?"

"Exactly. The Void is like a bubble. A bubble is empty in the center, but it's still a bubble, it has an outer core. *We* are that outer core, the material world. But our basic source is empty or, to put it better, unchangeable. To reach that unchangeable inner truth we have to find a place to contact it...."

"Point B, right?"

"Exactly. Now the Void-Truth has an energy, and that energy manifests itself as breath. Our minds are very attached to our breath and will go wherever we take it. The mind obeys the breath, and yet the mind makes the breath cooperate. That's the mystery of it all."

"So what do I do?"

"Shut up and listen."

"Oh," Sten said, his spine erect, eyes closed.

"Focus your mind on point B. Breathe deeply. Take your breath way down there and your mind with it. After a while they will begin to seem like one unit, your mind and breath. Do that for a while."

"I am..."

It would take time and practice before Sten's mind was conditioned to really cooperate, Capitan knew. But this was a start. He looked back, toward the boardwalk. The man was still there, and somebody else was approaching him, wearing something white on his head. A black man as best he could make out.

Monitor Five, code name "Ibari," nodded to the Zed A fire brother as he joined him at the railing overlooking the beach.

Their eyes did not meet. There was no reason for them to. The well-built Oriental continued to stare at the lifeguard station.

"I have news for you," the fire brother said. "A man was sent by Mantis to see our Big Sun."

"And he wanted news of the child?"

"Yes."

"The child is well?"

"Very well. He will grow to be a great warrior."

"That is for Time to decide," Monitor Five said. "Your master realizes now that Mantis was behind the terrorists?"

"Yes."

"The man who was sent as a spokesman—who was he?"

"One of our former brothers."

"Did you let him go?"

"We had him under escort," the fire brother said. "He escaped." Ibari looked up in concern.

"Where did he go?"

"That we don't know. We have his family with us again, however."

"Yes, but the man ... ?"

"His name is Oman."

"Whatever his name—you are not to take him back if he returns to you."

"The Big Sun believes that Mantis has killed him."

"No—I disagree."

"The Big Sun is all wise."

"Listen to me—"

"I listen to nothing against the Big Sun," the fire brother said, backing away.

"Perhaps not, but you are ordered by your Big Sun to obey what commands I have until he says different."

This is so difficult, Ibari thought, dealing with this kind of cult fanaticism. But I have to leave the child with them. I only pray that this fellow Capitan proves worthier than either Habib or Mantis of the Master's training. He turned once again to the fire brother. "Listen to me. This man Oman cannot be permitted to go anywhere near Habib or the child. Do you understand that?"

"I understand that I will tell the Big Sun all that you have said."

"You are to impress on him the point I just made. You are to tell him how serious I am. It is an order that I give to him as a long-time brother."

The Zed A glanced reproachfully at the Oriental. Evidently, the word "order" did not sit well with him.

"Where is the Big Sun now?"

"I cannot tell you."

"I order you to tell me," Ibari said. "I have that right, remember. The Big Sun gave me that right."

"He is en route to our farm in Kentucky, with Oman's family."

"And the boy, Aquila—?"

"He is at the farm."

Ibari cursed. "Can't you see that this is exactly what Mantis is counting on? I want you to contact the farm immediately. You are to make sure that Oman is not permitted anywhere near the grounds. You are to make sure that the Big Sun knows that Oman is a walking time bomb."

Capitan alternated his gaze between the pounding surf and the heavily muscled body of Sten as the *karateka* conducted his breathing exercises.

"Take longer on the exhales. You only need a few counts to inhale," Captain said. "Feel the mind and the breath as one now, seeping in, down to point B, flowing around it. Think of the breath as it comes in as the hand of something mighty, your mind grabbing onto it and flowing, flowing…"

"I'm flowin'," Sten said, his eyes shut tight.

"You can open your eyes. Aim them at point B."

"I'm seein' things…"

"What?"

"Cartoons."

"Then you're up in point A. Point A is a projector, like in a movie house. But it draws fuel from point B. Remember, let the breath flow in, and then let the mind join it so the two can dive down together to point B."

"My mind keeps on goin' up, though," Sten said.

"Right. It's not easy at first."

"It's not easy at all."

"Who said it was going to be?" Capitan asked, looking back toward the boardwalk.

It was empty. There was nobody watching now.

The early morning sun had begun to climb the Kentucky sky, casting its warm rays on fifty acres of cleared land that had been acquired by the Zed Advesta for its home base. Sentries, armed with automatic weapons and side arms, patrolled the gates leading into the complex—a complex that included, besides acres and acres of cultivated fields, several corrals filled with prize quarter horses.

Up on a hill, situated in the center of the farm, was the Big Home, residence of the Big Sun and his wives. It was a very active house with many children running about, all of them black, save for one, a blond-haired child not more than five years of age. One of Habib's wives watched with amusement as the little white boy maneuvered about with great skill, trying to mimic the acrobatics of some of the older children. She was trying to be as happy as she could, trying to block out the tears that were issuing from the next room.

Just beyond the door Habib, the Big Sun, was facing Oman's three wives and some of their brood. He shook his head. "I just got an emergency call from New York, from my old brother. He says I am not to let Kalil back in here."

"He is our man..." one of them pleaded.

"He is no longer the man you knew. He is now a victim of the same demons that took possession of Elijah and Omar."

"You tricked us into coming back here," another wife said.

"That is not true."

"It is," she protested. "You wanted us for yourself and now

you've taken Kalil from us. That was your plan all along."

"You should be happy the Big Sun even consents to let you back in," one of Habib's bodyguards said, "after the way you strayed from the path and reentered the world of sin and darkness."

"We only wanted to live our own life."

"And love our man."

"There's nothin' wrong with that," one of the wives said.

They were about to continue but Habib raised his hand, ordering them out into the yard. He wanted silence and time to think. Time to cover all the holes through which Kalil might slip back in. Monitor Five *had* to be right. Habib would never have thought that Kalil could engage in a suicide mission against his own people. But Kalil was no longer Kalil....

Habib turned to one of his men.

"Bring the eagle child to me."

As the man hurried off, Habib's thoughts drifted back—back to Irmgard, the lovely East German officer whom Mantis had captured. She had carried his son in her arms that day, looking on in tears as the grim commando stared at it.

"We shall call him ... Aquila," Mantis said.

"Aquila?" Irmgard asked.

"Yes. It is Latin for eagle. I am an insect. My son shall be a bird. But, a bird of prey—as I am an insect of prey."

Habib had watched as the tears rolled down her face, knowing all too well what thoughts were passing through her mind. Even he had despaired of finding any vestiges of Mantis's former self in this demented individual who stood before them....

Habib's thoughts returned to the present as one of his bodyguards entered with the blond-haired child. On seeing Big Sun, the little boy smiled and ran over as fast as his young legs could carry him. Habib brought him into his arms. He hugged him. The little boy pushed at his face in protest, then settled calmly into playing with the embroidery work on Habib's robe.

Such a strange child, Habib thought. Not like other children.

Not happy in the same way other children are happy. He is a boy who is in some ways ancient. An old spirit in a new body, yes...

And the son of a demon.

Habib thought back...

"I find it the most painful thing in my entire life that I cannot kill you," Habib had told Mantis. The vow he had sworn to Hoshima had become a terrible burden. "After what you did, there is no doubt that you must pay the price of a cruel, agonizing death."

"But not at *your* hand," Mantis said, smiling.

No, it would not be at my hand, Habib thought. Why Hoshima had willed it thus he could never figure out, but it was not his place to question the master's wisdom.

After Hoshima had taught Habib and Mantis the way to harmony of the mind, after they had both settled and had begun to become immersed in the roots of point B, Hoshima had begun to lecture them on ethics. The master was a great talker; he loved parables and he loved to relate the science of ethics and morality. It was here that he and Mantis began to part.

"Why should a man follow ethics?" Mantis asked.

"Because the more you settle into your primordial nature, the more you will need it. What does a giant of a man have to learn early in life? He has to learn how to be gentle or else he will walk through life like the proverbial bull in a china shop. It's exactly the same with Shin-Do. We acquire great mental powers that could be easily used to destroy others. Ethics directs those powers to noble purposes. To direct those powers to less than noble purposes is to tamper with the laws of nature. What did the prophet Jesus do? He healed. He did not use his powers to slay, since that would be to rebel against the order of the universe."

"You really believe Jesus had those powers?" Mantis asked.

"There's no doubt of it," Hoshima said. "He was a yogi, plain and simple. He had what the yogis call *siddhis*."

"'Powers,' yes, I know," Mantis said, familiar with the term.

"And so he used them, but with ethics attached. He healed. That was his power."

"If you believe he had it."

"Of course he had it. He had the power to enter a person with his own soul."

"Nonsense..." Mantis said.

What followed next Habib could only surmise, for as he sat there he was conscious of the master's aura expanding, asserting itself. Hoshima shut his eyes and turned into a cold rock. And then Mantis began to glow, to react, as if something had penetrated his inner being and was expanding inside it. Mantis's eyes widened.

"Christ..."

Then it all stopped, as if Mantis had let out a giant breath. Hoshima opened his eyes and smiled.

"That is a power, and nothing more. Had I not been versed in ethics, had I been a wicked man as you are by nature, my commando friend, I could have ripped you open from within."

Mantis sat there stunned, sweating profusely.

"After all," Hoshima continued, as if nothing had happened, "let us not underestimate the power, the danger, of the Egg."

"The Egg...?" Habib asked. Mantis listened but did not move.

"Yes. The Egg. As you develop your primordial nature, as you strengthen point B, you naturally reinforce point A. Point A draws its projectory power from point B, and point B can rechannel that mental power into the creation of the Egg. The Taoists called it the Egress."

"What is it?" Habib asked.

"It is your cosmic fetal body. It is what permits gods to become gods after death of the body. That is why you see gods when you meditate—they exist, in their astral form. They were once human, but they developed their Eggs and left, hatching them in the Celestial Sky of the Pure Land of the Innumerable Galaxies of the Taoist Monarchies...no," Hoshima said, shaking his head, "that's not the right term, no."

"Teach me..." Mantis said, regaining his strength but barely able to speak, "the technique...to the Egg..."

"I shall do nothing of the sort," Hoshima said. "You are an evil young man. A potential threat to those around you. Until you acknowledge the value of ethics, I will teach you nothing more."

And that was the beginning...of the end. The rift had been there all along, ever since that first day. Now the chasm widened, making rapprochement impossible. Habib's thoughts returned to the here and now.

He looked down at the little boy. He had fallen asleep.

Mantis wants to sacrifice him, Habib reminded himself. Like Abraham almost did with his son. He wants to do it because he thinks he *knows*.

But he's lost his mind.

Habib reflected on the fate of his own clan—a clan that had flourished in just a few short years. He had made arrangements that Zoroaster, his closest disciple, succeed him. Zoroaster commanded the security force that guarded the farm. It would be unwise to keep him in the same location as himself, Habib suddenly realized. If something happened to both of them, Zed Advesta would be in trouble.

"Tell Zoroaster to hand his post over to Fuman. Then have him come to me."

Habib ran his fingers through the golden hair of the sleeping boy.

He thought about poor Kalil, wondering where he could be....

In fact, Kalil was not very far off. Having killed the driver of a truck that was returning to the farm with supplies, Kalil was now steering a course for the Zed A headquarters, mentally repeating the orders that had been given to him: "Get to the Big Sun, at all costs, get to him and embrace him. Get to the Big Sun, at all costs..." Kalil sweated profusely as the truck barreled down the highway. His right arm felt sore, as if it had been recently cut open—as if there were something planted inside—but he could think no more about it. He could only think: "Get to the Big Sun, at all costs, get to him and embrace him...."

It was not long before the truck rounded the bend, appearing just below the hill of the first security post where Fuman had positioned himself. He pointed at it.

"Who's coming?"

"That's Young Elias. He took the bread truck in early this morning," another fire brother said.

"Young Elias, huh?" Fuman said, his automatic slung casually over his shoulder. "Youngster's drivin' awfully fast, isn't he?"

They watched as the truck bounded along the road, heading toward them, increasing in speed. Fuman exchanged nervous glances with his men. One of them held up his hands and motioned for the truck to stop.

But it continued, only faster.

"Shit...!"

They lowered their weapons.

"Stop!"

Fuman fired a warning shot, but the truck continued.

"Hit it."

All four men opened up with their automatic rifles, but it was too late. The truck crashed through the guardpost, hitting one of the guards and sending him flying. Fuman and the two remaining guards swung around, firing. They began to chase after it, shouting in frustration as the bread truck speeded up the hill, rounded the horse track, and then opened up full speed down the gentry-styled lane. Fuman ran back quickly and made a hurried call to the second guardpost.

"Stop that truck!" he told them.

But the second set of guards didn't need any warning; they were already firing as the bread truck zoomed down on them suddenly, crashing through the gate, through the second and last barrier that stood between it and the Big Home.

"Hit it!"

Shots peppered the van left and right, the truck's tires collapsed, but on it rolled, creeping up the hill, moving slowly but steadily....

"To the Big Home..." Kalil groaned, shot in a dozen places and bleeding badly, "at all costs, see...the Big Sun..."

Zoroaster was walking down the opposite side of the hill with Aquila when he heard the shots and the truck approach. He was at a safe distance from the vehicle as he watched it roll to a stop, the guards move in and blast it, and Habib emerge from the house. *He* was at a safe distance—but Habib and the Big Home and the guards were not, and—

The truck exploded with such force that Zoroaster was sent flying back, the little boy held tightly in his arms. Half stunned, Zoroaster sat on the ground and watched as the truck exploded again, this time unleashing a gigantic fireball that consumed everything within fifty yards.

"Good God..." the new Zed A leader exclaimed, looking at the scorched remains. Then he thought of the boy.

"Aquila, are you all right?" Zoroaster said, picking up the child.

Aquila wiped away a tear, then buried his face in Zoroaster's chest.

CHAPTER EIGHTEEN

ABE had read the headlines. He was disgusted with the headlines, the violent headlines.

"Black cult leader goes up in smoke," he read aloud.

He threw the paper down as Charlie slowly cruised south on Riverside Drive. Eddie and Billy were in the back seat. Billy opened his suit jacket and looked at his revolver.

"What're you doing?" Abe asked.

"Gettin' ready," the apprentice gangster said.

"For what?" Abe asked.

"I don't know—trouble."

"Don't be an asshole or I'll send *you* in, let Mantis feed *you* to his snakes.

Abe chucked the paper at him and looked out the window. Charlie looked on in concern.

"You're goin' in alone?"

"Sure, why not?" the old-timer said. "Don't worry. If Mantis wanted to hurt me, he would have, secret-like. That's his style. But he won't hurt me. You want to know why?"

"Yeah, why?" Billy asked, opening up the newspaper.

"Because I'm big time. For him, I'm useful. I'm a prestige connection who knows lots and lots of dames."

"You do?" Eddie asked.

"Sure..." Abe said.

"You never told us," Billy said.

"That's because you wouldn't know what to do with 'em."

"With who?"

"Broads, you asshole," Charlie said, looking back through the rearview mirror.

Billy read the headlines. "Shit. All these stupid niggers are blowin' each other up. Did you read this, boss?"

"I read the headlines," Abe said.

Billy read on. "High-powered explosive ignited, killing cult leader...assassin believed to be former cult member, Kalil Oman—"

"What was that?" Abe asked. "What was that last name you just read?"

"Uh, let's see..." Billy said, glancing over the paper.

"Come on, come on," Abe said, his mind racing.

"All right, here! 'Ka-lil O-man.' You want me to say it again?"

"No, just shut up and keep on reading."

"I thought you read this, boss?"

"Shut up and read," said Charlie.

Billy continued reading the article, which went into further detail concerning the explosion. Abe's mind drifted back into the file he had obtained at Al's request....

"This is it," Abe said, pointing at the ivy-covered building up ahead. Billy lowered the paper and glanced out as the car rolled up in front of it.

"Shit...place gives me the creeps."

"You sure you want to—"

"I'm sure," Abe said as he opened the door. "Just wait."

"How long you gonna be?" Eddie asked.

Abe glanced at the two in the back. He snatched the paper from Billy and hit Eddie with it.

"Hey, why you wanna go do that?"

"You two are fired," Abe said, slamming the door and heading toward Mantis's building.

"You're not serious, are you, boss—?"

There was muffled laughter from the car. Abe hit the buzzer.

Mantis motioned for his visitor to sit on a soft zabuton cushion. The champion had just lit some incense. It burned away, smoke trailing up from the dais toward one of the jade insect statues. Abe looked about, then watched as a leopard emerged from the garden jungle and made its way over to Mantis.

"Cats don't scare you, Mr. Goldman?" Mantis asked.

"Not especially," Abe said.

"Just insects?"

"Yeah, like your last present."

"Ah, yes," Mantis said, rubbing the leopard's chin. "I remember that. I picked him myself. Just for you."

"How sweet."

There was a pause, Mantis looking at his cat, examining it, glancing through its fur. He looked back at Abe and smiled.

"Mr. Goldman, Mr. Goldman, Mr. Goldman—it's been so long since we've been together, face to face."

"Yes," Abe said dryly, glancing again up at the statues.

"You like them?" Mantis asked.

"Yeah. In an odd way, sure. They remind me of...something. A Vincent Price movie—that's it."

Mantis turned somber. His face was all business.

"Funny old guy, isn't he?" Mantis said to his cat.

"No, not really. Curious old guy would be a better way of putting it."

"Curious? About what?"

"Kalil Oman."

"Ah...yes. Mr. Oman. Poor Mr. Oman. He did his duty and then, poof! Up to his mighty Fire Chief in the sky. Yes..."

"What did you do to him?" Abe asked.

"I did the same thing, more or less, that I did to the man at

Grand Central, the man at the Houston bank, and the man who got shot down outside the White House. I, well, I hypnotized them. I hypnotized them and then I gave them orders." Mantis smiled. "The first three were not as effective as the last one—which you helped supply, incidentally. Thank you. But then again, the last one was fitted with something that would make him more effective, and he had a much more concrete mission than the other three."

"Like killing twenty innocent people, most of them children?"

"Now, now—Mr. Goldman. You are no one to lecture me on the subject of innocent blood."

"I apologize," Abe said sarcastically.

"And I accept." Mantis rose to his feet and circled the old-timer, the cat in his arms. "But, back to your question. I hypnotized all four of them and sent them out. The first three were not as effective as I had hoped they would be. I didn't program them well enough. The bank robber was supposed to rob the bank. But then he became confused, he didn't know why he was there, so he...well, he blew himself up. The second man was ordered to shoot any member of the Triumvirate, but he fused out just before he got on the White House lawn, and that was that."

"Let me get this straight," Abe said. "You were gonna have him kill one of the Triumvirate?"

"Sure."

"The President?"

"Or the Vice President, or the Secretary of State, yes."

"Why?" Abe asked.

"Why not?" Mantis said. "It seemed like an interesting thing to do. And quite in keeping with my primary goal, which was to destroy the Zed Advesta—to thoroughly discredit it." Mantis laid the cat down and examined his right hand. "Then came the man on the train. He was programmed to go to Central Park and just shoot anybody at random, it didn't matter, just kill, and proclaim the Zed A vision of the sun. But, as you probably know, he met up with a certain somebody on the train, and his programming went off kilter. He ended up shooting it out with the police instead.

Do you know who that certain somebody was, Mr. Goldman?"

"No. Tell me."

"It was Sten Johnson, your old employee. He was the big white man the report described. Didn't he tell you that?"

"No, that part I didn't know about."

"You know, it would be very easy to have Mr. Johnson arrested for his role in that incident. That way I wouldn't have to trouble with him in the ring."

"Then why don't you do it?"

"Because, quite frankly, he's caused me so much trouble at this point that I thought it would be satisfying to kill him, with my own hands. He is point A, and point A is going to lead me to point B."

"Which is?"

"This fellow Capitan. Capitan is a part of a movement to which I myself belong."

Abe turned pale.

"You—"

"Yes, yes Mr. Goldman, *I* was the one who sent you that C.I. dossier on the Aiki movement. Most of it was complete fabrication, of course. But I had to find out about a certain monitor, as we call it, someone who operated in our area, who I didn't know."

"So you had me do the work for you?"

"Right. Exactly. Cagey, wasn't I?"

Abe softly clapped his hands.

"I already knew who the other leader was, our former friend Mr. Big Sun. He was a big nut to crack, but I had access to his old soldiers, the ones I hypnotized and used against him. Eventually I needed another fighter type, so—"

"You had me do more work for you?"

"Exactly. You're catching on fast. Oman came along. And now part of my work is done. There are only two monitors of any consequence left. Capitan is next on the list."

"And after him, don't tell me. The list of Japanese advisers, right?"

"You'd make a good detective, Mr. Goldman."

"I can even tell you which one—the good-looking Jap. What was his name, I—Ibur—i, or something like that."

"A very good detective…"

"And he's the head honcho, right?"

Mantis folded his arms and nodded. "I want him alive. I have something special in mind for him."

"I don't get you," Abe said. "If you're a part of this movement, then why are you trying to kill off everybody in it?"

"Oh, there's a simple answer to that."

"There is?"

"Yes. The answer is 'why not' and 'because.'"

"Why not and because," Abe mumbled, realizing that Mantis was mad.

"Exactly. We are a part of the same group, and a group implies unity, brotherhood—things I have little or no respect for. So, kill my fellow brother—why not? As to the second part, because, because with them dead I am the unopposed leader of the movement and its secrets—its powerful, powerful secrets."

There was a long pause as Abe digested everything. Then he turned to Mantis. "There's just one thing. If you're all members of the same group, then why'd you need me to help you contact one another?"

"Oh, a good question. That was because our master, a most disagreeable person, decided that we shouldn't be allowed to contact one another. I was the reason for much of the security. You see, I was the black sheep of the flock, the dangerous one. So our master threw a veil up, albeit a very flimsy one, that I have now penetrated."

"Who is this master? Hoshima?"

"That's him."

"And is he still alive, or what?" Abe asked.

Mantis's face changed expression. His voice took on a grave tone. "He is not dead," the champion said.

"And the Japanese officer, how can he be head of the movement if Hoshima's alive?"

"Hoshima's authority acts through this officer. In this conversation we have referred to him as Ibari, but actually he had many names. Now—" Mantis waved his hand to change the subject. "It is my turn to—"

"To ask questions?"

"To give orders."

Abe rose defiantly. "I'm too old for orders, sonny. Too old for orders and being intimidated by spiders and bugs and big house cats."

Mantis stared intently at Abe, his green eyes boring away. The piercing, psychic drills caught Abe before he could avert his gaze. Abe felt his own name fading, his own sense of identity dissolving before an invisible wave of power that seemed to wash over him....

Mantis laughed and sat down on the cushion. "Very good, Mr. Goldman," he said. "Your resistance is stronger than most."

"What are you, a vampire?"

"Something like that," Mantis said. "Only I don't suck blood." He clapped his hands abruptly. "I have some entertainment for you. Watch..."

He pointed toward the lush garden jungle. Suddenly a half-naked figure leapt out, hopping swiftly from one side to the other. It sprang onto one of the giant rubber plants, scaled it swiftly, and then jumped down, displaying all the agility of an ape. The figure ran back, to the center of the path, resting on its haunches, breathing heavily. It was young Bimbi.

"He thinks he's an ape," Mantis said with a bright smile. "It gives you some idea of the power I have. All I need is a defect."

"A defect?" Abe asked, glancing over at Bimbi.

"Yes. Everyone has mental flaws that constantly recur in the thought process. They're like loose screws. I enter there." He pointed at Bimbi. "Take our friend here. He had a desire for revenge, so I worked on it, entered his psychic system. Then, well, I took it over. Now he's mine."

"Very nice," Abe said. "I know that face from somewhere..."

"He was Capitan's old student."

"Ah..." Abe remembered that night at the Coliseum.

"That's the primary reason I took him in," Mantis continued.

"He's a weapon to use against Capitan. You see, moral people have soft spots."

"Soft spots?"

"Yes. They get attached or concerned for things, and this softens them, their defenses. Mental Boxing—it's a kind of sport, and I know how to play it well. I intend to strike a good blow below the belly—the psychic belly, of course—at Capitan through this ape." Mantis looked over at Bimbi, pursed his lips. "I also keep him because, well, he makes a nice pet."

"Yes, you do like pets," Abe said. "So why are you showing him to me?"

"You're my guest. I want to entertain you."

"And you want me to find a slot for him—in the arena?"

Mantis leaned back and laughed. "Ah, 'the monkey man.' I could see it. Or 'the Spanish Ape.' Yes. *'El mono picante.'*" He broke into a bizarre laugh that echoed throughout the studio.

Abe glanced at the apelike Bimbi staring out into space, and thought to himself, yeah, the crowd probably would enjoy it. It was their sort of thing.

Mantis must have been reading his thoughts because he shook his head. "No. I have something better in store for him. I showed him to you because I wanted to make you aware of a new world order that is about to be ushered in." The ex-commando rose, his right hand moving with strange reptilian motions. "Relax, Mr. Goldman. Relax while you are one of the first to hear of this new, great order of things."

This guy should be put away, in a jacket, in a cell, in the middle of friggin' Antarctica, Abe thought, as he watched the fingers of Mantis's hand jerk crazily.

"Understand," Mantis said, "that I have called you here for a reason. *You* are going to help me usher in this new order."

"How am I going to do that?"

"You are going to listen, first," Mantis said. "Now, after I kill Johnson, I want Capitan in that arena. You are going to help me get him there. You are going to clear the way for me. Getting this match with Johnson in direct violation of the rules has already been enough trouble. You are going to see to it that similar problems are not encountered in arranging a match with Capitan."

"But I'm U-2—"

"U-1 or U-2, it doesn't matter. The strings are all attached and you know how to pull them. So, that's done. Next, I want to... well, how shall I say it. I want to *publicize* this match with Capitan. I want to make a show of it. It is going to be an example. I am going to kill him as a way of introducing my New Order."

"New Order...?"

"Yes, I am going to indoctrinate the public in certain principles of my movement. I am going to teach the masses the law of Power. There are opponents of this Power, namely the other members of the Aiki movement. They must die. Capitan is going to be the first example. He is the example because he represents the theory of Universal Love, of Harmony. I am going to show the world that it is not Universal Love, this Aiki, that rules the earth, but Power. I am going to show everyone that no matter how much a man holds to this Universal Love, no matter how much he is guided by it, he is still no match for Power. He will be defeated by it, as I intend to defeat Capitan."

"And then what...?" Abe asked, not knowing whether to be shocked or amused or a little bit of both.

"I intend to teach the world my theory of Power. I intend to enter classrooms and teach children Power. I intend to start with them young and make them loyal to me, to my mind. My *mind* will become *the* Mind. I will become the World Mind. All other minds will focus and flow in and out of me..."

Yeah, just like zombies, Abe thought to himself.

"Have you ever studied the ants, or the bees?" Mantis asked abruptly.

"No, can't say I have."

"Well, they function on order, on power. And they function well. They are not concerned with emotions, with pleasure or pain. The workers serve the queen and everything runs smoothly. People, at heart, are insects, and I intend to make them more so, for their own good. It's a goal, and you are going to help me attain it."

"Insects, huh?"

"Exactly."

Abe looked up at the jade statues. "Is that why you have these?"

"They're symbols."

"And what about that Buddha out in the garden, the one that's slashed. What's he a symbol of?"

Mantis flushed angrily.

"Of everything I wish to wipe out." He rose from his chair. "You are excused now."

"You want me to bow?" Abe asked, amused.

"I will contact you, Mr. Comedian."

Mr. Comedian I may well be, Abe thought as Al escorted him out toward the elevator. But I ain't laughin'. God in Heaven, after what I've heard I ain't laughin'. And I'm plannin'. For the good of the future, I'm plannin'.

When Al returned, Bimbi was still sitting on his haunches. Mantis was at the dais, watching.

"What do you want to do with him?"

"I want to see if we can put some brains back inside his head. Did you get the X-ray on Johnson?"

Al nodded and handed Mantis an X-ray print. Mantis examined it. "Good shape. Big brute."

"Heavyweight. You oughta let me handle him."

"No. He's mine. They're *all* mine." Al nodded humbly. Mantis tore up the miniprint. He pointed at Bimbi. "Now, let's put some clothes back on that ape."

When Capitan returned that evening the army of reporters bombarded him with a series of questions concerning "the woman who had entered the studio." His heart leapt as he considered the possibility that Carmen had returned home. He pushed through them quickly and made his way to the door.

She was standing there, just standing, as he locked the door behind him. And she was looking at him—not staring, but watching....

If eyes could speak, he thought...

He wanted to speak, he was going to speak, but Carmen raised a finger to her lips to prolong the silence.

A tear rolled down her cheek, and then a tear rolled down his.

Her hourglass figure, the sweater falling over her smooth hips, the smart curve of her back and then the rise of her strong buttocks—Capitan took it all into his heart as if for the first time. Her long auburn hair, her almond eyes, her thick lips, her Indian smile—they were like balm to his bruised senses. Capitan drew closer, swimming across a sea of swift and sudden grace.

They embraced in mind, they embraced in heart, and then they embraced in body. And as the reporters mingled behind the closed windows, buzzing like bees, trying to draw the sweet nectar of gossip, Capitan held his love close, very close, feeling that somehow this was to be their last true moment together, not in body, but in peace. The future boded ill for peace.

CHAPTER NINETEEN

BROOKLYN, the Coliseum...

Carmen sat in the special front row seat supplied by Sten and looked with disgust at the program. She set it down and looked up. The video monitors were playing some old clips of famous fights. She closed her eyes.

People hooted and howled.

She had closed her eyes but she could not close her ears. A few rows back, some garishly dressed drag queens were nibbling away on sushi rolls and laughing.

"Ooooh! Tonight there's some of those big Amazon women who use long daggers."

"Oh, that ought to be splendid."

"And then Mantis is going to top off the evening with another of his bizarre kills."

"Yes, he's fighting that big blond brute we saw last month."

"Johnson's his name. He's become the...the..."

"The Champion of the People's Republic, or..."

"Or something like that, yes..."

They laughed and nibbled away. Carmen felt like cramming those sushi rolls down their throats. She looked up to the top of the Coliseum, to the thousands of Untouchables roaming about. She could see hundreds of security officers walking among them, making sure that order was kept.

Carmen had once been a big fan of all this. She had never told Capitan, but at one time she had even thought of entering the Arena League herself. Skilled female competitors, especially beautiful ones, could earn thousands of credits fighting. Capitan had saved her from all that, though. Thank God.

The crowd hooted and hollered.

The people began to stamp their feet.

Down below, down in the bowels of the arena, Sten sat with Capitan, the two of them silent, meditating as best they could. It was such an odd way to prepare for a fight, and then again, Capitan thought, perhaps not. He knew that Sten's fate was sealed. Perhaps this was just a way of having him make peace with his Creator, so to speak.

And Sten...

Sten was meditating as best he could, but his mind began to float like everyone else's, thoughts drifting. He could not help but see Elijah, the fire priest, smiling and talking about "sacrifice." Sten was there again, on the train, with the screams and the smoke. What was it the fire priest had said?

"When the real moment comes, life and death are the same."

Yeah, he had to look at it that way. He wasn't going up there to confront death, to stare it down. He was going up there to face life—life as it was.

Time passed. Up in the arena two large Amazon women, each close to three hundred pounds, were slugging it out. Bowie knives were positioned at either end of the ring. Abe watched, shaking his head. In the next aisle a cameraman turned to his assistant.

"Look at the muscles on those mamas."

Reporters had spotted both Carmen and Abe. They moved in on them simultaneously. Carmen pulled out a can of mace.

"I have the right to use it," she said.

"All right, we know. We just wanted to ask—"

"Ask and I'll spray."

People began to applaud. The reporters who attached themselves to Abe found the veteran a bit more agreeable.

"Didn't Sten work for you?" one of the reporters asked.

"Wait," Abe said. "Just tell me one thing first. Who's that broad up there?"

"Her? Alzerras's wife, we think."

"Ah."

"Now. About Mr. Johnson, didn't he work for you once?"

"Yeah. Now move—I wanna watch."

"But—"

"Sit down!" people yelled to the reporters.

The reporters crouched, mikes in hand. A beer container flew out and hit one of them on the head.

"*Christ!*"

"That'll teach 'em!"

Down in the arena pit one of the Amazons was suddenly thrown and then pinned. Bridging her back, she rolled out and grabbed her opponent's leg, flesh shaking as both bodies deadlocked and strained against one another.

"Kill her!"

"Which one—?"

"*Anyone!*"

Abe shook his head. "The crowd wants blood tonight." He glanced up at the clock and shook his head again. "Sten, Sten... your time is on the slide."

Capitan decided not to give Sten any advice as they walked toward the Waiting Station. It was the *karateka*'s fight—his show. But Capitan realized that it was *his* show now, too. He *also* was going to be facing Mantis, and in his capacity as Sten's coach he would be appearing once again in front of the cameras. Somehow the tides were dragging him deeper and deeper into this entire mess.

When they entered the Waiting Station, Capitan saw something

that made him stop short. Bimbi was there, dressed in a camouflage uniform, seated next to Mantis and Al. His face was distant,
impassive, like a zombie in a trance.

"Bimbi...?"

Capitan rushed over to him. As the cameramen jostled each
other for position, trying to get a good picture of the scene, Mantis
rose from his seat.

"Bimbi...?" Capitan asked.

No response. Bimbi stared straight ahead, eyes glassy. Capitan
looked closer and could see two marks on the young Hispanic's
forehead, impressed like a third eye. He turned to Mantis.

"What have you done to him?"

Mantis merely smiled and motioned to Al. Al quickly pulled out
a mini X-ray camera and flashed it over Capitan's body. Capitan
turned to Bimbi again and touched him gently.

"Hey, partner...it's me, you remember?"

Bimbi turned and looked at him. Then, suddenly, he spit into
Capitan's face. Capitan moved back, his face red with anger as he
focused on Mantis. The champion merely responded with a tight
amused grin. Sten barged over and aimed a finger at Mantis,
turning as he did to the cameras.

"This is the Big Machine's Man. This is their top dog. The
people out there in the Coliseum, they can hear me now—"

Sten's voice echoed throughout the Coliseum. Much to Abe's
shock, people *were* listening.

"—so listen. I was once a top man in my field. But the government, the Arena bosses, fixed it so I would be out of action for a
long time. They did the same thing to a lot of other competitors;
they even killed some people who stood in their way..."

Sten's voice echoed like thunder up and down the aisles as Abe
closed his eyes and shook his head. Sure, why not, he thought.
Let him sing before he meets his maker.

"We were put down the same way you've been put down..."

The Arena president could be seen inching his way down, toward the central audio box.

"This game here was created at the expense of other games so that you could pay with your freedom, your lives. This game was created so that men like him..."

Sten could be seen clearly on the video monitors, pointing at Mantis. The champion's arms were folded, his face placid.

The Arena president had reached the audio box now. He shouted at the sound engineer, *"Kill the sound."*

"...could lie to us and..."

The sound went out of the picture. Immediately, the crowd began to stamp their feet, the masses of Untouchables in the upper balconies chanting "AU DEE OOO. AU DEE OOO. AU DEE OOOO. AUDIO!" Security police could be seen scrambling into position. The Arena president motioned to the chief technician. "Some old clips—I want them on that screen, now!"

The stamping grew in intensity as the screen changed picture. Bits and pieces of garbage began to zoom down.

Sten was the last to know that the sound had been cut. Mantis clapped his hands.

"Bravo," he said, and Sten exploded.

"Killer! Monster!"

There was a slight pause as Capitan pulled the *karateka* back. Mantis burst into laughter just as the Chief of Security rushed into the Waiting Station.

"We're gonna have a riot out there unless we start the fight now."

"So, I'm ready," Sten boasted, his nunchakas in hand.

"You should be," the security chief said, "'cause you started this mess."

The *karateka* turned and offered Capitan his hand. "Here's to you, pal."

The next instant he was marching toward the Central Lift, and Capitan suddenly felt empty inside. He could not take his eyes off Bimbi, poor young Bimbi. Sten turned around as he entered the Central Lift. He aimed his thumb up at Capitan.

"And here's to the people!"

The cylindrical lift rotated shut. Mantis stared like a Cheshire cat at Capitan.

Mantis and Sten stood facing the Arena president's box.

The riot had stopped abruptly the moment Sten entered the arena. The mobs were just roaring now, waiting for the fight to begin. As the president appeared, the catcalls began to die down. The gaunt-faced man looked down on the two, eyes shifting from champion to challenger.

"You know the rules. There are no rounds. You cannot leave the ring. You *can* retreat to your corner, but your opponent can follow. The champion as always has the right to choose the opening means of combat. Hands to weapons, or weapons to hands?"

"Hands," Mantis said.

"Hands to *weapons*," Sten corrected.

"*Hands,*" Mantis said once again, backing off to his corner. Sten went to his own corner as Capitan took up his position in the Coach Zone, directly above. Sten looked up and gave him the thumbs-up sign once again.

The bell...

Sten and Mantis approached each other as the crowd roared. Both warriors kept each other at a distance of a few yards, neither committing to any form of combat stance. Puzzled, the crowds began to quiet down. Mantis casually walked around Sten next, sizing him up. Suddenly he threw a rapid-fire punch at the *karateka,* but Sten quickly deflected the shot and side-stepped away. Mantis smiled and nodded, then continued to circle around the challenger, baiting him, keeping his distance because of Sten's superior size. Then, very slowly, the champion stepped back and fell to his knees in meditative posture.

The Coliseum went silent.

Puzzled, Sten began to circle around the champion. Mantis was not moving, his eyes half shut. Sten stopped circling and returned to face Mantis. The crowd began to stir.

"Come on, big karate man!" someone yelled.

Sten had had enough; he attacked. Mantis quickly sprang to his feet and tripped his opponent. Sten went rolling across the mat, only to spring back swiftly onto his feet. He turned and opened up his arms, beckoning Mantis to approach. The champion moved around Sten cautiously, fists ready to lash out. There was a brief, inconsequential exchange of hands, Sten succeeding in driving the champion back somewhat, but it was ground that was quickly regained by Mantis as he moved in again and landed a series of punches to the *karateka*'s side. As Mantis drew closer, Sten suddenly leaped on him and grabbed him by the arm, swinging him around as the crowd roared and Capitan beamed in approval.

"If only..."

Mantis, however, was like a wet noodle. Sten had no sooner gotten hold of his opponent than the champion was wrapping his body around him. Both men fell over and began to grapple, Mantis moving swiftly out of Sten's large embrace, sending his knee into the *karateka*'s face. Sten went stumbling back, his mouth bleeding. He spat out the blood at Mantis, and the killer lunged forward. This time Sten managed to slip his foot into the champion's thigh and then fell back, flipping Mantis clean over his head.

The crowd erupted in cheers.

But Mantis was quick to recover. He swiftly rolled to his feet and then spun around as Sten charged, the two of them rolling over again. Mantis flew quickly to his feet and let loose with a flurry of fast punches that sent Sten stumbling back. The challenger shook his head in an effort to regain his senses and then punched back himself. Hands flew like lightning and then there was a deadlock, the two fighters tumbling down once again onto the mat. Mantis was quick to move in this time, the killer wrapping his limbs around the challenger's large torso and then pinning it abruptly to the ground. Sten struggled, bridged, then rolled over, only to have the champion tighten his bizarre vicelike hold. Mantis clung to Sten's back like a bee or a hornet preparing to sting.

Capitan turned away, disgusted.

Abe shook his head. Now he's just going to play with him, Abe thought. Poor bastard...

As Mantis began to tighten his hold with all four limbs, Sten felt as if he were in the grip of something inhuman, like a python. He could feel the power draining from his body. Mantis' arms slithered like snakes into position around the *karateka*'s neck. With a last burst of power Sten bridged himself and rolled over onto Mantis. But the move did not help. It only prompted the champion to begin his choke hold. Mantis slowly tightened his grip, cutting off the carotid arteries in Sten's neck, stopping the flow of blood. The mighty *karateka* felt himself growing dizzier and dizzier....

And then he was out...passed out.

Releasing his strangle hold, Mantis slowly repositioned his knee into the *karateka*'s back. Then, arching his body like a bow, he abruptly snapped Sten's spine in two.

"No!" the crowd cried out in horror as Sten rolled over in agony, conscious again, gasping for breath. Capitan fought back tears and Abe shielded his eyes. Mantis smiled and returned to his corner, picking up one of his sais. Then he began to parade around the arena pit, flashing the dagger, walking directly over to Capitan and pointing it at him. As Capitan fixed Mantis with a look of hatred, the cameras zoomed in on the two and recorded the tacit exchange. The crowd began changing: "Maantis! MAAANTIS! MAAANTIIIS!" as Mantis's face broke into a wild smile—the delighted smile of a child at play.

I don't believe what I'm seeing, Capitan thought. I know what I'm dealing with now....

Mantis aimed the sai at Capitan again, only firmly, very firmly, as he turned to the crowd. Then he sent a last glance at Capitan and began to walk toward Sten's writhing figure. Looking about, Mantis knelt down and placed his razor-sharp sai to the *karateka*'s throat. The mobs in the upper balconies began to go wild as they raised their arms in judgment: *thumbs up!* Capitan looked around to see everyone else joining in with raised thumbs, bidding for mercy. Gifts began to land in the ring. Mantis smiled with amusement as people began to scream: "Spare him!"

Get it over with, Abe thought. Quickly.

"Spare him!"

Throughout the Coliseum people rose to their feet with raised thumbs.

"Spare him!"

Sten gave a limp smile, his head raised like a bull awaiting sacrifice.

"Spare him!"

Mantis smiled.

Then he abruptly cut Sten's throat from ear to ear.

"Oh, Lord, God no…" Capitan turned away in horror as the crowd roared its disapproval and missiles began to dart down. Mantis kicked the now lifeless body aside and walked back over to Capitan. He pointed his bloody sai at him. And their eyes met again.

CHAPTER TWENTY

"**W**ELL, what do you plan to do?"

Carmen paced the studio as Capitan sat in front of the hearth. She glanced out at the army of reporters encamped in the alleyway.

"Well...?"

"I intend to do nothing," Capitan said.

"You're just going to sit there?"

"If I have to, yes."

"Those guys out there want to talk to you," Carmen said. "You've been challenged, honey—world-wide, on TV. And they want to talk to you."

"I'm aware of that."

"So you're not gonna go out?" she asked, her voice cracking.

There was no answer from Capitan at first. Carmen sat dejectedly by his side.

"You're sorry you came back," he said.

"No. I'm not sorry. I know you're confused about all this. But, look—we can split. We can beat it out west somewhere. I'm not afraid to start over."

"I have no intention of running, or going anywhere."

"Well, are you just gonna sit here forever? That Mantis wants your head."

"He wants my head, but it can only be on certain terms: in the ring. He wants me in that ring for a certain reason."

"Yeah," Carmen said, "to kill you."

"No. He can have all the victims he wants. He wants me in that ring for another reason."

"Why? To play patty-cake with you?" Tears were running down her cheeks. Capitan put his arm around her.

"Listen to me," he said. "Last night, when he killed Sten, I noticed something. Mantis is not just a killer. He's, well, *innocent.*"

"Oh, real innocent. Goes and cuts a guy's throat, ear to ear."

"*Listen.* He is like a giant child that wants to play. Killing is just a part of the fun. Last night he flashed that blade at me just like a child would have. Back and forth it went, like a toy. Don't you see, that ring is a sandbox. Life and death to him is just a game. And there's no one in there to teach him about it."

"Well, you're not gonna go in there and try, are you?" Carmen's emotions crested again and became all the worse as Capitan closed his eyes and refused to answer. "You *are* gonna go in there and try?"

"I didn't say that."

"No. But that's what you're thinking. I can see it," Carmen said. "It's the old warrior in you. A month ago, when Sten offered you those tickets, you didn't have to accept them. You didn't have to see Savinien. When Sten wanted you to coach him, you could have said no. But you didn't, because you really want to go in there."

"That's not true."

"Then what is true?"

"That I'm confused. That I stuck my neck out on a limb and the limb was booby-trapped."

"Because you went to see Savinien?"

"No. Because I played that game with Goldman. Ever since I did, things have gotten worse. I played my hand in the wrong direction. And I'm confused, very confused."

Carmen drew closer to him. The reporters could be heard, buzzing outside.

"I never heard from any Monitor Five," Capitan continued. "But I have been hearing from Mantis."

"You don't think—?"

"What?"

"I don't know," Carmen said, shrugging her shoulders. "It was just a crazy thought..."

"Let's hear it."

"What if Mantis was involved with the movement? In some strange way..."

Capitan nodded as he thought on this. It was a strange idea. Yet with Hoshima's odd way of seeing into people, who knew? The master had an odd way of picking people out. He even had an even odder attitude concerning his own Shin-Do.

"Unlike other techniques that are kept secret," he had once said, "my techniques should eventually be spread to everyone. Especially to those who are evil."

"Good God, why?" Capitan had asked.

"Because, in the Absolute there is total peace, but here, in the Relative, there is constant discord. That is the basic nature of this Relative plane: asymmetry. Mother Nature doesn't make any one thing the same. It's the same thing with minds. Now, to teach my Shin-Do to only good people with clear, pure minds would be a tiresome bore. A little evil is needed to spice things up and give a clear interpretation of the whole picture. After all, what is really good, and what is really evil? Would Jesus have been able to die for the sake of man without the treachery of Judas? No. So a little evil is good for flavor. There is nothing more boring than a thoroughly pious saint, because no one is thoroughly pious or free from evil thoughts. And that's because of the asymmetry I spoke of. Nature produces the mind, and nature does not lean toward the symmetrical. A clean-cut, completely proportioned mind?

Nonsense. Any clean-cut mind would be half evil. Symmetry is based on the equal proportioning of opposites."

"I don't fully understand," Capitan had said, expecting Hoshima to respond with his usual "neither do I."

"That is because you are not enlightened like I am," he said instead. "My mind is the Grand Computer of the Junction of Buddhas at the Crossroads of Messiahs of the Fifth Galactic Quadrant... yes, I like that."

Hoshima would have been crazy enough to take in evil-minded people just for the fun of it, but Mantis? Mantis had been stationed in Japan, and so, Capitan had found out, had this "Big Sun." Could he have been a monitor, too? And Mantis as well? Damn. Why hadn't Hoshima ever informed him? He told Carmen what he thought.

"All this leads us back to where we started," she said.

"Yes."

"Which leads me to ask the same question, what do you intend to do?"

"Take each minute for what it's worth and pray. As for the media masters, and Mantis—I'm going to use them as best I can to my advantage. I have a plan worked out, but I need to stall for time."

"How will that help?"

"It will give Monitor Five a chance to show his face."

"And where is this Monitor Five?" she asked.

"*That,*" Capitan said, "is something I would very much like to know."

"If he exists at all..."

"I have to believe he exists," Capitan said. "If he doesn't, then I don't know what I'm going to do."

Mantis sat back on the dais and watched as young Bimbi performed kata, form work, his body moving in clear, perfect motions as he passed a pair of nunchakas over and then around his head.

Al entered from another path in the studio. Mantis did not take his attention from Bimbi's kata.

"What news?"

"The boys have spotted Ibari roaming around near Capitan's studio. He's a cagey bastard, a real fox."

"Tell me about it," Mantis said.

"No sooner is he trailed, then—poof! He's gone. Vanishes. And he knows we're watching. He finds it funny."

"Yes," Mantis said, nodding. "He would…"

"Some of the boys want him. They're getting irritated and want to hit him."

"That would be their grave mistake—their grave, grave mistake."

"Why? He's here to finish you."

"Yes. But I need him as a witness first, then I'll handle him. The boys would only find themselves dead if they even consider tangling with him alone. Enough of that, what else?"

"We've also intercepted calls he's made…"

"About Aquila?"

"Right. Zoroaster, this new guy, he has him safe and sound."

"I already knew that. The boy's safety is not of concern to me, only his death."

The champion fell silent. Al watched him study Bimbi's kata as it mounted in speed and intensity, the young Hispanic passing the weapon faster and faster over and around his head. Everything always fell silent when the boy was brought up.

"Then…let's move in…kill him," Al said a bit hesitantly. He was still confused about killing his boss's own son.

"You don't understand…" Mantis said, watching Bimbi.

"No. If you ordered me to kill the boy, I would kill him. But I don't understand."

"I will be the only one to kill, to sacrifice Aquila. As to the reasons why, I have told you. Time and again I have told you. There is an alien spirit inside the child. If I do not kill him, if I do not kill him in sacrificial fashion, then he will kill me."

Mantis fell silent again, watching as Bimbi's kata became even more intense. The young Hispanic was sweating madly now, his eyes glassy, animal-like.

Animal bodies...

Sweating bodies...

Mantis remembered Irmgard's animal, sweating body. He remembered mounting her, riding her like a horse, running his hands along her smooth, broad thighs, hanging on to them like a saddle...

"...*du sollst mir alles geben*..." she panted. Give it all to me. The East German wrapped her long legs around him, running her fingers through his blond hair. He, in turn, ran his tongue between her firm breasts. "*Gibt mir alles*..." she panted again and then their lips united, Mantis pressing his tongue into her mouth and Irmgard arching her back and shaking with pleasure as the commando thrust into her, thrust in, again and again...

"I will pass through your seed and then destroy you..."

Hoshima's vow ran through Mantis's mind as he held Irmgard tighter.

And then it was forgotten.

He was invincible. Leaning back, he drew Ingrid on top of him, the lovely East German releasing her long legs and then falling onto her knees as she pivoted around his sex.

"...*alles...zu mir*..."

"I will pass through your seed and then destroy you..."

She began to rock in passion, her large breasts swaying. "...*alles*..."

"'Your seed'..."

Hoshima's words fled as he closed his eyes. No, he was invincible now. He had known that for weeks—ever since he had experienced the Moment, the great glorious Moment. He had sat like the Buddha and had awaited the Moment. He had always thought Hoshima was wrong and the Moment had proved it. Like Buddha he had sat in that forest and had watched as life passed by him— life, the struggle.

Life, the great struggle...

Life, the battle, not of good versus evil or evil versus good or pain opposing the virtues of pleasure and happiness...

No, life the battle for survival, he thought, watching as a cat began to tear apart a wounded bird.

Life, a contest for power, the meek submitting to the strong, the strong laying down the order.

Watching everything from point B, he saw the worms and ants shrink from the birds, the birds take flight at sight of the cats, the cats slink under cover from the tread of man. All of it a natural march of power, the great primordial power acknowledging no prayers...

Watching, watching, from his tree he saw the natural march of power take its grip upon every living creature, placing each and every one into its respective niche, birds to the sky, fish to the sea, and man master of the land.

Power, power, rising up through the sap of the tree and then branching out and blossoming in a thousand directions. Power, and only power. Truth and ethics were all man-made inventions, he realized then. He had always realized it, Hoshima had always been wrong...

Mantis' reverie was broken suddenly by Al's rasping voice.

"We processed the X-ray on Capitan," he heard Al say. "You want to see it?"

"Not now," Mantis replied curtly. He motioned for Al to leave.

Mantis rose and clapped his hands. Bimbi stopped and fell to his knees, his body exhausted, his mind numb. The ex-commando motioned for his new student to approach the dais. The terrarium was there. Bimbi sat in front of it and stared inside, mesmerized.

"Your training is almost finished," Mantis said. He took the praying mantis out of the cage and placed it before the young Hispanic. The insect rested passively on the table. Bimbi stared at it. "Now listen to me," Mantis said. "Listen to me as you focus on this insect. A man perfectly trained in the great way of combat is just like this creature. He moves and reacts by instinct. He perceives neither right nor wrong. He merely acts. The way of thinking, of combat, of death, thinks through him. He is a vehicle. A *vehicle*, Bimbi. An instrument. When the moment of challenge comes, when he is threatened, he does not hesitate, he does not stop to think right or wrong. He acts. He kills. Tomorrow you shall fight the man who killed your brother. And when that moment comes you must not hesitate, or your training, like your life, will have been in vain."

Mantis positioned himself a few inches from the insect. He raised a hand. "And remember, as I have told you: whether we hesitate or not, whether we kill or not, we are all insects in the end. We are all expendable."

Mantis slowly lowered his hand and crushed the insect. Bimbi started, as if suddenly awakened.

"Hey," he said. "What are you...that was...?"

"That was an insect, Bimbi," Mantis said firmly. "And insects are expendable. We are *all* expendable."

Capitan proceeded down the street, grocery containers in hand as an army of reporters surrounded and followed him. Most of the reporters were armed with only minimikes. Capitan handed a food container to one of them.

"Here, you're not doing anything. Carry this."

"Mr. Capitan," they started up again, "do you have any comments about Mantis's challenge to you?"

Capitan continued along, smiling at the cameras. "Was it a challenge?" he asked.

"Why, certainly," a reporter said. "I mean he kept waving that dagger in front of you."

"What else would you call it?" another reporter said.

"I'd call it—" Capitan stopped short, the army of reporters waiting.

"Yes?"

"What—?"

Capitan turned to a cameraman. "Do you think you could get me from this angle, this side?"

"Please, Mr. Capitan—"

"The last name is Alzerras," Capitan said.

"You were saying—"

"I was?"

"Yes. What about his challenge? You said it wasn't a challenge."

"Right. You were going to call it something, though."

"I was."

"Yes."

It was fun to torture the media masters, he thought.

"I was going to call it, well, the behavior of the five-year-old who had no one to play with."

This response caught the reporters off guard. They looked at each other quizzically as Capitan walked on.

"Hey, wait a minute—"

"What do you mean 'five-year-old child'?"

"Are you saying that Mantis is a five-year-old child?"

"Something like that, yes."

"Well, would you care to elaborate?"

"Certainly, but—" He pointed at the cameras. "Are people watching out there?"

"All over."

"You're sure?"

"Of course."

"Yes. Now please, explain."

"Well, Mantis has issued no public statement concerning me," Capitan said. "I mean, nothing that concerns a challenge. All he did was flip that dagger of his at me, back and forth, just like a plaything. He seems to want someone to play with—someone to share his sandbox."

The cameras inched closer. Capitan bowed politely and slid out of view.

Mantis watched on TV as the reporters pursued. Al was there watching, too.

"A real funny man," Al said.

"Let me see that X-ray on him."

The lieutenant handed it over. Mantis scanned the film.

"Dislocated shoulder," Al said. "Tournament accident."

Mantis rolled up the film. He watched as the reporters cornered Capitan in front of his studio.

"Please," Capitan said. "I've already said enough."

"Couldn't you clarify just a little?"

"What's to clarify?"

"You've accused the champion, one of the most skillful fighters in history, of being—"

"Juvenile?"

"Exactly."

"Well, he is. Look at his record in the ring. Each and every time he asks the crowd to render their decision, then he goes parading around like a little boy with those daggers of his and does exactly the opposite. He's a child, albeit a very violent one. No one wants to play with him. I certainly don't want to play with him."

Capitan headed toward the door. "Please. Let me pass."

"Does that mean you don't intend to fight the champion?"

"Fight? I have no intention of getting anywhere near the man."

"Does that mean—?"

"Could you—?"

"Gentlemen, please. What I have said, I've said. I don't think I need to clarify anything more."

Some of the reporters began to disperse. As they did, Capitan happened to spot a Japanese gentleman in the crowd. The man smiled mysteriously. Puzzled, Capitan awaited further signs of recognition, but the Oriental simply turned around and walked away. Capitan quickly ducked inside the door. As he did, Mantis abruptly switched off his TV.

"Get the car ready," he told Al. "We're heading to Brooklyn with Bimbi."

"What about last night's big phone call?" Al asked.

"What about it?"

"They were pretty firm, the three of them. They want you to cool it with this guy Capitan. They don't want you making any more martyrs in the ring."

"Sten was no martyr, he was a sap. As for Capitan, he's a sacrifice. This is my game, not theirs."

"They're still the Trium—"

"They're nothing," Mantis said. "I'm the only one who directs the people now. I, and I alone." There was a slight pause, Mantis in lotus position, plotting his next move. Then he rose and added with an air of finality: "Now—to Brooklyn."

Enrique, Tomaso, and their gang were not hard to locate. Being warrior chiefs on the block, it was their job to stand out, to show the kids and the frightened tenants who was who and what was what. They were so consumed with their misguided conception of their own power that they didn't even bother to notice the black sedan as it rolled down the street. The sedan stopped finally alongside a fire hydrant that was issuing a steady stream of water from its mouth.

"That's him," Bimbi said eagerly, tightening up in the back seat of the car. "He's the thin, long one."

"Smoking a cigarette?" Mantis asked.

"Yeah."

Enrique was busy puffing away, drinking a beer and gesticulating amorously to some neighborhood señoritas. Tomaso and the others stood nearby, laughing and drinking. Mantis watched the scene, then motioned to Al.

"Go get him."

"What about Tomaso?" Bimbi asked.

"What about him?"

"He's the big one, the one that fought my brother. I want him, too."

"You can fight only one. Al..." Mantis motioned to his lieutenant again, gesturing something. Al smiled his no-smile and left the sedan with another bodyguard.

They headed down the street in their business suits, looking distinctly out of place and drawing immediate attention. Enrique threw down his cigarette and stepped back, wary.

"Hey, what's this...?"

Al approached him.

"We want to talk with you," he said.

Enrique panicked. "Tomaso..."

The entire gang of seven hoods stood ready—ready to either run or fight.

"We don't want trouble," Enrique said.

"No. But *we* do." Al smiled and motioned to the other body-guard. He went over and grabbed Enrique. Tomaso stepped in.

"Hey, that's my bro—"

Al swiftly dashed over and scooped up Tomaso, lifting the large Hispanic off his feet.

"Hey, what is this?" Tomaso said. He tried to break free of the man's grasp, but got nowhere.

Abruptly, Al hurled Tomaso against some steps. The big His-panic hit head first and immediately snapped his neck.

There were screams as the rest of the gang fled. People living in the neighborhood tenements dashed inside and locked their doors. Enrique looked wide-eyed at Tomaso's big body, slumped on the tenement steps.

"Jesus..."

"You see," Al said. "We *do* want trouble."

"Please...please don't kill me," Enrique begged, his thin body beginning to shake.

"*This* is a fight-guru?" the other bodyguard asked.

"Slim pickins," Al said, and they both laughed as Enrique tried to get loose. As they walked back to the car, Mantis and Bimbi opened the back doors of the sedan and stepped out.

"Pendajo—"

Mantis held Bimbi back with a mysterious, subtle touch of his fingers. Meanwhile, the two Hispanics stood silently and eyed one another.

"Well, there he is," Mantis said to Bimbi. "He's all yours."

"Hey," Enrique said."What kinda fair fight is this?"

"The same fair fight you gave my brother," Bimbi said, starting to move forward.

Mantis held him back again with a mysterious touch of his fin-gers.

"Patience, my little cockroach."

He motioned to Al. A leather case was soon brought out of the car.

"It's going to be a fair fight," Mantis told them, taking the case himself. "Now, both of you know how to use these, right?"

He opened the case. Inside lay two pairs of nunchakas. Enrique looked at Bimbi and sneered.

"Oh yeah..."

"Well, go ahead, take one—both of you."

Mantis and his men watched as the two Hispanics chose their weapons, neither one taking his eyes off the other. Mantis smiled and reached into his pockets.

"And, just to make things a little more amusing, I'm going to give each of you one of *these*."

He flashed open two large switchblades, then handed them over. Mantis and his two men backed off as Bimbi and Enrique eagerly faced one another, both of them placing the blades between their teeth. They prepared to fight, then briefly engaged, a challenge issuing from both sides as each of the warriors flashed their nunchakas. People began to watch from the tenement windows. An elderly Dominican lady came to the door of the tenement, a porto-phone in her hand. She aimed the receiver at Mantis and his men.

"You white boys shouldn't—"

Al whipped out a revolver and fired at the doorway, chipping off a piece of wood and sending the old woman scurrying in fear back into the building. He turned and watched with his boss as the two Hispanics continued to bait each other with the weapons.

"This is even more pleasurable than I expected," Mantis said.

A patrol car appeared at the end of the street. Mantis calmly raised his hand and waved it away. Then he clapped abruptly.

"Destroy."

Suddenly, without notice, Bimbi opened up with almost inhuman force, swinging his nunchakas madly and driving Enrique back—back toward the tenement steps. Enrique broke in confusion, a bar of Bimbi's nunchaka connecting and sending the gang leader crashing onto the cement. He curled up like a caged animal, his switchblade ready. Bimbi stood over him in stunned triumph. The two Hispanics began to stare at one another, breathing heavily.

Mantis flushed. "Don't hesitate."

There was panic. Enrique and Bimbi lashed out at one another at the same time. Bimbi's blade caught Enrique in the throat, but Enrique managed to slash his attacker across the eye. They both fell back, screaming wildly.

"Shit—my eye!"

Bimbi fell to his knees in front of Mantis. Mantis merely kicked him away.

"You hesitated," the ex-commando said. "You failed."

"*My eye!*"

"Scream all you want, you've disappointed me." He looked over at Enrique, then at Al. "Finish him."

Al took out his revolver and went over to Enrique. He pressed his gun to the back of the gang leader's head and pulled the trigger. Mantis tapped the other bodyguard on the shoulder and pointed to Bimbi, who continued to scream and hold his bleeding face.

"Put a blanket over his head so he won't bloody up the car. We're taking him home to his friend, Capitan."

The bodyguard nodded. Al put away his gun.

The sedan could not get down the alleyway, but that didn't displease Mantis in the least. With reporters everywhere he knew he'd get the audience he wanted. He motioned for Al to open the door. Unceremoniously, with the blood-stained blanket still over his head, Bimbi was dumped out onto the pavement. There was a mad rush around the car, the attention focusing first on Bimbi and then on Mantis, who sat at the window calmly examining his fingernails.

"Capitan—!" Bimbi screamed. "CAPITAN!"

Capitan was quick to recognize a true alarm. He dashed out of the studio.

"Oh, my God..."

He knelt down and embraced the young Hispanic. "Oh my God, no..."

Mantis pointed at Capitan, a sly grin on his face. "Okay, Mr. Funny Man. I'll be seeing you, and you know where."

He nodded his head as the sedan drove off. Capitan nodded grimly in return.

CHAPTER TWENTY-ONE

CAPITAN sat that night, alone, at the lifeguard station on the beach, bundled up. The sky was lit with stars.

Stars shining over New York...

Yet Capitan didn't see any of them. In his mind he was still at the hospital, in the emergency ward, sitting with Carmen, watching as the reporters stood at a distance. Carmen had threatened to spray them again. He remembered a doctor approaching.

"Bad?"

"We had to remove the eye," the doctor said.

The reporters rushed over. It was madness, and the comedy routine Capitan had used with them before was now void.

Everyone wanted a confrontation. An answer.

And so he had worked out a plan with Carmen. She would stall, hold them off and shoot the bull with them, while he escaped. He had to escape.

And as it turned out, he had escaped here, to the lifeguard

station, escaped to a place where there was no more Sten, no crippled Bimbi and no world ready to breathe down his neck through the face of Mantis. These last two months Fate had slammed its mighty hand down on him, hit him with such force that there was a part of him, he knew, that would never recover. He huddled close as the winds howled.

"What to do?" he said aloud.

He looked up to the heavens, looked up feeling betrayed. What hurt most of all is that he had been abandoned by Hoshima and by Monitor Five. When he most needed them, they were not there. For eight years now he had played a game, a simple little game, and now, suddenly, a series of bizarre events had ushered him back into the real world, the all too real world, and he didn't know how to cope, didn't know what to do.

"What to do?" he asked again. "What to do?"

The winds howled. He huddled close under the blanket, shaking his head, beginning to cry, crying for Bimbi, and for Sten, and for the entire mixed-up world that wanted to see his head stuck on a pole.

Or did it?

Am I supposed to search the heavens for an answer? He looked up to the sky, seeking an omen. There were so many stars, so much vastness. It made him feel small, made him feel as if he counted for nothing.

No, the answer would not be found in the heavens. He must find the answer here in the real world, somewhere in the dark, dusty streets, somewhere amid the throngs of people. If he looked hard enough, he knew he would eventually find someone who would tell him what he needed to know.

Capitan turned over as morning struck. He was hunched up in the lifeguard stand, seashells raining on him.

Seashells?

He awoke, and shook his head. Another seashell landed in his lap. He looked down to see a man kneeling in the sand, a sheathed samurai sword in front of him. Capitan recognized him. The

Japanese man in the crowd. The stranger motioned for him to climb down.

A moment later they were both kneeling and facing one another, the sword between them.

"I am Monitor Five," the man said. "I have gone by the name Ibari. But from now on you are to call me *sensei*."

"Why?"

"Because I am to be your new teacher now that Hoshima is no longer of this world."

Capitan turned numb. "Dead?"

"In a sense, yes."

"When?"

"Years ago. Mantis killed him. Mantis is Monitor Six."

"Why—"

"You have many questions," Ibari said. "My silence, my distance has been for a reason. But all along I was aware of what you were going through, your doubts. Faith is often tested. Perhaps you resented the silence."

"Yes. Can you blame me?"

"Blame you? You make it sound like you've been victimized."

"You might say I'm in a very delicate situation at present," Capitan said. "One that has nothing to do with me."

"Oh, it has everything to do with you," Ibari said.

"I don't understand."

"You are the one who is going to stop Mantis."

"Stop him, how?"

"Why, in the arena, of course."

"He'll cut me down like a piece of grass."

"You don't know that."

"I have a good premonition that he will."

"Premonitions are abstractions. This," Ibaria said, pointing at the sword, "is no abstraction. Take it."

Capitan hesitated. He looked at Monitor Five, the new *sensei*. "Who made it?"

"I made it. You made it. The Great Buddha made it. Don't ask stupid questions. Take it."

Capitan picked it up and examined the *kanji* symbols written on the sheath.

"Aiki sword."

"Yes. The sword of truth."

"Poetry's not going to help me stop Mantis."

"No, but virtue will. You are in virtue of the Way. You shall win. Even if the sun were to rise from the west, victory is yours."

Capitan just sat there, his knees dug into the sand, the sword in his hands, his head shaking.

"I am lost...confused."

"No, not at all. You were, in fact, chosen for this task."

"By who?"

"By Hoshima. He never contacted you again because there was no need of it. You were one of his early students, sent off to bloom on your own. He tried your loyalty by isolating you. I went along with the plan. That's why you were forbidden to write letters back to him."

"What happened to Hoshima?"

"I told you," Ibari said.

"Yes, but how?"

"Mantis cut off his head."

Capitan closed his eyes. "Oh, God..."

Ibari nodded grimly. "It was horrible to watch."

"What—?" Capitan looked at him, aghast.

"Yes, I was there. So was Habib."

"And...you...*you just stood there?*"

"We were ordered to," Ibari said. "The master ordered us not to lay a hand on him."

"Why? *Why?*"

"If I had the answer to that, I would not be here now. And Mantis would long have been dead. There is more to this than you know, and there is more for me to tell you, but not now."

"But I—"

"Be silent for now," Ibari told him, raising his hand abruptly. "Just focus on the sword."

"This is madness. I don't know if I trust you, and *this* is an instrument of death."

Ibari smiled, amused. "It is an instrument that you are good with," he said. "And it is an instrument that you must use."

"Me..." Capitan said, his head lowered, shaking in disbelief.

"Yes. That should be rather evident now that the cameras are on you. Mantis wants you. It was inevitable from the beginning."

"The beginning? What beginning?"

"The beginning, when Hoshima first met you and when he first met Mantis. He saw in you and Mantis a polarity that had to be played out. 'Good versus Evil' is the way I think you Christians like to put it, though of course it's more complicated than that."

Capitan digested Ibari's words carefully. "I had considered the possibility that Mantis may have been at one time a student of Hoshima's. But there's something I still don't understand. Why, if the Master was on the side of good, would he have taught his technique to an individual committed to evil?"

"Mantis would have arrived at his own self-realization even without the technique. By reaching him, Hoshima bound Mantis to his spirit, as you and I are bound to Hoshima's spirit. It is very important that you understand this point."

"I do not."

Ibari leaned closer, his thick hand raised to accentuate what he had to tell.

"Mantis is a very, very powerful spirit. One like the world has not seen for many ages. His course is the course of power and the enslavement of others. It is a blind course that rolls over anything in its path. Our master saw this immediately, he saw that it was only a matter of time before Mantis's own demented form of enlightenment took place. A wrench had to be thrown into Mantis's corrupt moral machinery. Hoshima did that by taking Mantis on as his student, by teaching him, by imprinting his spirit into Mantis's mind."

"And then he let Mantis kill him?"

"It didn't matter whether Hoshima maintained his human form

or not. He now lives with the devas, the gods, though Mantis thinks otherwise. It is this nagging thought that the master still lives that will destroy Mantis. All that is needed now is an instrument."

"Me."

"Yes."

"Why not *you*?"

"Because Mantis will not agree to combat. Because I am Asian and you are white. Because the day is light and night is dark. It is not easy to explain."

There was a long silence, the waves crashing on the beach and the gulls cackling, soaring overhead. Capitan just stared at the sword and shook his head. Ibari folded his arms.

"Your duel with Mantis is unavoidable."

"I cannot kill," Capitan said.

"Do not think about killing. The Great Way shall kill for you. Remember that."

Capitan ran his hand over the sword and nodded.

Mantis sat in front of the TV set, the head of his pet leopard cushioned in his lap. As the beast purred softly, Mantis and Al stared at the screen, watching as a pack of reporters converged on Capitan's studio. Mantis was anxious to see what new approach Capitan would use after the incident with Bimbi. A new approach was unavoidable. A statement of some sort was inevitable. Capitan would have to fight. As the young warrior appeared on the screen, Ibari at his side, Mantis smiled.

It is all falling into place, he thought.

The reporters surrounded the two men.

"Mr. Alzerras..."

"We feel that viewers and the fans out there would like to know—"

"Do you or don't you have any intention of confronting Mantis in the arena?"

Capitan raised a hand to quiet them down.

"Gentlemen, the answer to your question is yes. I will be meeting Mantis in the arena, at his pleasure."

The reporters had already begun their follow-up questions when Ibari inched between them, aiming a finger at the camera.

"Mantis!" he shouted. "Beware the Aiki sword."

Ibari and Capitan backed off. The reporters surged forward but the two men managed to slip the bolt on the studio door just in time.

Mantis abruptly turned off the TV. Al noticed that his right hand was writhing again, that he was in pain. The breathing, the strange breathing, would start soon and he would be in greater pain. He watched as Mantis rose slowly, inching the leopard off his lap.

"Bring me my sword," Mantis said.

Al nodded, knowing what was about to happen. Mantis walked past him, his hand writhing. He proceeded down the tile path, through his garden-jungle, out onto the terrace. He approached the slashed statue of the laughing Buddha. He stared at it, his hand writhing. Then the breathing began, the intense abdominal breathing. He began to double up; he fell to his knees. Al came up behind him, holding a sheathed samurai sword.

"Leave it," Mantis said, closing his eyes, his very bowels contracting.

Al nodded and walked off. Mantis stared up at the statue—at the slashed, laughing face. The face was Hoshima's. The killer could not shake the face from his mind. He thought back...back to that day long ago...

Mantis had returned after his great vision—his vision of the exaltedness of power—to the dojo. Hoshima was there with Ibari and Habib. It was time for a session. Hoshima lit some incense while Ibari and Habib knelt down upon the tatami. But Mantis stood, looking on in disdain. The teacher looked up at him.

"You have seen something."

"Yes," Mantis said. "I have seen that you are wrong, old man.

They say that the moment of realization is hard to attain. That is because the holy men lie, because they are searching for the wrong thing."

"I see," Hoshima said. "You're saying that all the holy men, the sages and great saints are all wrong?"

"I am," Mantis said. "You are wrong."

"Thousands of years of tradition are wrong, too, I assume."

"All lies," Mantis said. "Truth is a lie."

"Then what *is* the vision?" Hoshima asked, his eyes calmly floating from Ibari to Habib then back to Mantis again. "What is the Moment?"

"The Moment is Power," Mantis announced. "Power is All. Power and Power alone. And not just brute power; water has power, fire has power, the snake with its winding body has power. But it is Power and Power alone that is the All."

Habib prepared to speak, but Hoshima motioned for him to remain silent. He looked at Mantis calmly, then at the sword that hung upon the wall. Ibari caught his glance, as did Mantis. Hoshima lowered his eyes, focusing them on the floor.

"And what of ethics?" he asked.

"I have told you about ethics."

"And now your great Moment reinforces your former opinion?"

"All the more. Power has showed me that ethics are the feeble invention of timid men."

"Ethics prevent men, my son, from doing bad things."

"Do not try my patience. There is nothing bad, or good—only Power."

"Murder is bad," Hoshima said.

"Murder is a relative term."

"And a negative act."

"If you choose to see it in relative terms," Mantis said. He knelt down and prepared to joust verbally with his former teacher. He folded his arms, waiting. Hoshima remained silent for a moment, pursing his lips, running a hand across his bald head.

"So, to you," he finally said, "murder is nothing more than killing with a negative edge to it." Mantis gave no reply. He watched as Hoshima glanced at the sword, then turned to him again. "What about the law of karma? The law of cause and effect? How does that apply to your Power?"

"It is voided by power," Mantis told him.

"Ah," Hoshima said. "There you are wrong, very wrong. Everyone within the six realms of existence is subject to the law of cause and effect."

"Can you prove it?" Mantis asked.

"Certainly. Habib, do you see that sword up there?"

"Yes, *sensei*."

"Take it down." Habib rose and went over and got the sword. He turned to Hoshima. "Now, place it in front of Mantis." Habib hesitated slightly, then obeyed. Hoshima looked at the commando. "There is a sword. You may kill me with it if you like."

There was a sudden exchange of glances from Ibari and Habib. Hoshima raised his hand to indicate silence, his eyes not moving from Mantis.

"I have no wish to kill you...at present," the commando said.

"Presently you will."

"Why?" Mantis asked, amused.

"Because you are a dirty spirit and, what's more, an ignorant one," Hoshima said, his tone suddenly reproachful. "One that has never learned and that has been sent back over countless lifetimes to crawl like a snake until the law of karma is understood. Still, now, in a human body you fail to learn the lesson, you fail to see that whatever you sow you shall reap. If you kill, you will be killed, if not in this lifetime, then the next."

"That is all gibberish," Mantis said.

"I will prove it to you. Kill me now, strike off my head—and my spirit will return through your own seed to destroy your spirit. I will ride on the tides of karma and haunt you, then confront you, and I will send your spirit back to the hell where it belongs."

"Old fool..."

"Take the sword."

Mantis rose abruptly. Habib and Ibari stood ready.

"Don't worry," Mantis said. "I'm leaving."

"You are to stay and accept my challenge," Hoshima commanded. He turned to Ibari and Habib. "And you two are to watch. You are to do nothing. You are never to lay a hand on Mantis."

Habib jerked forward. "But—"

"Silence. That is an order, vow to it, now."

The two other students watched as Hoshima's face took on an aura they had never seen. His eyes pierced them and set words onto their tongues.

"I vow..." they each said.

Hoshima took the sword by its sheath and offered it to Mantis.

"Accept my challenge. Strike off my head and my spirit will return through your seed to send your soul back to the very bowels of hell."

Mantis took the sword and smiled. He held it by the sheath, limply.

"You're playing with your life," the commando said.

"My life means nothing if it cannot serve as a sacrifice to knowledge, to the light that you fail to see with your juvenile, childish little game of power. Power, bah!" Hoshima burst suddenly into laughter. "How many tyrants have been seduced by that illusion? Caesar, the Khan, Hitler? And yet you have the audacity to believe that you have reached self-awareness?"

Everyone watched as Mantis' grip on the sheath tightened.

"You have reached self-delusion, and nothing more," Hoshima continued. "You have taken mind technique and twisted it, molded it according to the shape of your own crippled brain. You have opposed the laws of karma, of virtues. You have dispossessed the Lord within you, all for the sake of an ego as hard as a nut shell, refusing to crack, to give way, to—"

"Enough!" Mantis shouted. The sword burst out from its sheath and Ibari and Habib made ready to rise from their knees, watching as Mantis' eyes flashed an intense green, every nerve in his body ready to strike. Hoshima looked up, laughing.

"Through your seed..." he said, rolling his eyes back into his head, and then Mantis slashed the sword down in a clean arc.

"God no!" Habib cried.

It was a clean cut, Hoshima's head rolling from his body and facing Mantis with a smile on it, the eyes still fluttering Habib began vomiting as Ibari closed his eyes in pain and Mantis stepped back in awe.

The head...

The head with a smile...

It was so long ago, and yet Mantis remembered that head with a vividness that would not fade. He was on his knees now, in pain, facing the statue of the smiling Buddha.

The Buddha was laughing...

Hoshima was laughing...

Mantis gripped the sword and drew it. He approached the jade statue and began to slash it with the sword, the blade chipping and Mantis crying angrily as his abdomen contracted in mad rhythm. He slashed the belly, the neck, the arms. But he could not slash that smile. Not even with his "Aiki sword."

CHAPTER TWENTY-TWO

THE hospital...

Bimbi was sitting with his back to the door when Capitan entered. He heard Capitan come in, but he did not move. There was a large bandage over his right eye. He was ashamed of the bandage.

"Hey, kid," Capitan said. "I brought something for you."

He handed the young Hispanic a package. Bimbi looked at it, then began to open the package halfheartedly. He refused to look at Capitan. When he had finally taken the last of the wrapping paper off he realized that there were two rattan fighting sticks inside.

"The best I have," Capitan said.

"Thanks," Bimbi mumbled, and then there was silence for a long time. Bimbi finally shrugged his shoulders. "A lot of good they'll do me now."

"You still have another eye."

"I'm blind," Bimbi said, beginning to cry.

"Only on one side," Capitan reminded him. There was another

256

gap of silence as Bimbi wiped his nose and shook his head. Capitan sat stoically. Then he added: "Mantis is evil, Bimbi. Like it or not, you have to face facts: for a time you went and sat at his side, you were filled with anger, you were confused, so you chose Mantis's way, which is an evil one."

"And you're good, right?"

"I'm not saying that. It's never that simple. But I have always been committed to life and not to death. As I said, let the facts speak for themselves: you went and trained with Mantis and that training was based on anger, and now that anger has partially blinded you. Let that teach you something."

"Teach me what?"

"That you can't put the eye back, so use the loss as knowledge." Bimbi considered this as best he could. "Take that knowledge and put it on the side that you can see with."

Capitan watched as Bimbi mulled over the situation. He saw the tides of self-pity begin to draw the young Hispanic back into his shell. Bimbi began to shake his head again, ready for tears.

"I can't."

"Can't what?"

"I just can't..." he said, sobbing.

"Listen to me," Capitan said. "You want to be the big warrior. Then stop crying like a baby. Warriors used to lose their arms or legs without even uttering a sound."

"I've lost *my eye!*"

"Because you were a punk," Capitan said. "Face facts, Bimbi, you were a punk. Jumping here, jumping there, with no gratitude. You had only one person you wanted to listen to in the end, and that was yourself. And look where it got you."

Capitan rose and looked at his old student. Bimbi would not look up. He slung his head to the side.

"Yeah..." he mumbled.

"Think on these things. I'm still here to teach you. I'm not God, I can't put the eye back, I can't bring José back. All I can do is teach you. All you have to do is listen."

Bimbi nodded, halfheartedly. He would not look up. Then he

began to cry. Capitan hesitated for a moment. The kid had been through a lot, he realized. He had undergone Mantis's bizarre forms of hypnosis. Now he was partially blinded and besieged by reporters. Perhaps the hard line was wrong.

But the hard line always made people think.

Capitan backed off toward the door. "I'll be at my studio. The doctors say you'll be ready to go by tomorrow. You're welcome back. Take care."

Bimbi nodded. Capitan was about to say a word of encouragement, but he decided against it and left.

The door closed and Bimbi wept.

Abe had thought twice about it all, about the risk he was taking, but it didn't seem to matter anymore. When Sten's throat was cut something bled out of the old-timer as well. Perhaps it was a will to live, to survive, or to just basically go on playing the same foul game. He had returned home that night after the talk with Mantis, had taken a shower, and as he sat there drying off, looking at his flabby old bullet-ridden body in the mirror, he saw in himself an antique, something that was found on the back shelves of dusty old shops, bartered for, and then put on display.

I'm a dinosaur, he thought with amusement, running the towel along the back of his head, staring at the old wounds that were reflected in the mirror. And dinosaurs have a way of becoming extinct.

He had never married, never had children; it had been strictly business all his life. He could remember all the vacations he had taken; he could count them on his hands.

If his life had been successful, it had been successful in wasting other people's lives. His success cast a grim shadow. Perhaps that was why he had hired two idiots like Eddie and Billy. They made it amusing—the whole game. With them he could walk through it all with a comical edge and not have to think back on all the crimes he had committed.

Crimes...Abe was not one to be riddled by guilt, but waste

bothered him. And the Arena was becoming more and more of that, a waste, a simple game that had started as a device to get people thinking the government's way and ended up showcasing sadistic murder. Sten's death had disturbed him, disturbed him deeply. The memory of the poor brute just bleeding there, his life breath flowing out of him...God, what a waste.

The following morning Abe prepared a series of statements for the press. Mantis had instructed Abe to roll out the red carpet for him, for his vision of world power. Well, he would present that vision to the media as instructed, but with some of his own editing attached.

Despite Charlie's plea to tone down what he would say, Abe faced the media masters and their snub-nosed cameras as scheduled, and started off with a detailed description of his dealings with Capitan and with Mantis. He described the phony dossiers the Arena champion had sent him, revealed the threats that had been made, and implicated Mantis in the two Brooklyn killings of Enrique and Tomaso. It was the issue of moral confrontation, though, that excited the press, that really started the questions flying. The picture that Abe presented of two men, taught by the same master, possessed of the same powers, vying to determine whose vision was stronger, was one that the press immediately embraced. As Abe continued to talk it became apparent to those viewing at home that Capitan was a virtuous underdog and that Mantis—the champion so many had perversely looked up to— was out to misuse the power of the Aiki movement for his personal designs. The fans began to feel duped. It was one thing for Mantis to flout their decisions in the arena, to go ahead and do as he liked—that was his prerogative; it was all a part of the "fun." But it was another thing to proclaim a new order, a new vision of things that cast the common man in the role of an insect. *That* was an insult. And so the fans—the great masses of people who followed Sport Arena—began to embrace the vision of Capitan. The interview with Abe had not been more than a few hours old and already a new chant had started. *"Capitaaan! Capitaaan!"* The name of the challenger echoed throughout the surrounding ghettoes and into the very heart of Manhattan itself. A new hero was being proclaimed.

Rather than be distressed by this new state of affairs, Mantis showed total disdain a few hours later when he made his statement to the press. Facing the cameras, the champ raised a hand to indicate silence, then held up a samurai sword.

"To Capitan," he said, "to the public. Beware my Aiki Sword. It is *this*," he told the cameras, unsheathing the weapon, "this weapon here that shall sever Capitan's head from his shoulders. Capitan is the people, his head is their Will. I intend to destroy that Will. And it is *this*," he added, flashing a sai dagger, "that shall parade that head, that Will, about the arena."

The reporters bombarded the champion with questions.

"Are you saying that—"

"I am saying that no more need be said." Mantis turned and abruptly walked off.

Ibari shut off the TV.

He was in the studio, with Capitan and Carmen. They had all listened to Mantis without saying a word.

"Quite a speech," the Oriental said. "As you Americans say, the devil is catching up with him."

Capitan had told Carmen everything that Ibari had related to him, and Ibari had described to them both the actual moments of Hoshima's death. But there was more, much more, that the Oriental had yet to tell.

"Where does the child, Aquila, fit into all this?" Carmen asked.

There was a long pause and then Ibari turned to them.

"Have you ever heard of the Egress, the Egg?" he asked.

"It's a Taoist term," Capitan said.

"Exactly. It is something that Hoshima never fully taught any of us, something that only the master knew and that Mantis later learned about, and that he is perhaps developing himself."

"Well, what is it?"

"It is the ability to take your life force, your very essence, and turn it into a fetus."

"A fetus?" Carmen said, not sure whether Ibari was serious.

"Yes. When we meditate we are nurturing the process without even knowing about it."

"And this fetus—it has a womb and all?"

"Not a real womb, more like an incubator. After all, it *is* an Egg, it has to be hatched. The incubator is point B, the food is breath and meditation. The life force—your sperm, your breath, your mind—gather in this incubator and slowly form a body, a fetal body."

"Your spirit?" Capitan asked.

"In a sense, yes," Ibari said. "It is a living creation, a subtle body-creation. And this creation is called the Egress, or, as the master preferred, the Egg. This Egg eventually hatches and leaves point B, the abdominal region, just as a child leaves home. It then matures and functions through point A between the eyes and then prepares for the moment of death, when it exits through the crown of the skull up into the realm of astral bodies and celestial deities—the land of the devas, the gods. From there it is able to watch the transaction of material life, our corporeal world. It is capable of judging when and where to reenter the human world, what parents to pick. All these things."

"And the master—he did this?"

"Of course. You don't think he was letting Mantis snuff him out for good, unprepared, do you?"

"But still," Capitan said, "to die like that. To give up one's body..."

"Why not? Hoshima's early sake years as a cadet and warrior had lacerated his kidneys. The Hoshima-Body was deteriorating, slowly but surely. He had grown bored with it. Then there was the situation with Mantis, which I described to you. Everything just fell into place. Hoshima ensnared Mantis in his aura, then exited his own body."

There was a long pause as Capitan and Carmen sat there, trying to digest it all.

"There's something I still don't understand," Capitan said. "What about Aquila, and Hoshima's vow to come back and destroy Mantis 'through his seed'?"

Ibari smiled. "Now we enter the truly mysterious part of which even I am not sure." He rose from his chair and walked over to the weapon rack. "Shortly after the murder, Mantis impregnated Irmgard, an East German officer who had been wounded and captured by his commandos. The two had undergone treatment together in Tokyo and had grown quite close. The conception was a show on Mantis's part of his power—a demonstration of his great vision. It was also done in defiance of the master's threat, to return 'through Mantis's seed to destroy him.' But that defiance turned to doubt. Mantis learned later about the actual process of the Egg. He began to see Aquila as a threat, as the reincarnation of Hoshima, ready to grow and then kill him. He had begun to triumph in the arena and his mind was growing more distant, madder. Eventually that madness drove Irmgard to suicide, but not before she made sure Aquila was safely in my hands. I turned him over to Habib and his clan, and there he has remained ever since."

Capitan looked at him quizzically. "And what do you believe? Do you believe the boy is Hoshima, reincarnate? And if he is and the omen is true, then things don't look good for me."

Ibari took down two wooden swords from the weapon rack and examined them. "The omen says 'through his seed to destroy his spirit.' It says nothing about Mantis's present body. One may also take the term 'through his seed' to be a trap for Mantis."

"How do you mean?" Capitan asked.

"We are all one another's seed in the end."

"Ah…" Capitan was beginning to understand.

"It is my belief that Aquila shall have another future. As for his father, it is our duty to make sure that the process of the Egress is halted, if indeed it has begun. Otherwise Mantis's spirit will surely return."

"How is the process stopped?" Carmen asked, not sure of what to make of all this.

Ibari smiled and pointed at Capitan. "Capitan must kill Mantis before the astral fetus is allowed to exit his body."

"This is madness," she said.

"Oh, yes, very much so," Ibari replied. "This and the Arena and everything else we are experiencing in this present age." The Oriental was standing directly over Capitan now, the two wooden swords in hand. He offered one to Capitan. "You have a job to do. Remember, the man is stronger than you, he is in far better shape. He is probably only an equal swordsman, though. And he has accepted our bait about using the Aiki sword. He also functions through one great defect..."

"Which is?"

"Exactly what we've been discussing. He expects any true attempt on his life to come from his own blood, not from you. He is predisposed, and that is a distinct disadvantage for him." Ibari motioned for Capitan to rise with the sword. "Attack me, or—" he lunged swiftly at Capitan, only to have his blow parried, "—or I attack you. Good."

They began to circle one another, swords ready. Carmen moved back, out of the way. Capitan attacked but the older warrior quickly pivoted and struck, hitting Capitan on the wrist, disarming him. He aimed his wooden sword at Capitan.

"Mantis will use real steel. Had you been in the arena, you would have lost your hand. Pick up your sword."

As Capitan reached for it, Ibari attacked again, showing no mercy. Capitan quickly rolled out of the way, then sprang to his feet, ready. The Oriental smiled.

"And so the training begins." Ibari attacked once again.

CHAPTER TWENTY-THREE

ABE had not expected Mantis to come to his office, not at noon at least, during broad daylight. He told him that when he entered with Al, watching as the lieutenant pushed Charlie out the door. Mantis just smiled.

"Ah, but business is business, what better time to arrive?"

Abe leaned back in his seat. He knew he was in trouble.

"Did you like my spot on TV?" the old-timer asked.

"I was shocked," Mantis said, tongue firmly in cheek. "*You* were supposed to do some work for me. That's why we had that whole big, giant conversation at my place."

"The one with all the entertainment?" Abe said. He hit the automatic switch for the blinds, permitting sunlight to flood in. "That poor little monkey got his eye plucked out, didn't he?"

"Yes. Well, he—he disappointed me." Mantis leaned over and hit the switch, closing the blinds, shutting out the light. He shook his head and handed the switch back to Abe.

"Horribly," Al added.

"Just like you've done," Mantis said. "Why, the *idea* of accusing

264

us of killing those two Hispanic chimps down in Brooklyn. I had the police at my door," Mantis said, "and God, the questions, and the insults. I almost cried..."

Abe pulled a hankie out of his pocket. Al grabbed it abruptly. "Wiseguy."

"Let's all be peaceful now," Mantis said.

A slight ripple of silence passed through the office. Abe summed up his opponents.

"You know, there was nothing else I could really do," the old-timer finally said. "I mean, what'd you want? You asked me to clear the way with the league so you could fight Capitan. That was bullshit. The media masters have already arranged that. The league couldn't stop you from fightin' that chump any more than it could stop the sun from risin'. You think—"

"Be nice," Al cut in.

"Ah, buzz off," Abe said. He turned back to Mantis. "Look, everything's a setup for you. You don't need me to pull strings. I don't owe you nothin', and don't give me any rap about Sten, either. Sten acted on his own, you got to play with his head in the ring. You got to cut his throat, poor bastard. So don't play with me. You wanna kill me, kill me. But respect me, I'm old, so don't be a perverted maniac bastard, all right?"

"Don't insult him," Al said. "He'll cry."

Abe shook his head. He looked at Mantis.

"Really. I told them what you told me. Did you expect the people to love you after they found out you thought they were all insects?"

"They *are* insects," Mantis said. "As for their love, I never wanted their love."

"Well, in any case, now they got Capitan."

"Who they're going to lose, shortly."

"You don't know that," Abe said.

"You wanna bet on it?" Al said, smirking.

"Sure," Abe said. "How much time do I get to place bets?"

"About five minutes," Mantis told him, looking at his watch.

Abe glanced at the top drawer of his desk. He had a gun in there. It would be nice to go out fighting. Perhaps he could even win. But then he thought back—way back to all the wounds and his nine lives. He had only one life left, he realized, and it was fading fast. He watched as Al leaned against a file cabinet.

"Say, don't you ever sit down, relax?"

"I don't like to relax," Al said.

"You know, ten to one my assistant there is callin' the cops."

"That's okay," Mantis said."We already spoke with the police. They're not coming up."

"Disappointed?" Al asked, biting into a piece of gum.

Abe leaned back and glanced at the top drawer again. Mantis watched him closely, a broad smile on his face.

"You bring any snakes or tarantulas this time?" Abe asked.

"Nope. Just me."

"Just you and Baby Huey here," Abe said, nodding toward Al. "Right?"

He watched Al's jaw tighten. Mantis looked at his fingers, ignoring it all, then he looked up at Abe. "You're probably wondering why I came to visit you, right?"

Abe just shrugged his shoulders. "Shoot."

"Not yet," Al bit out.

"Well, it's because you've become like a, well...a big brother to me. Someone I can talk to, confess to."

"Confess? You want me to bless you 'cause you've sinned?"

"Father Goldman, haha!"

Abe glanced one more time at the drawer, then at the switch for the blinds. Sunlight and then the gun, he thought. He went to press the switch but Mantis swiveled around in the seat and scooped it up.

"No, no confession," he said. "I just, well, feel bad."

"Ohhh, why?" Abe smiled with mock concern.

"Well, because it's all going to end."

"What, your life?"

"Don't be funny," Al said.

"Feed him some biscuits," Abe told Mantis.

Mantis motioned for Al to simmer down. He swung around in the swivel seat and aimed a finger at Goldman. "'It' is going to end," Mantis said, hitting the switch. The blinds unfolded and light flooded into the room.

"What does 'it' mean?" Abe asked, ready to move for the drawer.

"'It' means a whole, well—series of circumstances," Mantis said. He abruptly closed the blinds, leaving the room very dark, a tomb. "I knew you, you knew Sten, Sten bumped into me, Savinien came along, I met Capitan, then the chimp Bimbi. I killed Sten, the eye got plucked—"

"And what about 'it'?"

"Well, like I said, it's all going to end."

"Dear me, you sound sad."

"I am," Mantis said, placing the switch on the desk.

"Why?" Abe asked, looking at it.

"Because I, well—"

"You want new playmates. Is that it, little boy?"

Mantis just laughed and shook his head, pointing at Al, telling him in one silent gesture to relax.

"Mr. Goldman, I could kill you so easily now. Why are you—"

"Bugging you?"

"Exactly. Why?"

"Maybe because I'm afraid," Abe said calmly, glancing at the drawer. Oh, how sweet it would be, he thought, one bullet, point blank, right between your pea-green eyes.

"So—"

"You're sad, because it's all going to end, you think."

"It is."

"Oh, now—you don't know that," Abe told Mantis. "I mean, you assume that you're going to defeat Capitan."

"And why shouldn't he?" Al asked.

"I thought you was eatin' biscuits."

"Be nice."

"What makes you assume that?"

"Because," Mantis told Abe as he examined his well-manicured nails, "my destiny cannot be threatened by anyone other than my own seed."

"How intriguing."

"Yes," Mantis said, his eyes lighting up in good humor. "It makes me rather immune."

"From what?" Abe asked.

"Danger."

"Invincible, eh?" Abe asked, reaching for the switch.

"Exactly," Mantis said, inching the switch away.

The drawer, Abe thought, the drawer, damn if only I could reach the gun in the drawer...one bullet—pow! I'd send your skull screaming to Mars....

"So like I said," Mantis continued. "It's all going to end. And I'm sad. I've had so much fun maneuvering things into place. And you've been so much a part of it. I've had fun using you. Now, it just seems a matter of time before my plans unfold and I take over completely..."

"And that's not good?" Abe asked.

"Oh, it's good. But no one likes to come by things too easily. Everyone needs a few obstacles in life."

"Capitan will be an obstacle," Abe said.

"Here we go again," Al moaned.

"Where'd you dig him up?"

Mantis gave Al another "sit-tight" look.

Abe could hear strange breathing. He watched as Mantis' right hand began to writhe.

"Hey, you know," the old-timer said. "There's somethin' I've always been wonderin' about."

"What?" Mantis asked, swiveling around in the chair.

Abe pointed at Mantis' right hand. "Why is your hand always doin' that, jumpin' around like a Mexican bean or somethin'?"

Al gritted his teeth. "I oughta—"

"Enough," Mantis commanded, raising his hand. He waved it in front of Goldman. "*This*, my friend, is a war wound. Along with this, too," he added, opening his shirt and revealing his bizarre, contracting abdomen. Abe looked at it, slightly shocked, watching as the very silhouette of Mantis' spine appeared with each and every exhalation of breath. "I got this in Tibet."

"That when you disappeared for a while?"

"Exactly."

"Some rumor had it you were hit by a—"

"A neutron grenade. Yes, I was. It is a slow process of radiation. It eats through you." Mantis watched as his fingers writhed with a will of their own. "But in my case, I reversed the negative effects. I turned my wound into a power. Anyone can do it, with any wound. Mother Nature adapts things through us. And so this radiation adapted through me. It is a part of me that is evolving."

Abe glanced at the desk drawer again. "A part of you that is evolving...I don't get it."

"It's much easier if I show it to you." Mantis said, opening up his shirt a little closer. "Look. Focus."

Abe leaned forward, glancing once again at Mantis's abdomen, at the mad contraction and then—something else.

He quickly went for the .38 in the drawer.

When Billy and Eddie stepped into the office, they found Charlie sitting at his desk, shaking. They drew their guns.

"Too late," was all Charlie could say.

Eddie opened the door to Abe's office. The old-timer was there, slumped over his desk, the handle of the .38 in his hand, the muzzle in his mouth. The back of his head had been blown off. Billy stepped in next.

"Shit..."

"He shot himself..."

"You assholes," Charlie said, coming up behind them, "since when do you slump forward after you've blown your brains out?"

They looked up to see blood all over the closed blinds.

"Yeah..."

"What happened?"

Charlie told them in a shaky voice. "I don't know what really happened. All I heard was the shot. Then Mantis and that ape came walkin' out, laughing. Christ..."

Billy looked at Abe's body, and at the blinds again.

"Whatever happened, they weren't messin' around," he said.

"No," Charlie said, reaching for the phone. "They don't mess around."

Back in the studio Capitan, Carmen, and Ibari watched as Charlie appeared on the TV screen, giving his version of the story. There was someone else watching, too. Bimbi had joined them. He was still somewhat in shock, but he had pulled through; he had returned to join Capitan. Carmen gave him a big hug as she looked at Ibari. The Oriental shook his head.

"Goldman's demise was long in coming. He knew what he was doing when he crossed Mantis that way, publicly humiliating him."

"Do you think his death'll change things?" Carmen asked.

"It means nothing. Nothing can stop the fight tomorrow. Goldman's death, if anything, is just another thrill for the public. They want the fight, they want blood."

"Mine?" Capitan asked.

"Anyone's," Ibari said. "Anyone who walks into the arena pit is fair game. Your friend Savinien went in there handicapped by his own outsized conception of himself, and so he fell. Sten followed next because he was misguided enough to believe his concern for the people would invest him with added power. He fell, too. Now it is your turn to enter the arena, but you'll step in there with neither Savinien's arrogance nor Sten's sorrowful illusion. It will make all the difference."

Despite himself, Bimbi began to cry. Carmen held him close. Ibari nodded.

"Yes, you weep," he said. "How many people are weeping now because of what Mantis has done, the murders, the torture."

"Can any spirit be so evil?" Capitan asked. "Why can't we look at him as something—misguided or—"

"There are spirits, my friends, that are very ancient and very old. That have learned to adapt to even the most painful experiences and to work with them until they are almost pleasurable. Mantis is one of these. No matter how great the punishment, his spirit returns to earth to gain control, power. He is lord over the hungry ghosts. The object is to send him back further, like the master said, into the bowels of hell. Otherwise, he will return even stronger."

There was silence as they sat and continued to watch the screen. Charlie was being interviewed by another media master now. Suddenly he broke off and looked into the cameras.

"Capitan, kill Mantis. Please, for all of us—kill him."

Capitan looked away from the screen. "Shut it off," he said.

"For everyone's sake, kill him. Cut his throat!"

Capitan abruptly pulled the plug.

Cut his throat, stab him, gouge his eyes out, choke him—my God, he thought. He looked over at Ibari. The Japanese officer nodded and pointed to the Aiki sword.

Unavoidable, his eyes seemed to be saying.

Mantis laughed when he saw Charlie screaming on the TV. But he could not be humored for long. He was in great pain now; the bizarre breathing had mounted and the ache in his abdomen had caused him to fall over at one point, directly in front of the slashed statue of the Buddha. He had never experienced pain like this, but he was fast to rebuke Al for even considering a postponement of the fight. Everything had fallen nicely into place: Ibari was here to watch; Habib had been taken care of; and now Capitan would serve as a splendid sacrifice preparatory to seizing Aquila and sacrificing him. There didn't seem to be anything that could possibly stand in the way.

Capitan...?

He had to laugh. The man was a puppet—a marionette suspended on the strings of sugar and spice. What could he possibly know in terms of combat that could threaten or even abuse his position as world champion? There was nothing to know, nothing that Capitan could even learn that would approach his vast knowledge, his enlightened state of power within the arts of death.

No, what these ridiculous media masters had contrived was a Sunday school fantasy, an archaic Hollywood screenplay whereby the pseudo-"righteous" underdog would suddenly defy the odds and prove the victor. It was an amusing fantasy, but one that had been played out too many times. The media masters had to be taught a lesson, too, Mantis decided, and Capitan's head would do nicely. It would teach them; serve as a sacrifice. Capitan's head was going to put everyone in their proper place.

Mantis knelt before the Buddha. The pain came in cycles. He had been lucky. The neutron grenade was a living death, but he had survived the final stage. The radiation had seized him, and flowed through him, but Mantis had conquered it.

And he had used it.

It was the radiation that had given him the power. The power to see the Power. Yes. It was the radiation that had taken him beyond Hoshima's shallow view of ethics. The radiation had been the guide; it had seized him, his bowels, and it had run clear through his spine up to his head and beyond, showing him a view of Creation that no one else had yet seen. He had looked down upon the universe, and when he returned he was the center of all things. Power, he *was* the Power now, he...Mantis.

He looked up at the statue, and its laughing face. How he hated it, now it reminded him of Hoshima—Hoshima and his silly, comical behavior. Hoshima who had reincarnated himself through his seed, his very own loins.

Mantis smiled back at the statue. He smiled and thought: old man, you never considered the possibility that I would learn the secrets of the Egg. My son who is no son but who is you, you who will soon be dead. You are in a child's body, you won't be able to fly back to your deva-land, your land of the gods. But I will. I can....

He looked up to the heavens now on this, the night before the fight. The sky was clear, a canopy of stars hanging overhead. Capitan, on the other hand, would be in a little Brooklyn studio, hiding and waiting like an insect. Another insect to step on, to put in its place. He smiled to the stars. The stars were *his*.

Still, there was the pain....

Mantis suddenly doubled over, his bowels, his loins, his abdomen contracting, alive, separate, alien and yet a part of him. For him the Egg was to be a painful process. For him the Egg was very much alive.

CHAPTER TWENTY-FOUR

THE night of the fight was like no other in the history of Sport Arena. Mantis had irrevocably changed the nature of the game when he first fought Tanaka in Tokyo. Now he was changing it even more by determining where the sport was ultimately going. Mantis had laughed at the rules, had castrated the power of the Arena League, had undermined the concept of major and minor leagues, and had personally rearranged the scheduled season to suit his own interests. The Arena had always been his playground; now he was making it formally so. It was a fact that did not go unnoticed, either on the part of the public, or the press, or the Arena League itself. Mantis was beginning to take things out of context. He had to be stopped, and nobody was very secure with the idea of some greenhorn like Capitan doing the job.

Still, assassination was out of the question. You couldn't just remove a figure as potent as Mantis's from society's delicately balanced hero-worship structure without finding someone to take his place. For the time being, then, Capitan would have to do. If the odds were stacked against him as far as Mantis's superior strength and experience were concerned, the newcomer had one thing in his favor: everyone wanted him to win. This one factor alone might be worth its weight in gold.

The security officers who had driven Capitan to the Coliseum that night supposedly worked for the Arena League, but as the challenger drove along—Bimbi, Carmen and Ibari at his side— he and his crew found out otherwise.

"We represent certain interests that send you their support," one of them said.

"Tell them thanks."

What more could be said? Sport Arena had never been the kind of competition where you could take a dive. The only dive possible was to the grave.

"They send their support," one of the "security officers" added, "and they send an open invitation for you to examine the possibility of—"

"Just wait a second," Capitan cut in, "I don't know who you guys are. But tell whoever it is that you represent that if they want to help me, then just shoot Mantis the moment he steps out, have someone shoot him for me. Okay? Either do that or shut up. I don't need this...."

The media masters had been no better. They attacked in waves once Capitan and his crew made it to the lower bowels of the Coliseum. They were everywhere, posing as attendants, police, security. One had even managed to hide himself within Capitan's dressing room. The situation had grown absurd.

Since Ibari had disappeared en route to the dressing room, Capitan decided to make an early peace with Carmen and Bimbi. He said a few words and then asked them to withdraw so he could meditate.

"It's best this way," he said.

"Yeah, well, where's that Chink, eh?" Bimbi asked, wondering about Ibari. "He just did the kung fu split routine, man."

"*Sensei* is not needed now," Capitan said. "I'm the one that has to fight Mantis, not him."

"Yeah, well how do you plan to beat him, if you don't believe in killin' nobody?"

"By appealing to a higher power," Capitan said, closing his eyes.

"What?"

Bimbi looked at him, thoroughly confused. Carmen took Capitan's hand. She pressed it firmly, then went to hug him. But he was hard, like a rock. She backed away, teary-eyed.

"Go now," she heard him say.

"I love you..."

"If you love, then believe that I will hold you once again."

She began to sob as she backed away. He looked at her, his eyes pleading for her to leave quickly so that he would not weaken.

She turned to Bimbi. Capitan turned his head away, and a second later, found himself alone. Not just alone in a cold-walled room at the bottom of a Coliseum devoted to a sport whose goal was death, no—he was more alone than that. He had been singled out. He thought back to the old poem by Donne. "No man is an island..." How true. But there were two sides to every coin, if not to every poem. Every man is an island, he thought. I entered life alone, I shall leave it alone. And this fight...I must face this alone. All things considered, it has been a good life. I have always tried to do well, so let the fates judge me as they wish. I pray to the Way, to God, to all the angels and saints and whatever exists. Please judge me fairly.

Capitan straightened his posture and lowered his eyes. He began to focus on his breath. In time everything grew calm. Everything but the cries from up above in the arena. The killing had started.

Monitor Five, the man known as Ibari, was not far off. He had business to attend to. A security officer had announced his presence to Al, and Al in turn went in to Mantis.

"He's outside. Says he wants to see you."

"Let him in," Mantis said, eyes staring dully at the floor. It was not long before the two of them were face to face. Mantis turned to his men. "Get out."

Al stepped forward. "Don't you think—"

"*Out.*"

Al joined the other men, reluctantly. There was a long pause as Ibari stood before the champion, Mantis staring at the floor, not looking up. Finally he smiled.

"And so, here we are."

"Yes."

"How is the boy?"

"Well."

"Sacrifices should always be well fed," Mantis said.

"You shall fall tonight, soldier."

"That is doubtful. Remember the omen, the threat."

"Yes, I remember it well," Ibari said. "But I have never misunderstood it."

The heavy, rhythmic breathing began. Ibari listened attentively.

"Me, misunderstand? You are an insect. You never saw the day you comprehended things the way I do. I have even gone beyond the techniques of the master."

Ibari listened closer, to the pulse of breath, thinking—By the gods, no! He has it. He realized that he had underestimated Hoshima's omen as much as the killer who now stood before him. If by some ill fate Capitan should fail, he thought, then I will have to act. My vow applies to Mantis, not his spirit. Again he listened closer, to the breathing. And he looked at Mantis.

"If only it could have been me to fight you," Ibari said.

"Yes. I would have enjoyed that. It would have made better sport than the execution that awaits."

"Do not underestimate Capitan, old soldier. He is good. And he has one thing in his favor."

"What's that?" Mantis asked, amused.

The Oriental pointed to his heart. "He is in virtue of the Way."

"He has no concept of Power," Mantis said, scoffing.

Ibari backed off toward the door. "You shall fall tonight, soldier."

He walked out. Al returned to the room. Mantis did not speak. He merely stared stoically at the floor. In a very short time the sound of rhythmic breathing filled the room.

When they met at the Waiting Station, Capitan and Mantis had nothing to say. Media masters babbled around them as cameras popped and flashed, but the two fighters merely stood face to face and stared at one another. It was the kind of showdown the fans loved.

Carmen had taken position in the Coach Zone with Bimbi. She did not want to watch, but she did not want to run away, either. Her lover was a warrior; she had to face this fact now, the same as Capitan himself had to face it.

"Oh, but he does strike a handsome pose," Carmen heard someone say about Capitan, who was visible on the video screen. She looked up, a few rows higher. It was a member of the Drag Queen Tribe.

"Yes, a handsome pose—just ripe for the grave."

"Shut up," Bimbi heard Carmen say. She pointed up at them. "Just shut your mouths."

The painted faces looked down, ugly, clownlike.

"Gonna make us, honey?"

"Try me," Carmen said.

Bimbi nudged her. "Hey, those are drag queen warriors. They'll beat us up."

"No they won't," Carmen said, rising. She watched as the largest of the drag queens inched his way down toward the Coach Zone, the others hooting like owls.

"Teach her a lesson, Babby."

"Pinch her good."

They giggled away, the large queen approaching Carmen and sneering. "Wanna run that by me again?"

"Yeah—shut up."

The big queen went to grab Carmen, but she seized him by the arm and then spun her hips. Before Bimbi knew it the queen had been thrown over the edge—into the arena.

There was applause from the crowd.

Cameras zoomed in from all angles to cover the scene as security guards rushed down to seize the paint-faced intruder. Bimbi turned to Carmen, amazed.

"Shit, you're tough."

"I used to be a pretty fair wrestler," she said.

"*Used* to be?" Bimbi laughed.

The taste of blood was flowing through her now, too. It was like an infection—an infection that spread from one person to the next. She stood up and aimed a finger at the other drag queens, demanding, "Anyone else?"

"Sure—why not?"

The rest of the tribe rose in unison.

"Now we're in trouble," Bimbi said.

"We'll see," Carmen said, drawing out a mace gun.

But she didn't have to use the gun. Security officers blocked off the Coach Zone, and the drag queens returned to their seats.

Blood, she thought. So easy to flow, too easy to draw. She looked up to see all the old video footage of Mantis and his kills. First Tanaka, then another, and another, the faces of the dead mounting until she recognized Savinien and then Sten. She held Bimbi's hand firmly.

"Oh God," she said aloud, "I've never yet made a wish 'til now..."

The blood was still being sponged up from the previous fight when the central lift ascended, admitting Capitan into the ring. He had never seen things from this angle before, let alone been greeted by hoots, howls, and cheers of blank faces hiding behind bright lights. The initial feeling he had as he stepped out, sheathed sword in hand, was that he was a bird, and that the walls of the arena were a cage. In this cage, though, he was a bird without wings, unable to take flight. A big bird, grounded.

If I have to go, Capitan thought to himself, I'm going out fighting and with a sense of humor. What else is there? What else is left to do?

He watched as the lift descended. He looked about, attempting to get his bearings, to adjust himself. There were lights and beacons and things flashing and he could see himself on video screens mounted along the breadth of the arena zone. He wanted to look for Carmen, but he thought better.

Chanting had begun. Slow, steady chanting.

"Capitaaan! Capitaaan! Capitaaan!"

Now I feel like I'm in a jungle, he thought. He watched as the central lift ascended into the arena.

"Maan-tiis! Maan-tiis! Maan-tiis!"

The cylindrical turret opened and the green-eyed champion stepped out, sheathed samurai sword in hand, sai dagger case under one arm, The chanting had become deafening now; there was something wrong with the audio system, and feedback began to echo across the Coliseum as the beacon to the President's Box flashed. Mantis motioned with his hand for Capitan to proceed, to approach the box.

Capitan felt numb; his legs felt weak, as if they were about to give out from under him. He turned toward the direction of the President's Box, then took a step, then another, and Mantis's eyes stayed on him all the time.

He's on home turf, Capitan thought.

They stood before the President's Box. The guant-faced official rose, preparing to read the rules, but Mantis aimed a finger at him dramatically.

"We don't need an announcer for this," he shouted.

"I must state the rules," the president said.

"You must state nothing. He knows the rules, everyone knows them. There are none. But it's still my right to choose how we start the fight."

"So choose," Capitan said.

"The sword," Mantis said, smiling. "I'll give you the edge, you're dead just the same."

He shoved Capitan aside and walked over to his corner. Once there, he removed his sai daggers and dug them into the floor. As he began to unsheath his sword, Capitan did the same. Champion and challenger slowly approached each other then, blades held low. Casually they began to circle, eyes focused on one another. A silence began to take hold of the Coliseum—a deepening silence that traveled with great deliberation across the length and breadth of the building. The only sounds that could be heard were the muffled tones of the media masters and the low buzz of the cameras and screens. Everyone watched as champion and challenger prepared to engage.

Mantis suddenly attacked, flashing his blade twice at Capitan, who dodged the blows and then cut back. The impact of steel on steel produced sparks.

"Jesus."

The feedback from the sound system echoed across the arena. The fans sat stunned, deafened by the blast of sound. Mantis looked about and then laughed.

"Just like the old days," he cried. "Blood and thunder."

He laughed again and then lunged at Capitan. Capitan quickly pivoted away and then cut, but his blade greeted only air. Mantis attacked again, catching his blade with Capitan's and sending up a flurry of sparks. The sound system once again erupted in a deafening wave of feedback. Carmen and Bimbi covered their ears in pain as they watched a quick burst of action from the arena below. Mantis and Capitan were still attempting to hack away at one another, and the feedback roared like thunder. A technician cut the sound on the central audio panel. The crowds began to recover as a stalemate arose, Mantis and Capitan locked swords for the first time. Suddenly Mantis pulled away, pivoted, then struck—

A hit!

Capitan quickly swung to safety and spied the wound: a cut below the shoulder. Blood began to flow...

No fat there, Capitan thought, as he recouped his strength. Mantis smiled and moved in. The champion opened up with a series of cuts, beating Capitan back as the challenger parried each blow with swift skill.

"He's beatin' him back to the wall," Bimbi said, watching Capitan retreat. Mantis slashed away and and beat down on the blade of the challenger.

Capitan was cornered. As Mantis paused to catch his breath, the sudden thought occurred to him that *he* was hesitating. He struck like lightning—

A hit!

Mantis was hit! Capitan had pivoted on his heels like a top and dove with his blade through an opening, cutting the champion across the torso. Mantis struck back with rapid instinct but missed. He stepped back and examined his wound. He began to smile. It was a good cut. It had hurt him, but not enough. He aimed his blade at Capitan.

"Not bad," Mantis said. "But can't you do better?"

"I'll try," Capitan said with a curt bow, senses wary.

"You'll have to," Mantis told him as he prepared his blade. Blood flowed now from both of them. Silence descended on the arena once again as both swordsmen began to circle, anticipating. Chanting began.

"Capitaaan! Capitaaan! Capitaaan!"

Bimbi swung toward Carmen. "They want him. They're rootin' for him."

The chanting continued to mount. Suddenly Mantis charged, hacking away with his sword like a man possessed. Capitan parried each blow skillfully but found himself being pressed once again up against the opposite wall. Sparks issued from both blades as Mantis struck again, the tip of his blade slicing across Capitan's torso.

"Oh, God," Carmen cried.

The crowd went wild as Capitan jolted back, stunned. Mantis merely stepped to the side and twirled his blade playfully as if he were marking time.

Capitan examined the wound. He had been lucky. The tip had not gone deep, and Mantis had deliberately provided him with time to recoup his senses. He fixed his eyes on his opponent. Mantis aimed his blade at him and smiled.

"I'm drawing this out," he said, running his free hand over his own wound, taking the blood and examining it. "We don't want to disappoint the fans, after all."

Capitan nodded grimly, then opened his arms, motioning for Mantis to strike again. A broad smile began to form on the champion's face, his blade rising into position as he moved closer. Capitan checked his own breath and circled cautiously. Mantis lunged suddenly, but Capitan sprang back. And then Mantis attacked again, both blades sparking in an interchange that ended in a double hit. Mantis cut into Capitan's flank, but the challenger jolted back and struck with a swift counterattack that tore across Mantis's arm.

"He got him again," Bimbi yelled.

"Not good enough," Carmen said. Tears flooded her eyes as she watched her man stagger back. Mantis followed, blade ready, eyes glaring madly as he attacked and hacked away again. Capitan was still defending and parrying but his power was quickly fading now. In a few moments he was beaten back against another wall. Mantis continued slicing like a woodsman with an axe, but Capitan's blade bounced back each time, like a branch refusing to break. Enraged, Mantis slashed again and then dove in, both blades locking. The champion attempted to drive his knee up into Capitan's groin, only to be blocked. He turned in next with his elbow and struck a swift blow to Capitan's wounded side. Grimacing with pain, Capitan reacted sharply, hurling the champion back and slashing with his weapon. The wild slash produced an opening for Mantis. He sneered and then cut low—across Capitan's right leg, sending him crashing down on one knee.

"Can't be, man," Bimbi said, not willing to believe what was taking place. Carmen buried her face and sobbed as Bimbi held her tight.

Mantis began to circle Capitan as the crippled challenger rose painfully and attempted to limp away from the wall. Capitan's mind was reeling.

I'm really hurt now, he told himself. And I'm losing a lot more blood than he is. *A lot more.* He watched as Mantis aimed the blade at him again.

"Cat and mouse, my friend," he said. "Do you know the game?"

Capitan replied diplomatically, his breathing labored. "Maybe you can teach me..."

"That," Mantis said, "I have every intention of doing."

With blades in position, both warriors began to circle again, Capitan limping badly as the chants began to mount. The security police were out in full force now, especially in the top rows occupied by the Untouchables.

Cat and mouse it is, Capitan thought. He can afford to have me move first. But I can't afford to miss next time because it's all come down to a one-cut deal. One cut, that's all I get.

The chanting had completely died out. Dead silence fell over the Coliseum, cameras recording, spotlights burning, reporters and fans watching on the edge of their seats as Mantis playfully twirled his blade. Capitan was bleeding steadily now. He attempted to recover his breath, but his eyes danced around, losing focus. He had unknowingly positioned himself between Mantis's two sais. Feeling pinned by them he began to draw back, drawing Mantis closer. Then, suddenly, Capitan felt a strange numbness penetrating him as he heard Hoshima's voice say from within: "Never forget the Way. If you are in virtue of the Way, the Moment is yours, you shall win."

With that, the power faded, his legs went limp, and in an instant he was on his knees, Aiki sword still in hand.

Good God, he thought, what's this?

Everything spun like a whirlpool around his head as a new chorus of chants flooded the arena. Mantis slowly moved closer, coming within striking distance of Capitan.

"I thought you'd play longer," Mantis said.

Capitan looked up at him. "I'm not dead yet."

Mantis smiled. "You will be. Where do you want it? If the head goes, it's fastest."

Capitan tensed the grip on his blade. He smiled politely, quickly comparing Mantis' cutting distance with his own thrusting range.

"The head would be nice," Capitan replied, arms coiling, ready.

Mantis nodded stoically. "The head it is."

Mantis raised his blade high. Capitan sprung and lunged abruptly, thrusting his blade straight through the champion.

"*Capitaaan!*"

The Coliseum echoed and thundered as Mantis staggered back, the blade passing cleanly out of him. His own sword fell from his hands as he looked down and examined the wound. Stunned, he looked up, as if to heaven.

"I'm finished..." he said.

He fell to his knees, directly between his two sais, both opponents facing each other now from the same position, not more than a few feet apart. The fans screamed and roared. Missiles rained down. Security and medics began to enter the pit, forming into a tight circle so that no one could enter and interfere with the final kill. Mantis looked at Capitan and laughed. "You finished me, you bastard."

Capitan looked down at his sword, still in his hands, the blade covered with blood. He looked into Mantis's wild eyes.

"The omen..." Mantis said. "What about the omen...?" He ran his hand over the deep wound, then pointed at Capitan. "You're not my seed."

Capitan nodded. "*I am* your seed...and you are mine."

The killer sneered. "Hoshima's final joke."

"*Capitaaan!*"

"*Kill him!*"

Mantis and Capitan looked up, out, across the arena. The fans were raising their arms in judgment: *thumbs down.* Mantis looked at Capitan, waited for his attention, then nodded. Capitan shook his head, only to hear a voice among many—he was certain it was Ibari's—crying: "*Kill him! Cut off his head—now!*"

Mantis flushed angrily. "Finish me," he said.

"No," Capitan replied.

"*Finish me.*"

"No way."

The crowd roared: *"Kill him!"* Missiles and bracelets and food rained down on them. Mantis began to laugh, his abdomen contracting madly. He pointed at Capitan. "The kill is yours," he said.

Capitan threw his sword away and shook his head. "No," he replied, "the kill has always belonged to you."

Mantis began to nod, amused by the irony of it all, face lightening as if to say "you're right." He looked over at one of the sai daggers, then grabbed it, the same voice crying from below in the pit, behind the security, *"Cut off his head!"*

Mantis rolled his eyes back, his entire abdomen contracting madly. Capitan watched as the breath seemed to pass like a lightning bolt up the killer's spine, into his head. Then, abruptly, Mantis disemboweled himself.

"Cut off his head—now!"

Capitan could see Ibari struggling to break through the security ranks. The officers moved in closer and raised their riot shields as people from the lower balconies began to jump into the pit.

A moment later Carmen and Bimbi were at Capitan's side. The media masters hummed like bees as cameras flashed all around them. Capitan could hardly hold himself up. He looked over at Ibari, who was standing over Mantis's body.

"Why the head?" Capitan asked weakly.

"It doesn't matter," Ibari said. "It's too late. For now…"

Ibari looked down at Mantis's face.

There was a smile on it.